THE REVOLUTION:

Captain, Pirate, Heroine

Written by:

Cheryl Bartlam du Bois and Debra Ann Pawlak

A Place In Time.Press • Beverly Hills, CA

To all brave women
who have served their country,
faced war and took action

A Place in Time.Press
8594 Wilshire Blvd. Ste. 1020,
Beverly Hills, CA 90211
310 613-8872

e-mail: info@aplaceintime.press
Website: aplaceintime.press

Cover Design & Layout: Christopher Staser, brandweaver.tv
Map Design & Illustration: Steve Luchsinger

Library of Congress Cataloging-in-Publication Data is available on file.

Print ISBN: 978-0-9745414-4-0
Ebook ISBN: 978-0-9745414-5-7

Historical Fiction

Printed in the United States of America

Our books may be purchased in bulk for promotional, educational, or business use. Please contact your local bookseller or the publisher.

First U.S. Edition 2022

AUTHORS' NOTES

<u>Cheryl Bartlam du Bois</u>

In 1979, just after I graduated college, I moved to Florida to start a sailing charter company with my boyfriend. I had been on the water for years with my family and had enough experience to study for and take the United States Coast Guard Merchant Marine test for my six-pack Captain's license. I went to Jacksonville and took the written test, acing it and completing all qualifications to obtain my license. When it came time for my oral interview with the Commander, Lieutenant Lewis, in charge of licensing that day, I suddenly realized the mistake I'd made. Trying to look nice, I'd worn my best dress making me look quite feminine and young — I was all of a 105 pounds. It seemed he took one look at me and made the determination that I wasn't qualified to drive a boat for hire. It also seemed that the only woman to precede me on the east coast had been involved in a terrible accident, to no fault of her own, in which a passenger was killed. So it seemed I was to potentially be the second woman to ever receive my license on the east coast of the U.S.

I looked at him and demanded he name the deficit in my qualifications, which would prevent me from receiving my license. All he could come up with was that I was, a woman. My response, "Well since I don't plan to have a sex change anytime soon it seems to me that you are being very prejudiced and chauvinistic and I don't think that will look very good for the Coast Guard." He mulled that over for a bit, I'm sure considering how sexist that would look and he finally whipped out the certificate to fill in my name. However, when he got to the part where it read, *"This is to clarify that Cheryl Winifred Bartlam has given satisfactory evidence to the undersigned that 'he' can safely be entrusted with the duties and responsibilities of operator of...."* He looked up at me quite dumbfounded, uncertain what to do with the wording 'he.' I just said stick it in the typewriter and XX out the 'he' and type in 'she.' Without another word he did just that and signed it, shrugged his shoulders and shoved it at me. "Here you go," was his only comment. I thanked him and went on my way.

Now forty-three years later I hold my USCG Merchant Marine Master's Document for driving one-hundred-ton vessels with sail auxiliary and I have no intention of ever letting it go. I fought for my right as a female to do a man's job as I have done throughout my entire life in sailing, architecture and film and I'm proud to have accomplished what I have as a woman. When I look back on women such as the fictional Fanny Campbell and the very real Sarah Emma Edmonds who found it necessary to disguise themselves as men in order to pursue their destiny, I can fully appreciate their reasoning and their struggle to accomplish more than most men can boast, as well as more courage than any man I have ever known.

Debra Ann Pawlak

History is amazing and sadly, so much of it is forgotten. From the beginning, women have played an important role in many critical events. Often overlooked, it is important to remember their contributions. In the 1700s, opportunities for women were severely limited. They were not even allowed to own land. Yet despite these restrictions, many women stepped up. In between having babies, they carried on alone, taking care of farms and families while their husbands were either off fighting or running the new fledgling government. Some even ran successful businesses in their spouse's absence.

Although Fanny Campbell is a fictitious character, the Revolutionary War was very real and marked the beginning of America as an independent country. Rest assured, it was not an easy accomplishment or without controversy. Patriots versus Loyalists. Rebels versus Redcoats. Violence erupted from the Quebec Province of Canada all the way down to Nassau in the Bahamas. There were no guarantees that the Colonists would prevail as they were definitely the underdogs with their ragtag Army and newly formed Navy.

Daily life in the colonies was difficult as the citizenry dealt with many hardships including high taxes, food shortages, and demanding British soldiers who often took over their very homes. They resisted the idea of war as long as they could, but once begun, there was no going back. We live in a free country thanks to men and women who stood up for what is right. Is America perfect? Hardly. Could we do better? Most definitely.

Before we can move forward, however, we need to understand how and why we got here in the first place. Freedom did not come easy. It never does. We often forget that lives were lost and families shattered. Freedom comes with a heavy price and to appreciate that, we must look back upon the valiant men and women who were courageous enough to take those first steps. At the very least we owe them a nod of thanks.

TABLE OF CONTENTS

"We may destroy all the men in America, and we shall still have all we can do to defeat the women."

--British General Lord Charles Cornwallis

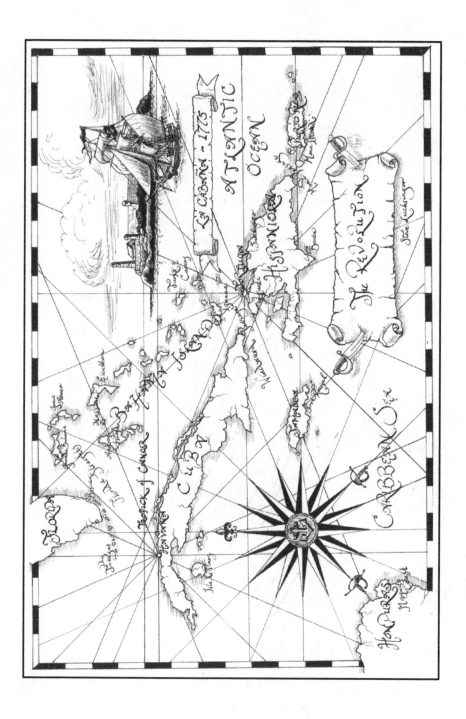

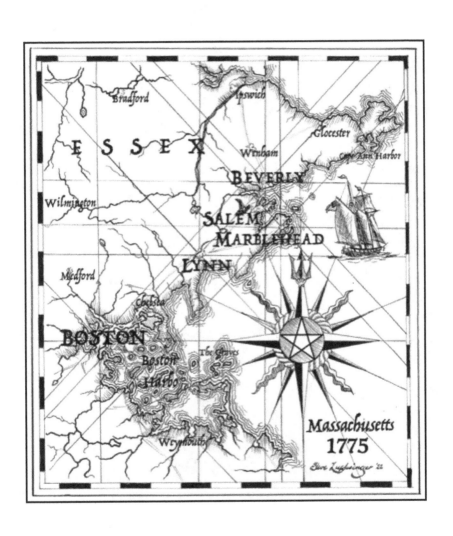

Massachusetts
1775

Steve Lughinger '22

PROLOGUE

Boston, Massachusetts - February 1, 1768

In protest of the recent Townshend Acts and the resulting taxes levied by the Crown against the American colonies, The Assembly of Massachusetts Bay responded with a circular letter written by Samuel Adams and James Otis, Jr. In part, it read:

> "...imposing Duties on the People of this province, with the sole and express purpose of raising revenue, are infringements of their natural and constitutional rights because they are not represented in the British Parliament, his Majesty's Commons in Britain...

> "This House is further of the opinion that their constituents, considering their local circumstances, cannot, by any possibility be represented in the Parliament; and that it will forever be impracticable, that they should be equally represented there... being separated by an ocean of a thousand leagues. That his Majesty's royal predecessors, for this reason, were graciously pleased to form a subordinate legislature here, that their subjects might enjoy the unalienable right of a representation..."

And so began the trouble between Great Britain and its American colonies...

⚓

Lynn, Massachusetts – June 30, 1768

Squinting in the summer sun, twelve-year-old Fanny Campbell was lost in a book of poetry as she strolled to the docks where her father was due in from the sea. Her long auburn curls were tied back and her ankle-length, gray skirt made a faint swishing sound as she walked. As usual, Fanny was to meet the old fishing boat, *Love Of The Sea*, and help unload the day's catch. Unlike most girls her age, the foul odor on the docks didn't bother her. She was used to the smell of freshly caught fish and the feel of their slippery scales. Best of all, she liked being with her father. Fanny adored Henry Campbell, who doted upon his only child and indulged her every whim. And then, of course, there was young William Lovell, who also worked the nets on her father's boat.

"Don't act as if you don't hear me, Fanny Campbell!" A woman's sharp voice interrupted her reading. "I've called you three times now, child."

Fanny looked up from the verse she had been absorbed in to find Moll Pitcher standing just inches away. Moll looked much younger than her forty-some years. Her eyes sparkled emerald-green and her long chestnut hair showed no sign of graying. She lived at the base of High Rock with her shoemaker husband, four children, and a large, black cat, something every witch needed to do their bidding, or so Fanny thought.

Mothers warned their young sons to stay away from the town fortune-teller. They whispered that Moll might turn their boys into mice and feed them to her fat feline. The townsfolk knew that Moll had unusual powers. She could see the future, as well as mix magical potions that could either heal or manipulate one's hopes and desires. They believed she inherited her extraordinary skills from her grandfather who was known as The Wizard of Marblehead. It was said that he guided far-away ships through the deadliest of storms while pacing in a nearby cemetery.

Despite their misgivings, the good people of Lynn didn't hesitate to visit Moll, or buy a vial of one of her mystical brews, elixirs, or potions when facing hardships or illnesses of their own. In fact, Moll's efforts nicely supplemented the family income, since her husband's wages weren't enough to provide for a family of six. Although she charged a modest fee for her services to the colonists, she made the British pay double. A true patriot, she never accepted British gold from the king's soldiers, only colonial coin.

That particular June afternoon, however, Moll wasn't thinking about her paying customers. Instead, she was focused on Fanny and caught the young girl off guard.

"Sorry, ma'am," Fanny mumbled. "I didn't hear you."

"That's the trouble with you, Fanny Campbell," Moll shook her head. "You don't know what's going on around you… you always have your head in a book. You must pay closer attention, my dear. It may mean the difference between life and death someday."

"I'm sorry," Fanny repeated herself as she closed her book politely, giving Moll her full attention. "Sometimes, the words just take me to another place. I meant no disrespect, ma'am."

"I know you didn't, child." Moll smiled as if she were talking to one of her own daughters. "There's nothing wrong with learning all you can about the world. Mark my word, it could even come in handy someday."

"What do you want with me, Mrs. Pitcher?"

"Come to my house tomorrow at noon and you'll find out. The children should all be napping by then."

"I'm not sure my mother would like it," Fanny hesitated. "She says you consort with the devil."

"Agnes has always been a good Christian woman," Moll sighed. "But she's never once hesitated to buy a potion from me when she needed one."

Fanny's jaw dropped to hear that her own mother had patronized the sorceress.

"Close your mouth, child," Moll chuckled. "It's not becoming. Now get along with you and don't tell Agnes or anyone else that we spoke. Just be at my house no later than noon tomorrow!"

Now unsettled, Fanny watched Moll walk away. She couldn't help but wonder just what this strange woman wanted from her.

Fanny's gut told her to stay away from Moll Pitcher, but her curiosity soon got the better of her. Late the next morning, she slipped out of the house once her mother left to run an errand. As Fanny walked toward High Rock, uncertainty crept up her spine and fluttered through her stomach. Was visiting a fortune-teller— even one as renowned as Moll—a good idea? After all, Moll Pitcher was surrounded by tales of ill-fated lovers and unfortunate events. There were other rumors, as well. Some said that Moll cooked small children in her large, black kettle. Fanny thought she was far too large to fit inside even the deepest of kettles, so at the very least she wouldn't be eaten. She hoped. With growing trepidation, she slowed her pace when she spotted Moll's little wooden shack poised at the bottom of High Rock. If Agnes found out where her daughter was, Fanny knew that she would be in serious trouble.

"Fanny Campbell, is that you?" Moll opened the small front door, wiping her hands on her worn white apron.

"Yes, ma'am." Fanny came closer, but stopped just short of the entry.

"Afraid to come in?" Moll smiled. "Scared I might eat you for lunch?"

"N...no, ma'am," Fanny stammered.

"Well, don't you worry, lass." Moll waved her inside. "I don't like little girls—they are not tasty enough no matter how long you boil them. Besides, I just had some frogs and lizards that filled me up fine." She chuckled at her own joke.

Still frightened and unsure, Fanny steeled herself before stepping inside. Once her eyes adjusted to the dim light, she saw shelf after shelf filled with bottles of all shapes, sizes, and colors while strange herbs and plants hung from the rafters. Their scents blended into a musky odor that filled the room. A large, black kettle with a bubbling concoction hung inside the fireplace. Moll's black cat lay stretched across a dark orange rug in front of the fire. The eerie place reminded Fanny of a witch's lair—something she once read about. She wondered whether Moll could really cast a spell or lay a curse upon someone. Her thoughts were interrupted as the old cat slowly got up and ambled towards her, stopping at her feet. He arched his back and rubbed himself against her leg, purring.

"That's Percy," Moll told her. "He seems to like you, though I'm surprised...he doesn't like many."

Fanny hesitantly bent down and stroked the cat. "I've seen him in the garden catching mice."

"That's because he knows I like the fat ones for lunch," laughed Moll.

"Why did you ask me to come here?" Fanny straightened, leaving the cat alone. "What do you want with me?"

"I wanted to tell you about some visions I've had—the most recent one just this morning."

"What visions?"

"You are sweet on a boy. I've seen the two of you climb High Rock together on many a day. His name is William. Is that right?"

"Everyone knows that William and I are going to be married one day," Fanny began. "If that's what your visions are telling you--"

"--of my visions you best take heed my girl," Moll interrupted in a stern voice. "They tell me that you will indeed one day marry your William for it is your destiny. But first there will be many trials including a war and battles at sea. You must prepare yourself, Fanny Campbell, for I see pirates and mutineers in your future! There will be bloodshed, rough waters, and storms like you've never seen before. Take care to save your love, but most important, make sure you save yourself!"

"I....I don't know what you're talking about." Fanny's voice shook.

"But you will, my girl," Moll assured her. "All in good time. One day, Fanny Campbell, you will find yourself in the eye of a storm with only your wits to rely on. You are smart and your education will serve you well. Just be certain to prepare yourself since your life and William's will depend on you and you alone.

"I don't believe you! I should never have come here! You don't know what you're talking about!"

"I know what I see." Moll stepped in front of the girl. "And one day, you will come back here needing my help."

"It all sounds ridiculous!" Fanny took a step back in a small effort to distance herself from Moll.

"Mark my words, Fanny Campbell! You will do important things in the years ahead. Things that even the strongest man wouldn't do. There's a rebellion coming and you will play a part in it. Prepare yourself with knowledge of the sea for you will need it!"

"I….I don't understand," Fanny gasped.

"The time will come for guns and blood and when it does, don't say that Moll Pitcher didn't give you fair warning!"

Filled with fear, Fanny ran from the cottage as Moll called after her. "You'll be back here one day, Fanny Campbell! As sure as I live and breathe, you'll come calling on Moll Pitcher, begging for my help!"

The very same day that Fanny visited the famous fortune-teller of Lynn, the British Parliament responded to the circular letter by dissolving the Massachusetts Legislature. Shortly thereafter, 4,000 British troops arrived in Boston to police the city. Their interaction with the colonists failed to improve the already strained relations with the Crown.

CHAPTER 1

The Homeland

A mere eleven miles northeast of Boston lay Lynn, Massachusetts, a small manufacturing town comprised of quaint white cottages, industrious tanneries, and facilities where fine leather was made into shoes. Lynn's hard-working inhabitants went about their daily routines, laboring, worshiping, and raising their families. They could be counted on to nurse the sick, bury the dead, and in between give birth to babies who renewed their spirits—if mother and child survived. Even the four seasons were predictable. Snow-filled winters were harsh and unwelcome after which spring coaxed brilliant blooms from the once dormant dogwood trees. The summer sun encouraged gardens to grow before the crisp fall air signaled the coming of another winter. There was nothing extraordinary about the place— except, perhaps, its view of the sea and, the fact that in 1756, the remarkable Fanny Campbell was born there.

British brothers, Edmond and Edward Ingalls, sailed together across the Atlantic and, in 1629, were the first to settle in the area. Soon, the men were joined by other colonists and the group established a settlement called Saugus, the name given to the region by local Native Americans. Several years later, Reverend Samuel Whiting of King's Lynn in Norfolk, England arrived to become the first pastor of the village's Congregational church. A much respected man, the town was eventually renamed Lynn in Whiting's honor.

Due to its location along the eastern seaboard, Lynn was also home to several fishing families, like the Campbells and the Lovells. Henry Campbell and William Lovell were both loyal to the Crown and veterans of the French and Indian War. They served under the leadership of a very young George Washington when the conflict first began in 1754. Their adventures on the battlefield were short-lived due to dysentery and after recovering at the newly built Fort Necessity in Farmington, Pennsylvania, both men were discharged. Their shared military experience, and the fact that they each came from a long line of fishermen, sealed a life-long friendship.

After they left the army, the two men bought a fishing boat together.

They named it *Love Of The Sea*, and settled in Lynn. They also built a large wooden structure—big enough to raise two families. They shared a central kitchen and dining area that connected two separate dwellings on either side. Each home had its own front door, small living area and two bedrooms.

William was already married to a fine girl, Sarah Herriman. She'd given birth to William, Jr., during her husband's absence. While William sent for his wife and son, Henry married Agnes Smythe and the two families blended well in their new home. While the men went out to sea, Sarah and Agnes took care of the daily chores. Two years later, Agnes bore Frances, but everyone called the girl, Fanny. Other children were born to the Campbells and Lovells, but none survived infancy.

William Lovell passed on to his son not only his name, but also his love of the sea. He routinely took the youngster out on the large, wooden fishing boat where he taught him the trade. The boy took to sailing from his first day on the water. The only thing he loved more than navigating the waves was his best friend, companion, and confidante, Fanny.

Growing up in the same household the children knew each other well and, at a very early age, simply understood that they would spend the rest of their lives together. William particularly admired Fanny's adventurous spirit. She was fearless and always eager to accept a dare—something William encouraged, while most boys of Lynn often laughed at her antics. Unlike the other girls who giggled and flirted with any young man who happened by, Fanny was always busy riding horses or fishing and, thanks to her father, she could also handle a gun. At times, Fanny intimidated the other children, but that didn't matter to her. She found the girls rather silly and when it came to the boys, well, she only cared for William.

Henry knew his daughter could not be a fisherman, for that was a man's job, but he did insist that she get an education. During the winter months, he sent Fanny to Boston where a kindly old reverend taught her to read and write. When she was home, Henry allowed her to run free, taught her to shoot and encouraged her independent streak. Occasionally, he took her out on his fishing boat so he was able to spend more time with her. Agnes disapproved of Henry's approach to parenting and they often came to loggerheads over the topic. As it turned out, Henry usually got his way, allowing Fanny to grow independent and tough—traits not readily admired in a proper young lady of the time.

"You're making a hooligan out of our daughter." Agnes frowned at her husband one Sunday afternoon after he'd sent the girl out to hunt quail for dinner.

"I'm doing no such thing, woman," Henry argued. "I'm teaching the child how to take care of herself."

"That will be William's job one day." Agnes wagged her finger at him.

"William's a fine lad," Henry agreed. "But there's no harm in teaching Fanny a few necessary skills."

"Fanny should be learning the skills of a lady—cooking, sewing, and keeping house."

"Yes, dear," he smiled. "And that's where I rely on you."

But Agnes knew that none of those womanly duties were of any interest what-so-ever to Fanny.

⚓

As Fanny grew so did her love of books and her fondness for the sea. If she could have spent every day on her father's fishing boat, she would have. Aside from being close to William, she relished the galloping feel of the waves beneath her and the gusty wind that blew her auburn curls. Unfortunately, she also understood that, as a woman and the daughter of a fisherman, it was her destiny to dry and preserve fish. This was an unexciting, yet respectable, domestic occupation for a young girl in 1770s Massachusetts, at least until she married and had children of her own.

If only she'd been born a boy like William. Then she could have spent her life on a ship and experienced escapades at sea. This inequality seemed unfair to Fanny, but it did not stop her from daydreaming about giant whales, cutthroat pirates, and sea beasts with long white fangs. She craved freedom and found solace in the adventure stories she read. To Fanny's great disappointment, however, the heroes were always men whose dutiful wives waited patiently for their husbands to return from the sea.

William especially liked it when she read aloud to him and he expressed an interest in learning to read and write himself. This delighted Fanny and she made a fine teacher. William was an enthusiastic pupil and their evening lessons often ended in fits of laughter—especially the time he mispronounced the word 'igloo' saying instead 'eye glue'.

In 1765 when William was eleven and Fanny nine, an underlying fire began smoldering between the English colonies and the mother country. The British government passed The Stamp Act – a direct tax requiring that magazines, newspapers, and legal documents in the colonies be produced on stamped paper, which was manufactured and embossed only in London. To add insult to injury for the colonists, only valid British currency, not colonial paper money, could be used to purchase this vital paper. According to the Crown, the proceeds from this tax paid for the king's troops that remained in America after the French and Indian War, which had officially ended in 1763. The colonists were furious. They believed that the money went to British officers whose wages and pensions should have been paid by London. Being taxed without their consent only served to rile American resentment and birthed the slogan "No taxation without representation."

Later that year, an underground group of rebels banded together in Boston to form The Sons of Liberty. Both Henry Campbell and William Lovell joined in, attending clandestine meetings and public rallies to protest the unfair treatment by Great Britain. Alliances were formed throughout the colonies and, for the first time, the British subjects now permanently living in America united in an effort to diminish the Crown's control.

Young William often accompanied his father to these political gatherings, but Fanny was not permitted to attend—no matter how much she begged—because she was a girl. Women were simply not allowed. She had to content herself with secondhand news and that was scarce as the men rarely talked about their covert activities. Even William was tight-lipped when it came to underground politics. She couldn't even discuss the matter with her mother. According to Agnes, real ladies didn't talk about such things. Much to Fanny's dismay, Agnes believed that the fairer sex should run the home so their men could mind the rest of the world.

To make matters worse, the Townshend Acts soon followed forcing the colonists to pay even more taxes—this time on lead, paint, glass, and tea. Americans retaliated by limiting these British imports even though life in the New World proved difficult without them. Things came to a fatal head in Boston on March 5, 1770 when British Private Hugh White used his musket to strike young Edward Garrick, a wigmaker's apprentice, after Garrick insulted White's commanding officer. The altercation escalated resulting in the British soldiers killing five men and injuring another six. The infamous incident became known as The Boston Massacre. The Townshend Acts were repealed the very next month and most taxes lifted on British imports, but it was too little too late.

Despite the reprieve, relations remained strained between the English and the American colonists. The settlers viewed King George III as a tyrant and their resentment of the British soldiers, who maintained a weighty presence in the colonies, increased. This climate of unrest spurred a bold and rebellious determination in many Americans including William Lovell and Fanny Campbell. They were not too young to understand their parents' concern as they discussed each distressing turn of events around the dinner table.

"There's a meeting on Saturday morning," Henry announced over the evening meal, which was almost always shared by both the Campbells and the Lovells. It was understood by those present that Henry was referring to The Sons of Liberty.

"We'll go together," the elder William said as he plucked a piece of fish with his fork.

"I'd like to go." A hopeful young William looked to his father.

"Of course," Lovell nodded. "We need all of the able-bodied men we can get."

"I'll go," offered Fanny, pushing some boiled potatoes on her plate.

"Hush, child," Agnes admonished her daughter. "You're a girl and it's time you remember that."

"That's not fair!" Fanny retorted. "I am able-bodied and I can shoot a gun. That should be enough."

"Well, it isn't," Agnes frowned. "Let me remind you that we ladies belong to the Daughters of Liberty and we have important work to do, too."

"Boycotts and textiles?!" Fanny complained. "There's no adventure in that. I want to be part of the real action. I want to fight the British and show them how American girls can--"

"--that's enough, Frances!" Agnes interrupted with a shake of her finger. "Why must I always remind you that you are a lady?"

"Lady!" Fanny spat out the word. "Why a lady has no rights at all! It's the men who get to march and fight and make all the important decisions. What's right about that?!"

"Fanny," Henry tried. "Your mother is right. Proper ladies don't get involved in politics."

"Well, maybe I'm just not a proper lady!" Fanny sighed and then tried another tactic, smiling sweetly at her father. "What if I dress like a boy? Could I come with you then?"

"NO!" Agnes and Henry answered in unison.

"But I could borrow some clothes from William," Fanny tried once more. "No one will know."

"William, can you please talk some sense into this girl?" Henry waved his knife in the air.

"It's no use," William shook his head. "Fanny is always wishing for adventure so I guess it's up to me to find enough excitement for the both of us!"

⚓

By 1773, several Committees of Correspondence were created by American leaders throughout the colonies. These shadow governments kept citizens informed of the unstable political climate and roused them to unite against the unfair practices of the Crown. These committees also promoted patriotism and coordinated efforts between the colonies to defend their rights. For the first time, thousands of colonists joined together to strengthen American resistance.

While rebellion mixed with nationalism, blue-eyed, dark-haired William grew into a handsome, strapping nineteen-year-old, as well as an experienced sailor. Like his father, he had an energetic spirit that left him unafraid to challenge danger and yearn for adventure in faraway places. He often wondered what lay beyond the horizon—were there treasures to be discovered; sea creatures to slay and pirates to battle? Someday, he wanted to sail around the world if only to regale Fanny, his children, and grandchildren with stories of one-eyed buccaneers, gold doubloons, and deserted ghost ships that drifted blindly upon the seas. Thanks to his mother, he was also a gentleman, and always maintained an air of chivalry. Local maidens eyed him hoping that he might take note of their charms. Although he was amused by their attention, William always left the ladies disappointed. He cared for only one young girl—Fanny Campbell.

At seventeen, Fanny was tall and slender with a well-endowed figure. Her unruly auburn hair and large brown eyes made her irresistible, not only to William, but to other suitors as well. She carried herself with confidence and lacked the coquettish mannerisms that most delicate belles her age practiced. She would rather row a boat, shoot a pistol, or tame a horse, than giggle, or bat her eyes at a would-be beau. Besides, she had given her heart to William years ago when they were still children. A voracious reader, Fanny never went anywhere without a book in her pocket. She also wrote poetry and, like William, often dreamed about exotic lands far outside the limits of Lynn. Society dictated that she stay at home helping her family, but her heart longed for something more—to live in the world, not just dream of it. And that shared love of adventure is what made William and Fanny kindred spirits.

Fanny's wanderlust, as well as her teachings, deeply affected William. He took everything she said to heart. He pressured his parents for permission to sail from Boston to the West Indies on a merchant vessel. With war looming over them, Sarah and William reluctantly agreed to let their only son go, knowing full-well that from the Caribbean, he hoped to travel even further. Both the Campbells and the Lovells, along with Fanny, prayed that William would find a safe haven far from the rebellion that was sure to come. Better to be a long way off than a soldier at home facing war, they all agreed. They would welcome him back once the fighting was finished.

William only wanted to make Fanny proud and become the worldly husband she deserved. Since being a female barred her from experiencing great adventures herself, she encouraged William to leave. At least one of them could lead a life of intrigue, if only for a while. Admittedly, she looked forward to one day hearing about his escapades at sea. Meeting real cutthroat pirates sounded so much better than simply reading about them. If only they could make the journey together.

William didn't fear buccaneers or sea bandits, but he did have one worry—Captain Ralph Burnett, a British naval officer who was American by birth. Burnett was in charge of a royal cutter, called *The Dolphin*, which was docked in Boston Harbor. An older, successful, and sophisticated man, he was attracted to Fanny's lack of pretension and intrigued by her independence. Fanny shared Burnett's love of the sea, but had no romantic feelings for him. She treated him like a favorite uncle, or as the older brother she never had. Nevertheless, William felt inferior to the more experienced captain and was somewhat jealous of the time Fanny spent with him. One day, William vowed to himself, he would be like Captain Burnett—a man who could tell rousing tales of glamorous places and curious people.

What troubled William most was Burnett's habit of visiting Fanny when he wasn't home. Hence, the two men had no occasion to officially meet face-to-face. Common sense and Fanny's pretty face, however, told William that Burnett wanted more from the girl than simple friendship. Besides, his mother had let him know how Burnett shamelessly flirted with Fanny every time he was around her. To her credit, Fanny always made it clear that she was devoted to William. Regardless, William knew that there was one thing the girl and the captain, who was a staunch Loyalist, would never agree on—England's treatment of the colonies.

⚓

The evening before William's departure, he and Fanny walked toward High Rock hand in hand as they had done many times since childhood. William didn't notice Moll Pitcher peering out of her front window from behind a curtain as they passed, but Fanny caught a glimpse of her smiling as she looked upon the lovers. An uneasy feeling took hold of Fanny as she remembered the fortune-teller's warning of rough seas ahead.

The pair climbed to their favorite spot, where they gazed at the Atlantic, watching it consume the reflections of the setting sun behind them. When darkness fell, the moonlight shone across the calm water creating fairy-like sparkles as far as the eye could see. Ever since they were children, they had found peace in this place, but tonight, despite the serene surroundings, Fanny was anxious.

She thought of the old sailor's saying: 'Red sky at morning sailors take warning...red sky at night sailors' delight.' The man she loved was about to sail off and the possibility of never seeing him again was more than she could bear. She wondered if the morn would bring him red skies or fair winds; pirates or mutineers; bloodshed or storms...all of the things that Moll had once warned her about. The night air held a bit of chill for it was still early June. Fanny shivered and nestled closer to William.

"By this time tomorrow, I will be many miles away." William held her close. "But I promise that wherever I go my heart will still be yours."

"And mine yours." Fanny closed her eyes.

"Leaving you is the hardest thing I have ever had to do, Fanny."

"Are you having second thoughts?" She looked up at him in surprise.

"I want to go." He hesitated and then took her hand. "But these are such turbulent times what with all of the troubles between our colonies and the king. And now the new tax on tea has made everything even worse. What if there's a war? I couldn't live with myself if something happened to you while I was away."

"William Lovell!" Fanny straightened. "Have you forgotten that I can take care of myself?!"

"Even when Captain Burnett comes around with all of his sweet talk?"

"Oh, now the truth is told," Fanny grinned. "Your worries have nothing to do with the unrest. You're a wee bit jealous of my seafaring friend!"

"Need I be?" William's unsmiling gaze held steady.

"William, you know I have never had eyes for any man but you." Her smile faded and her voice took on a more serious tone as she again moved closer to him. "Make no mistake. I will be here waiting when you return next year."

"If you are sure."

"I am sure that you mustn't have regrets, my love." Fanny stroked his face. "Leaving Lynn is exactly what you must do….for you.…for us. I envy you your chance to learn about the world. Had I been born a man I would be going with you, but I am a woman and we are not allowed such privileges or adventures. We must stay home. And knit…and sew…and patch men's undergarments."

"My dear girl," William grinned. "I have never known you to patch any of my undergarments, nor sew a stitch, but I am eternally grateful that you were born a woman so you can be my bride as soon as I return."

"And I will live by that dream until you come home, William."

"Fanny," he tried one last time. "Are you absolutely sure you want me to take this journey? Just say the word and I will stay here with you."

"No, I would never ask that." A single tear betrayed Fanny's resolute voice. "Follow your dream and go…I'll keep busy. I have a trousseau to gather and a wedding to plan. All of that will be much easier to do if you are not in my way."

"But will you miss me, Fanny?"

"I will miss your touch and your smile, but knowing we look upon the same sun and the same moon will make me feel closer to you no matter how many miles are between us."

"Let's not talk anymore." William embraced her. "Let's just savor this moment and the love that will bring us comfort when we're apart."

They remained in each other's arms overlooking the Atlantic until midnight. For any other couple such behavior would have been considered scandalous, but Fanny and William had both grown under the watchful eyes of the townsfolk—none of whom could deny the youngsters these final moments. When they finally parted at Fanny's bedroom door, as they did every night, she retired to her room and wept—afraid that rough seas or murderous buccaneers might claim William, preventing his return to her.

She couldn't imagine living without him and she feared loneliness might consume her. She had known no other life.

Different thoughts kept William up that night. He lay in bed wishing that he had married Fanny before his departure. As much as he wanted to hold her beautiful, naked body in his arms and make love to her, he also wanted to keep her from being tempted in his absence by an established man like Burnett. Deep down, however, he knew that marriage at this point would be wrong. If something happened to him, he would leave behind a young widow—maybe even a child.

And that would be unfair to Fanny.

CHAPTER 2

Pirates

William Lovell always liked visiting the port of Boston since it was much larger and busier than the docks at Lynn. When he arrived at the harbor that June morning in 1773, he took in the sights and sounds of men loading and unloading the many cargo ships moored and docked there. It was back-breaking work, but he heard no complaints other than a few low grunts from those who strained under their heavy loads. He noted with some satisfaction that Captain Burnett's royal cutter was missing from its berth in the harbor where it was meant to protect the waterfront from marauders. At least the good captain wouldn't bother Fanny for a while.

The sun felt warm and seemed to welcome William as he searched for the USS *Royal Kent*, a smaller schooner built right there in Boston. Once he spotted the regal vessel, he laid down his small, black bag and stopped to admire the ship's appearance from the well-kept wooden decks to the intricate rigging, and the tall wooden masts made from old-growth, New Hampshire white pines. He knew that the largest trees were declared protected by the king for exclusive use by British ship builders. In fact, King George's broad arrow emblem, a vertical line tipped with an upside down V, was visible on the foremast. Lovell looked forward to seeing those magnificent sails unfurl and the ship head out in a southerly direction toward the horse latitudes—somewhere between 30 degrees north and 30 degrees south, where the tradewinds still blew.

William had mixed feelings about this maritime journey and the unknown adventures that awaited him. He wasn't worried about the sea. All of the days he had spent on the water with his father had made him a knowledgeable and able-bodied sailor, but he had always come home to a warm supper and the comfort of his own bed…and Fanny.

"Say, Will!" A familiar voice interrupted his thoughts. "What are you doing down here?"

"Jack?!" William quickly turned to discover a young friend, also from Lynn. He too carried a bag. "Jack Herbert?!"

"In the flesh." Jack showed a toothy grin while offering his free hand.

"I can't ever recall seeing you at the docks." William gave him a mighty handshake. "Do you work here now?"

"Not exactly." Jack nervously ran his fingers through his blond locks. "I'm boarding the *Royal Kent* and going out to sea today."

"What about your mother?" William asked. "She'll be all alone."

"It was her idea," Jack shrugged. "She thought I might be better off sailing away on a ship versus staying here and fighting in a war."

"Well, I'm heading for the *Kent* myself."

"You don't say?!" The young man seemed genuinely surprised. "I never thought I'd see the day that you would up and leave Fanny."

"Fanny encouraged me to go and get a little adventure out of my system before the wedding. So here we are."

"Then what are we waiting for?" Jack whooped, smiling. "Let's climb on board and have ourselves an adventure!"

The *Royal Kent* had been privately commissioned by a wealthy plantation owner to carry fur pelts to his business partner in the Dominican Republic. At least that's what William and Jack had been told, though they both wondered why anyone would need fur in such a tropical climate. Neither asked questions--they were just happy to be part of a real crew and anxious to set sail.

About a dozen tars were already on board along with their captain, James Tobin, and his three officers. Captain Tobin was a paternal sort of man who took a keen interest in his crew, making the men loyal and devoted to him. Behind his back, they usually referred to him as 'Father Tobin'. He knew, of course, but never let on and secretly enjoyed his unofficial title. He offered praise and criticism in equal amounts, encouraging the old salts to mentor the greenies.

The crew wore no specific uniform, but Tobin and his officers donned bright red jackets with navy blue trousers. Only Tobin sported a matching three-cornered hat. All men were armed in case of attack as they only had room for two six-pound cannons, which wouldn't provide much defense against a larger ship. Each crew member was required to learn all jobs and work started immediately—even before they sailed. First, however, William and Jack were taken below decks and shown their assigned bunks. The berths were tight, but neither man minded the lack of space. It was a small price to pay for the experience of a lifetime.

⚓

When the *Royal Kent* sailed out of the Boston Harbor that fine summer day, all aboard anticipated they would dock in a fortnight at Puerto Plata, which was located on the northern seaboard of the Dominican Republic. Aside from William and Jack, there was one other newcomer on board—Samuel Breed, a young man from Boston with thick black hair that hung well past his collar. His dark-colored skin gave away his Native American roots. He had been raised in the city by affluent parents who took him in after the French and Indian War left him orphaned. He knew nothing about life on the sea, but had dreamed of being a sailor ever since he was a lad. He had often gone down to the docks just to watch the ships as they sailed to and from the harbor. Breed was a quick study and the three trainees soon bonded as they worked together learning the rig and the ship's nuances, not to mention the crew's peculiarities. Since William was the most experienced, both Samuel and Jack looked to him for guidance.

For the most part, life at sea was good as the sturdy vessel cut through the calm water on a port tack, with an east/southeast wind of 10 to 15 knots. The small ship moved along at four to six knots depending on the waning tradewinds. Being June already, it was late in the shipping season and the *Kent* was sailing south into the Gulf Stream. Hurricanes were about to make their annual appearance as the hot summer months gave way to unreliable winds and the crew was anxious to reach Puerto Plata before any storms developed.

'June too soon; July stand by; August come it must...,' sailors would say about hurricanes in the lower latitudes, but no hurricane could scare William. He had experienced some of Mother Nature's worst storms off the coast of New England, where weather could get vicious even without a hurricane. He even sailed in a few 'perfect storms' when the weather caught the fishermen by surprise. Now, he secretly wished for at least a minor squall. Heavy winds and high seas would make a great story for Fanny, even if he had to embellish a bit.

While the ship sailed steadily over the insignificant three and four foot waves of the Atlantic, trimming and maintenance were ongoing with sails in need of repair, as well as, rigging to resplice. The younger men with the best eyesight shared look-out duty in the crow's nest. During daylight hours, Jack Herbert was given the important task of turning the marine sandglass every half hour as soon as it emptied. Another crew member relieved him after dark. This apparatus not only kept track of time, but along with the ship's log, helped the navigator stay on course. Food was kept in barrels and the crew often dined on such fare as groats and pickled herring—even for breakfast, but no one complained. When nightfall crept in, those sailors not on duty slept well, as their bunks gently swayed to the tranquil summer seas.

Unlike the long transatlantic passages that took months to complete, this voyage was a relatively short one so sickness was not a major concern. The *Royal Kent* suffered no rough seas and enjoyed a fair wind that kept her moving along at a fair clip, even as she cruised through the northern horse latitudes—an area notorious for becalming ships--sometimes as long as several weeks. Some say the horse latitudes earned their name from the many Spanish ships that stalled in the area due to a lack of winds. These ships often carried horses meant for their colonies in the West Indies, as well as America. While the sailors remained helplessly afloat, their fresh water supply dwindled. As a result, the horses were the first to go. Thrown overboard to drown, some miraculously survived and swam to shore on the Outer Banks and atolls of the Bahamas and Eastern seaboard where these hearty beasts created small colonies of wild horses on several nearby islands.

The *Kent* had no horses and their adequate water supply made the men grateful for their easy voyage. Their biggest fear during this trek were the ruthless pirates who posed a constant threat to any ship on open waters. These wicked freebooters made no exceptions when choosing their targets. They were always on the lookout for easy prey, making mariners of all nations fair game. The outlaws sailed under various flags—the white lily of France, the crescents of Turkey, the red cross of Great Britain and sometimes even the banner of the church callously displaying the

'Keys of Heaven' from high atop their masts. Their true pirate flag, a blood red pennant, was only raised when an attack was imminent.

The *Kent*'s voyage remained uneventful until they reached the Greater Antilles--a few day's sail from their final destination of the Dominican Republic. Shortly after sunrise, William who was manning the masthead or crow's nest, spotted a suspicious vessel on the horizon. He watched with a sinking feeling as the craft tacked and set sail straight for them. His anxiety eased momentarily when he caught sight of the British flag billowing from the ship's stern, but he kept the ship in his sites.

"Ahoy, mates!' William shouted as the ominous vessel continued toward them. "A ship dead on our starboard bow!"

The men stopped what they were doing to assess the situation. Their curiosity turned to horror as they watched the British flag descend and an ominous crimson flag rise in its place.

"We're under attack!" someone hollered.

"Down on deck, Mr. Lovell!" the captain ordered. "All hands on deck now!"

While William scurried down the mast and the rat lines, the pirate ship gave chase and the *Kent* fell off the wind hoping to outrun the enemy. The *Kent's* two cannonades were loaded and the officers brought out their brace of pistols and cutlasses to ensure that every man was armed. As the pursuing vessel closed in, the marauders fired their guns across the *Kent's* bow signaling Captain Tobin to heave-to, which he did not. Within minutes, the buccaneers fired their cannons, as well as their pistols on the *Kent*, which fired back with its six-pounders. The men choked as thick black smoke and the putrid smell of gun-powder filled the air.

The pirate ship outsized the *Kent* by several hundred tons. Nevertheless, the *Kent's* crew severely damaged the crowded deck of their assailant. It was apparent to Captain Tobin, however, that their attacker was better fitted for battle than the *Kent* and was gaining on them. He watched in despair as the pirates rammed the *Kent's* starboard quarter and then quickly hooked them with several grapnels.

In less than a minute, the pirate captain ordered half his crew to follow him as they stormed the *Kent*. Their formidable leader was a frightening hackneyed pirate who sported a red bandana in lieu of a hat. His long black coat covered his knees and his black leather boots were cuffed over his ankles. One long scar reached from his left eye down to his jaw. The man brandished a sword in his right hand and a pistol in his left as he spat out a flurry of orders to his men. "Kill them all! Take no prisoners! Find the spoils and then waste no time in sinking this poor excuse of a ship!"

The American crew was no match for the raging cutthroats who besieged them. Outnumbered and out-armed, the sailors fought hard to hang on to their ship as well as their lives. There was one brief moment of hopeful victory as Captain Tobin shot the enemy captain. A single bullet struck the sea bandit's forehead, blowing most of his brain onto the deck. The stunned man teetered for a moment and with a look of shock fell dead in his tracks. His men watched in disbelief, then returned a burst of staccato gunfire, leaving Captain Tobin dead as well.

The battle lasted another twelve minutes and when it was over, six sea bandits were killed and, only three American sailors remained alive, but wounded—Jack Herbert, Samuel Breed, and William Lovell. Jack had taken a bullet in his right thigh, while Samuel suffered a severe cut to his face. It was William, however, who had the most serious wound—a shot to the left shoulder just inches from his heart.

The three bloody men were dragged to one side of the deck and held at the point of a pistol by one of the marauders, while his cohorts looted the *Kent*. The bewildered prisoners were surprised to learn that the *Kent* carried no fur, but several chests filled with gold. They had been lied to, but none of that mattered now. Once all of the valuables were transferred to the enemy ship, Jack, Samuel, and William were forced aboard. The pirates then scuttled the *Kent* right where she lay. William watched in pain as the stately merchantman sunk to her watery grave.

⚓

"Welcome aboard the *Crimson Blade*, mates!" A poorly dressed man with dirty brown hair and yellow teeth waved a pistol as he paced in front of Jack, Samuel, and William, who lay bleeding and huddled together on the pirate ship's damaged deck. "Your lives have been spared today because we need replacements."

The three men remained quiet—afraid to speak for fear that they might say the wrong thing and be murdered for it.

"What will it be my good men? Life on the *Crimson Blade* or death at the end of my blade? As I said, we need replacements—not prisoners—so it's your choice. Either way, it makes little difference to us."

Dying was not on anyone's list of preferences after all the three men had just been through. Jack was determined to get home to his mother while Samuel believed that if he could contact his parents, they would pay any price for his safe return. William could think only of Fanny and his promise to return to her.

"We'll join your crew," William spoke up for them, still holding his shoulder as blood oozed between his fingers. "We'll work hard on your ship, but we're not murderers."

The man gave a hearty laugh. "You'll be what we say you'll be! And the minute any one of you refuses, you all die!"

"We can sail and loot," Jack said with a quick glance at

William. "And kill or be killed."

"I see one of you has some brains. "The man marched over to Samuel pointing his pistol directly at the young man.

"We haven't heard from you yet!" he hollered. "Are you willing to be a pirate of the *Crimson Blade?*"

"Yes, I'll go along with my friends, but my parents have money and will pay a fine ransom for all of us if you just let me contact them."

"A ransom?" The man threw back his head and laughed even louder. "Do we look like kidnappers?" he demanded. "We are pirates, my man! We don't negotiate. We plunder. We kill. We rule the seas! Are you three with us or not? I won't be asking again!"

"I wouldn't mind plundering some British ships," William spoke up. "They seem to carry the most cargo."

"Good." The man nodded and put his pistol down. "Aye, aye mate…. the boy's already thinking like a pirate! We like the British ships best! They carry the most treasure, but know that we'll be watching everything you do. One mistake and you're dead men. Understood?"

Jack, Samuel, and William nodded, knowing they had to stay alive at any cost. They silently hoped that one day soon they would have an opportunity to escape and return home.

They were given bandages and allowed to bind their wounds. No further medical attention was offered. They were then assigned the duties of the dead crew members and given their bunks, as well as their meager possessions.

It took some time to gain the trust of the sea bandits, but the three men kept to themselves and quietly did as they were told. Before long, Jack, Samuel, and William fell into a routine of sorts. They pretended to enjoy life on the ship, but were often horrified by the bloodthirsty ways of their wicked shipmates. The pirates were not selective—any ship that crossed their path and could not outsail them fell prey to their violence. Blood was shed and few lives were spared each time they attacked, ransacking all valuables before sinking what was left of the ravaged vessel. William and his friends found some consolation when British ships on their way to the colonies were captured. At least, their weapons and supplies would no longer be in the hands of the Crown.

After witnessing several murderous sprees, William soon realized how lucky he and his two companions had been to survive. For now, life on the *Crimson Blade* was better than no life at all. After a time, the pirates took their presence for granted and paid little attention to them. Still, they had to be careful lest someone overheard their plans to escape.

Jack was eventually assigned to assist the pirate who tended the cannons making sure they were always ready for use, while Samuel worked in the galley. Thanks to William's expertise with navigation—something he'd learned from his father—he was a seasoned tactician and his advanced skills did not go unnoticed on the *Blade*. Captain Pierre Boudreau, a French merchantman of the West Indies turned pirate, noticed William's proficiency one day when he was asked to aid the helmsman with a course for attacking a small Dutch merchant ship.

The vessel was sailing from the Golden Rock of St. Eustatia, the Dutch deep water trading port, and carrying supplies for the Americas. Following William's shrewd advice, the *Blade* stopped the Dutchman with nary a shot fired. From this point on, William replaced the usual tactician, Aime Bellier, who had fallen ill from eating rancid meat. This, of course, enraged Bellier and he quickly became William's worst enemy. William did his best to give the man a wide berth, but on a ship at sea it was often difficult to avoid him. Luckily, the pirate's code of no fighting aboard ship saved him—for a time.

All true pirates needed a hideout and the crew of the *Crimson*

Blade were no different. For their homeport, they chose the small, rocky island of Tortuga—just off the northwest coast of Hispaniola, which was technically held under Haitian rule. The turtle-shaped isle had long been an enclave for pirates in previous centuries, but their numbers had since dwindled. The crew of the *Crimson Blade*, however, were one of the few to still use Tortuga. It was there that they took stock of their spoils, hid from authorities, and waited out the hurricane season, which generally lasted from July through October. Jack, Samuel, and William reluctantly joined in the revelry whenever the *Crimson Blade* was ashore. They were careful to avoid any arguments, and never took sides when the men disagreed with each other—especially after swigging down several bottles of rum. In particular, William tried to keep his distance from Bellier who continued to carry a grudge.

And so it went, month after grisly month, while Jack, Samuel, and William bided their time.

CHAPTER 3

Rumblings of a Rebellion

Back home, tensions grew worse between England and its colonies. The unfairness of the Tea Act only complicated the matter and roused the colonists to retaliate. In New York City and Philadelphia, the imported tea was not accepted and was returned to Great Britain. In Charleston, the tea was left on the docks to rot. The colonists in Boston refused the tea's entry altogether. The trouble prompted Statesman Benjamin Franklin to publish his famous satirical essay: 'Rules by Which a Great Empire May Be Reduced to a Small One', which appeared in a newspaper known as The Public Advertiser on September 11, 1773—four months after William Lovell's departure. Franklin began by saying:

"An ancient Sage valued himself upon this, that tho' he could not fiddle, he knew how to make a *great City* of a *little one*. The Science that I, a modern Simpleton, am about to communicate is the very reverse.

I address myself to all Ministers who have the Management of extensive Dominions, their very Greatness are become troublesome to govern, because the Multiplicity of their Affairs leaves no Time for *fiddling*...."

Franklin went on to admonish the British for treating colonists differently than their very own citizens. He also criticized the Crown for placing governors in the colonies who had no interest in their charges, but only in their personal advancement and riches. In addition, he addressed the unfair taxes that benefited only the British—not the colonists who paid them. His words echoed what was on the minds of many.

While the beginnings of war started to boil, the Campbells and Lovells went on about their daily business—the men fishing, while the women dried and preserved their catch. Conversations about the coming winter and rumors of revolt swirled at their nightly dinner table, but Fanny's thoughts were elsewhere. No one dared mention it, but the family had not heard a word from William since he sailed away on the *Royal Kent*. For the sake of William's mother and Fanny, no one wanted to admit the obvious—William must be dead or they surely would have received at least a letter disclosing his whereabouts by now. Wedding plans were put on hold and talk of marriage came to an end. As each day passed and the temperatures grew cooler, Fanny's heart ached more and more at the thought of William being lost to her. Her only shred of hope was Moll Pitcher's long-ago prediction that William would one day claim her as his bride.

One crisp November morning, Fanny awoke from a dream where she and William sat upon High Rock gazing out to sea. She knew it wasn't real, but that peaceful moment between slumber and wakefulness rekindled her hope that William was alive and would one day return to her. As she lay in bed trying to clear her head, she thought of Moll Pitcher. In all these years since their first meeting, the two women had never exchanged more than a nod or a polite 'hello'. Maybe it was time to change all that. Maybe Fanny should seek counsel with the fortune-teller of Lynn and ask of William's fate. At the very least, Moll might know whether he was dead or alive. Fanny was desperate for news—one way or the other. She told no one of her plans, but she waited impatiently for an afternoon when she would be alone.

⚓

Several days later, while Henry and William prepared their boat for winter, Agnes and Sarah packed a basket of food for Bette Goodson. Mrs. Goodson had been recently widowed when her husband was killed by a British soldier who was too quick to draw his gun. The couple had three children and the fine ladies of Lynn were taking turns helping the family. As soon as the two women left for the Goodson home, Fanny covered her curls with a grey scarf and headed toward High Rock hoping to find Moll Pitcher at home.

Her heart beat even faster than the quick pace she was keeping. What if Moll told her William was dead? How would she cope without him? What if he were alive? How would she find him? Uninvited thoughts thrashed in her mind as she raced along the path. She hadn't come this way since William left. She couldn't bear to climb High Rock alone and none but the desperate paid a personal visit to Moll Pitcher, or so she thought.

When Fanny caught sight of Moll's house, she saw the four Pitcher children playing in the front yard. John, the youngest, held a large gray stone in his upraised hand. Fanny watched as he flung the rock at his three older sisters, who screamed and scattered. Fanny stopped for a moment to gather herself and her courage, while little John turned to study her. With a deep breath, she took several long strides past the boy to Moll's front door. Just as she raised her hand to knock, the door opened. Moll stood in front of her, holding Percy.

"I was wondering when you'd get here," Moll greeted the girl with a slight smile.

"You were expecting me?"

"I was."

"Then you know why I came?"

"I do." Moll stroked the fat cat who, like his mistress, never seemed to age. "Why don't you come in so we can talk?"

Fanny hesitantly crossed the threshold as Moll called out to her children. "Mind your brother, girls! I won't be long."

Fanny found everything the same as she remembered, right down to the black pot boiling in the fireplace. An uneasy feeling settled in her bones. Maybe coming here was a mistake.

"What's wrong, girl?" Moll grinned. "Cat got your tongue?"

"N-no, ma'am." Fanny tried to control her sudden trembling.

"I told you before, I don't eat little girls," Moll laughed.

"I'm not little anymore." Fanny found her voice.

"So I see." Moll motioned for Fanny to sit down on a small wooden stool. Percy jumped from her arms and sidled over to the young woman. He circled her twice and then laid at her feet. "I see Percy remembers you."

"May I pet him?"

"You may, as long as he doesn't mind. Percy doesn't like people much, but you seem to stir up his affections and if Percy likes you then I guess I should like you, too."

"Thank you." Fanny stroked the cat, who purred in contentment. The feel of his soft fur and gentle breathing somehow had a calming effect on her, but she wasn't quite ready to speak.

"While you're making friends with Percy, I'll brew some tea then you can tell me why you're here."

"I....I thought maybe you'd know."

"Well, I know it has something to do with that William Lovell of yours." Moll took five ladles of boiling water from the kettle and poured them into a pot. She then crumbled dark leaves into the vessel and let it steep. Her leisurely manner irritated Fanny until she was about to burst.

"William's missing!" Fanny stopped petting the cat as her words tumbled one over the other. "No one's heard from him since he left and I'm sick with worry. I was hoping that maybe you could tell me what's happened to him and where he is. That is, if he's alive. You see, I have to know or I'll go mad."

Moll closed her eyes, slowly rocking back and forth on her heels while the tea leaves turned the clear water into a deep brown color. Percy impatiently pawed at Fanny, demanding further attention. Still trembling, she reached down and scratched behind his ears and the satisfied cat returned to his supine position. Moll poured them each a cup of tea.

"Drink up, my girl." She smiled for the first time. "Your William is alive, but I'll have a look at your tea leaves before I say more."

He was alive! That's all Fanny wanted to hear, but she graciously accepted the steaming cup from Moll. Something about the tea and the cat calmed Fanny, as she enjoyed the warmth of the brew. The two women drank in silence and when Fanny was through, Moll peered inside her cup.

"Your William is still at sea."

"But he's alive?"

"Yes, but he sails with a crew of demons and cutthroats."

"Then he's in trouble? Tell me where he is! When will he come home?"

Holding up her hand to silence the girl, Moll put the cup down in front of her. "You and only you must bring him home, child, but the time isn't right yet. You must wait."

"But I'm tired of waiting. Why won't you help me?"

"You asked me if your lover was dead or alive. I answered

your question. Now it's time for you to go."

"But how will I know when the time is right and how on earth can I ever bring him home?"

"One day in the future a message will come from a country far away where English is not the native tongue. When you receive this news, come back to this house and I will help you prepare for the greatest challenge of your life."

"But how can I bring him home?" Fanny was confused.

"For now, learn all that you can about the sea."

"But women don't go to sea."

"Ah, but Fanny…you are no ordinary woman."

⚓

Following her visit with Moll, Fanny immersed herself in studies of the sea. She read books on navigation, sailing, and even ship-building. Whenever she went to Boston to study with the preacher, she insisted on learning all she could about the oceans. She researched practical navigation and weather cycles as well as the winds and tides. She borrowed as many books as she could find about maritime life and law and carefully read them, making notes to keep for later reference. With the fishing season nearly over, she could not set sail with her father, but she made him promise that in the spring, he would teach her to sail their schooner. Both the Lovells and Campbells were surprised at Fanny's new obsession, but they said not a word. They believed the poor girl was just trying to find something new to dwell on in place of William's probable demise.

Captain Burnett was another matter entirely. Since the Crown's enemy was ashore and not at sea, the British officer was assigned to guard Boston Harbor. This permanent duty gave him more time ashore and he ventured frequently to Lynn hoping to gain Fanny's favor now that William had disappeared. To Burnett's delight, the girl spent more time with him than she ever had in the past. Even though she still received him on the same terms—as a friend and intellectual companion—she seemed happy to see him. She always spoke of the sea, peppering him with questions about his cutter and demanding he share all he knew about nautical routines and maritime strategy. Encouraged by her enthusiasm he did his best to impress her with his knowledge. He even tried on several occasions to woo her, but each time Fanny silenced him with a reproachful look or a clever remark that quickly changed the subject.

One evening after being spurned yet again by Fanny, Burnett confessed to Henry that he would gladly give up his commission if she would only give him her heart.

"I believe to win Fanny," Henry advised the captain, "you'll have to turn rebel."

"And I would, sir, if I thought for a moment I had any chance with your daughter. Unfortunately, she still clings to Lovell, whom we all know must have fallen prey to pirates or man-eating sharks by now."

"I was always fond of William," Henry sighed. "Watched the boy grow up. Part of me wants to believe that he is still on some great adventure."

"No man in his right mind would willingly stay away this long from a woman like Fanny. If only I could find proof of his death."

"It might give Fanny and Sarah some peace of mind if they were to finally know the truth."

"Maybe then Fanny would stop pining for a dead man and agree to marry me."

Burnett remained hopeful and his visits to Lynn continued. He even confessed to Fanny that he thought the Continentals may be partially right in their discontent with the Crown. Though neither her parents nor William's ever interfered, gossip about Fanny and Burnett tittered throughout the town. Had Fanny given up on William? Was she falling for the handsome captain? If she did marry Burnett, what would happen if William returned? And what about her sudden passion for all things nautical? Her new fascination inflamed the good captain's desire. At the same time, her reluctance toward him did nothing to deter his efforts.

⚓

Six months after William's departure, Henry Campbell and William Lovell disguised themselves as Native Americans. They then joined Samuel Adams and other members of The Sons of Liberty at Boston Harbor on the night of December 16, 1773 in a rebellious effort of protest against the unpopular Tea Act. Under cover of darkness, the men stealthily approached Griffin's Wharf, boarded several British merchant ships and tossed more than 300 chests of tea into the salty harbor. What would later be called 'The Boston Tea Party' enraged the British.

As the new year began, a Loyalist named John Malcolm, who worked for the British customs service, found himself in a messy situation. The colonists disliked him because of his vociferous animosity towards them. On the evening of January 25, 1774, Malcolm was spotted by shoemaker George Robert Twelves Hewes (also a participant in the Boston Tea Party) as he threatened a young boy with his cane. When Hewes tried to stop the man, Malcolm knocked him unconscious. For his malicious deed, Malcolm was tarred and feathered by an angry mob of rebels.

When news of the colonists' insurrection reached England, Parliament enacted several more bills including the Boston Port Act, effectively shutting down Boston Harbor with a naval blockade until restitution for the lost tea was made to the king's treasury. To make matters worse, the British also passed The Massachusetts Government Act seizing control from the local authorities and relocating the seat of government from Boston to Salem. These and other discriminatory measures that followed further outraged the colonists who referred to these new laws as 'The Intolerable Acts'.

Now, there was no turning back—a rebellion was in the making. Blood would be shed and lives lost, but would a new country emerge from the rubble?

CHAPTER 4

<u>A Pirate's Life</u>

While the colonists pledged their allegiance to America, William, Samuel, and Jack were forced to place their left hands on a human skull and swear an oath of loyalty to the pirate crew. They were then made to sign the *Crimson Blade's* Articles of Agreement—a contract establishing the ship's rules and the allotment of any booty the crew might obtain. For the *Crimson Blade*, the Articles read as follows:

The crew of the *Crimson Blade* hereby agrees to the following:

--Compensation is given to the Captain for the use of his ship, and the shipwright, who takes care of the vessel.

—A standard compensation is provided for permanently injured crew members as follows:

--the loss of a right arm, six hundred pieces of eight;

--the loss of a left arm, five hundred pieces of eight;

--the loss of a right leg, five hundred pieces of eight;

--the loss of a left leg, four hundred pieces of eight;

--the loss of an eye or finger, one hundred pieces of eight.

--Shares of all booty taken are provided as follows:

--the Captain is allotted five or six portions of the spoils;

--the Master's Mate and senior men, two portions each;

--any new men, one portion each.

--Any man caught stealing, even the slightest of treasure, will be separated from the group immediately.

--Any man who tries to run away shall be marooned with one Bottle of Powder, one Bottle of Water, one small Arm, and Shot.

-- Any man who smokes tobacco in the hold without a cap on his pipe shall receive Moses' Law (39 lashes) on the bare Back.

--Any man, who meddles with a woman without her consent, will be shot.

--Every man has a vote in affairs of the moment.

--No man is to play cards or dice for money.

--All men must keep their piece, pistols, and cutlass clean and fit for service.

--No boy or woman is allowed on board; any man found seducing a woman or carrying her to sea in disguise, shall suffer death.

--Any man deserting the ship or their quarters in battle will be punished with marooning or death.

--There will be no fighting on board ship; quarrels are to be ended on shore, with sword or pistol.

William was surprised to find that these ruthless sea bandits actually had a code of honor. Their methods, as outlined, appeared far more democratic than traditional ships since all the men had a say in most activities on board. They even held elections to determine who would be captain. They could also vote their leader out at any time if they were dissatisfied with the way he ran things. The captain was required to fight alongside his men and, in battle his word was final so as not to cause any further confusion during times of action.

William was also startled to learn that a British medical doctor, George Carleton, was being held on board against his will. The physician was forced to treat injured crew members, but not allowed to give aid to William, Samuel, or Jack since they were not fully accepted into the fold just yet. Word on the *Crimson Blade* was that Dr. Carleton would most likely be released the next time they were ashore on Hispaniola—a common practice when it came to a prisoner they valued.

Slaves were another matter entirely. The crew of the *Crimson Blade* usually freed most slaves found aboard any ships they encountered. They did, however, keep two young boys as indentured crew after overtaking a slave ship near the horse latitudes several months earlier. These children couldn't speak English and were relegated to the galley where they helped with the men's mess—making them the only exception to the *Blade's* code of conduct concerning boys. It was obvious to William that the lads, who couldn't have been more than ten years old, were frightened, as they kept to themselves and did what they were told as best as they could. William was touched by their situation and befriended them, nicknaming them Josh and Levi. The youngsters, who were starved for affection, followed William around when they weren't preparing meals. As time went on, William spent some evenings reading to them and teaching them the English alphabet. The other men snickered at the sight of their lessons, but no one stopped them and for that William was grateful. Despite the language barrier, the children proved to be quick learners and William knew that Fanny would be pleased with his efforts.

That particular season, the crew weathered out several tropical storms and one weak hurricane in the small, protected harbor on the leeward side of Tortuga Island. The impregnable haven, fresh water, and safe anchorage offered the perfect hurricane hole in that part of the Caribbean. The head of the Windward Passage also provided the perfect vantage point to spot fully loaded ships heading to or from Europe. Canal de la Tortue, the channel located between the islands of Tortuga and Hispaniola, was less than eight miles wide. Should the men need more rum or gunpowder from the small town of Port-de-Paix, located on the opposite side of the strait, the trip over would be a quick one.

William reckoned that he could swim across the channel, but he was uncertain whether his two companions might go the distance. One night while most others were sleeping, William signaled to Jack and Samuel to join him in a secluded spot below decks. It was often their habit to stay up late so they could talk privately.

"What do you fellows think about swimming for Port-de-Paix?" William whispered as the three men huddled together in the dark.

"I'm not sure I could swim that far," Samuel admitted. "But I'd be willing to try. Better to be dead in the water than living with these barbarians. I've seen enough bloodshed to last an eternity."

"I think we should bide our time," Jack offered with a shrug. "Port-de-Paix is part of Haiti, which is still pirate territory so even if we made it there, they could find us."

"And then we would have hell to pay," William agreed. "Maybe the risk isn't worth it. They would never trust us again and probably kill us for being disloyal."

"I can't live like this much longer." Samuel's eyes looked weary. "There must be something we can do."

"How about we wait until the *Blade* gets closer to Cuba?"

William suggested. "Maybe we could swim to Havana for help."

"Much better plan." Jack smoothed his dark locks with his fingers. "I've heard talk that Cuba doesn't welcome pirates. Once we explain our situation, maybe the officials there will even help us get home."

"We can only pray they will." William closed his eyes. "I miss Lynn.... especially Fanny. What do you boys miss most about home?"

"I miss the freedom," Jack volunteered. "And I am terribly worried about my mother. For all I know, she could be dead by now."

"I miss everything about Boston," Samuel sighed. "Even the British soldiers."

"Then Cuba it is," William announced. "We will jump ship in the middle of the night once we are close enough to Havana."

With that being settled, William's biggest problem remained Bellier's continued wrath. It wasn't always easy to avoid the angry man.

⚓

While ashore and bored, the crew drank heavily to pass away the time. Gambling was not allowed on board or off, so the men contented themselves with friendly sharpshooting competitions or affable challenges like who could chop the most wood in a minute. No prizes were given—just the satisfaction of being the best, if only for a day. Hunting wild pigs introduced by the Spanish was another favorite sport as the pirates waited to sail. There was always meat roasting on the fire or smoking for later use. Their favorite part was the marrow, which they sucked from the bone of pretty much any animal they caught—a true pirate delicacy. In addition, native guinea fowl, chickens, and other wild birds were easy prey, as well as tasty.

The men rarely washed and the pungent odors that lingered around them were unbearable to William and his companions. Being a fisherman at heart, William inconspicuously bathed on a regular basis while swimming to spear fish. Since most of the pirates preferred meat, the three colonists usually had their fill of fresh fish, making them feel a little closer to home. William salted and dried any extra fish as they did back home—a skill he passed on to Josh and Levi. They prepared a nice store of saltfish for later use, which to the Americans was a huge improvement over the brittle hardtack and rancid meats served onboard at sea. Between the abundant fish, fruit, and coconuts, William, Jack and Samuel found life on the island to be much more pleasurable than life aboard the *Crimson Blade*, as they waited for their chance to escape.

Many of the sea bandits took prostitutes as wives—the women mostly willing to go along with buccaneers. The women stayed onshore, cooking and maintaining the settlement while the pirates were out marauding and stealing treasure. While most of these harlots came from Port Royal, Jamaica and were shared by several men, the captain kept the most beautiful wench all to himself. In addition, he claimed one of the few structures in the harbor as his private quarters. His 'wife' made certain that no other siren laid claim to her man, nor her house.

William, Jack, and Samuel were not interested in taking harlot-wives. They chose to stick together and spent hours practicing sword fighting. It was a skill-set they had yet to master and it helped them feel more confident when wielding a cutlass. They knew that dexterity and proficiency with these weapons would come in handy during a future battle and could likely save their lives. Although the three men were not big drinkers, they imbibed a little when prompted by the crew who especially enjoyed downing a deadly mixture of rum and gunpowder. Of course, the toxic concoction killed a few pirates here and there, but that did not deter them from consuming the hazardous brew—it only made them crazy enough to fight and kill one another when boredom overtook good sense on a monotonous afternoon.

⚓

It had been a long, hot, bug-filled hurricane season. The men grew restless—anxious to return to sea, where they could plunder unsuspecting ships filled with needed supplies, valuables, and gold. After hunkering down for several days while waiting out a moderate tropical storm, the men were relieved to find their ship damage-free and still safely moored in the harbor. The high winds, however, had stripped much of the foliage from the trees, leaving few places for the wild pigs to hide, therefore, a massive hunt was in order. When the men returned with their kill, they celebrated with rowdy abandon as meat sizzled on the spit and rum flowed freely. Unfortunately, a bit too much of the volatile black powder found its way into their drink and the men were, to say the least—crazed.

William, Jack, and Samuel did their best to avoid the mêlée, but these raucous men were ruthless when it came to testing the worth of the latest members of their crew. Only those who proved their mettle would be initiated into the 'Brethren of the Coast'—a loose league of outlaws that dominated the seas. This practice included the formal settling of scores since fighting between the men aboard ship was strictly forbidden. Once ashore, however, everyone was fair-game as long as the pirate code was followed.

After imbibing heavily in the gun-powder cocktail, a very drunk Bellier approached William as he sat with Jack and Samuel observing the boisterous men.

"It's time I regain my rightful place on the *Blade*." Bellier spat on the ground near William's feet.

"What do you have in mind?" William stood up, knowing what was to come. He was a head taller than the mangy Frenchman and much younger and fitter.

"I plan to finish our unsettled business, my boy," Bellier grinned up at him, baring toothless gums. He then turned to the larger group and hollered, "I challenge this man to a duel at dawn! The winner, which will be me, regains his position on board the ship. The loser, which will not be me, will find eternal rest on this godforsaken island!"

A loud cheer went up from the pirates and their women. The excitement of a duel was just what they needed to relieve their land-bound tedium.

William understood that the pirates upheld a strict code when it came to dueling, a fact that gave him some relief since a loose cannon like Bellier could not otherwise be trusted. As the rules went, the quartermaster oversaw the contest and placed the two men back-to-back with dueling pistols. He then counted off ten paces before giving the command to turn and fire. If the first shots did not end the matter, with one of the two wounded or dead, then the use of swords followed. William had been a crack shot ever since he was a boy and he felt quite confident that his marksmanship would trump this drunken fool's ability to even walk the ten paces. Jack and Samuel, however, fearful for their friend's life, tried their best to stop the clash.

"You know you don't have to do this," Jack told William. "Just give Bellier back his position aboard the ship."

"Backing down is not an option." William shook his head. "If I don't fight him now, he'll find a way to kill me in my sleep."

"What can we do to help you?" Samuel asked.

"Just promise that on the chance I'm mortally wounded, one of you will find a way to tell Fanny that I love her. And, if I linger suffering, then finish me."

"Your first request is a simple one if I ever escape and return home," Jack sighed. "But, I could never kill you, my friend... no matter the circumstances. How could I face Fanny and your parents knowing I was the one who ended your life?"

"It won't come to that," William reassured Jack. "I can handle a gun, but if my aim is off, I beg you not to let me suffer. Fanny will understand and so will my mother and father. I believe they will even thank you."

"How did we end up in this mess?" Samuel shook his head with a woeful face.

"If I remember correctly," William grinned, "we were all looking for adventure."

Word spread quickly around the pirate camp and by dawn, a crowd of voyeurs had formed on the beach. Most did not care who won and since betting was forbidden, they simply cheered for the duel itself. The air was already hot and stifling as Bellier and William stood back-to-back in the sand—each man holding a pistol on one side and a sword on the other. The men grew quiet as the quartermaster started his count. "One...two...three..."

William, who had not over-imbibed the night before, knew he held the advantage over the still inebriated Bellier as the two paced off. The few swigs of rum that William consumed earlier to settle his nerves had quickly worn off, considering the sobering circumstances, and sweat ran from his temples as he took each step. The quartermaster's voice remained steady—"Seven... eight...nine..."

William took a deep breath.

"Ten!"

William spun on his heel, aimed the pistol, and fired before Bellier could fully make the 180-degree turn. The single bullet bored directly into Bellier's left shoulder, missing his mark since Bellier was not yet fully facing him. This, however, did not deter Bellier from firing his gun. Luckily, the shot went wild, missing William entirely—nearly taking out a large monkey in a nearby tree. Fulfilling his duty, the quartermaster knocked the weapon from Bellier's hand, proclaiming William the victor. But, as William turned to Jack and Samuel with a sigh of relief, the now fully enraged, Bellier lifted his sword with his remaining good arm and sliced a shallow gash down William's back.

Unaware he was bleeding, William was quick to retaliate as he drew his own sword from its scabbard and with a blow to Bellier's right side, cut him deeply. The quartermaster tried to intervene and end the duel, but Bellier attacked him, slashing the officer's jaw. William had done his best to avoid killing his opponent, but now he had no choice. The months spent learning to wield his sword had paid off and within seconds William inflicted a mortal wound through Bellier's gut. The man fell to the ground, writhing in pain surrounded by an oozing puddle of his own blood. It was the worst kind of death imaginable.

"Finish me," he taunted William with a gasp. "Or are you not man enough to do it?" William stood over the wounded man considering the thought. He raised his sword for an instant before throwing it down in the sand.

"I will not waste another breath on the likes of you," he said as he turned and strode away, giving his friends a nod. Another man stepped forward, picked up William's discarded sword and in one swift stroke cut Bellier's head from his tortured body.

Now accepted into the 'Brethren of the Coast', William instantly became a well-respected member of the crew and by association, Jack and Samuel were treated with the same high regard.

⚓

Seven months into their unwanted service, William, Jack and Samuel once again set sail aboard the *Crimson Blade*. The Pirates were on a new mission to find unwitting merchant ships heading to or from the West Indies. The tradewinds had resumed their reliable breeze and many a mercantile vessel rode the waves through the Windward Passage. The sea bandits had also learned that, due to the growing unrest in the American colonies, many of these ships were now laden with a great store of munitions. The *Crimson Blade* had barely made it into the shipping channels along the north coast of Cuba when the pirate's lookout set his spyglass upon a schooner. Within seconds, the captain ordered the pirate flag raised and pursued the vessel, which was at a disadvantage due to the tonnage she carried.

"Ha!" the captain roared. "She'll be a rich prize with such a load in her belly! My guess would be gunpowder and rifles if me nose be right. I can smell black powder a mile downwind!" The men laughed with glee at the thought of all the weaponry that would soon be in their hands. Within minutes, the *Blade* overtook the schooner and fired once across her deck as a warning. Knowing they had little chance of escape, the schooner turned into the wind and sat in-irons as the outlaw ship slid alongside. The pirate crew threw grappling hooks over her port rail and it took only seconds for the marauders to swarm her decks and cut down most of the sailors aboard.

Within minutes, the decks were drenched with blood and the majority of the ship's crew lay dead. Replacements were still needed on the *Blade* so some of the younger, more trainable men were taken captive, much as William, Jack, and Samuel had once been. The captain had been right—the ill-fated ship carried tons of black powder, but the weaponry stowed aboard was the greatest prize of all. The schooner was making a delivery to the British soldiers stationed in Boston. This news gave William and his companions great pleasure to learn they had thwarted the delivery of much-needed munitions for the British army. They felt that they had at least played a small hand in aiding their countrymen back home. The British would never be able to use these weapons against the colonists. No doubt, the Sons of Liberty would be pleased.

While the men carried the booty to their ship, William and Jack were assigned the task of searching the officers' quarters for valuables. While William searched the quartermaster's cabin, Jack entered the captain's berth. He thought he'd heard a muffled cry and stopped to listen. There it was again! Someone was hiding behind an Oriental screen that had been dragged to one corner of the small room. Clutching his pistol, he strode over to the partition and flung it aside. To his great surprise, a beautiful, but terrified, young woman cowered on her knees before him. Her large blue eyes focused squarely at his gun, much like a frightened doe caught in the crosshairs of a hunting musket. Jack was speechless and it took a moment for him to find his voice. "It….it's all right, ma'am. I won't hurt you. Please don't be afraid."

"I will give you all my jewels and any gold I have if you would only spare my life." She spoke with a refined English accent. "I am on my way to the new world, where my father has arranged for me to marry a captain in the king's army—a man I have never met. In any case, my father has provided a generous dowry. You can have it all, I swear!"

"You needn't be afraid," Jack's voice softened as he looked down on the trembling girl before him. She wore her golden hair swept up on her head in a feminine bouffant and she was dressed in fine blue satin marking her as a woman of privilege and wealth.

"Then why won't you put your gun down?" she asked with a catch in her voice.

Poor Jack hadn't even realized that he was still pointing his pistol directly at her. He quickly tucked the weapon in his belt and offered his hand. She stood barely reaching his shoulder and a tenderness he had never felt before shot through him. He had heard about love at first sight, but never really believed it was possible—at least not until today. "I assure you, my lady, that I wish you no harm. You see, my friends and I are also being held against our will by this band of pirates. I promise to do everything in my power to keep you safe, but you must do as I say."

"I won't give up my virtue that easily," she peered straight into his eyes. "Especially to a buccaneer."

"Believe me, I am not a buccaneer by choice nor will I compromise your virtue and the pirates pillaging this vessel do have a code of honor when it comes to women. Now, please put together your personal belongings and I will escort you back to our ship."

"And then what will happen to me?" she demanded.

"I will personally ask the captain to put you safely ashore in Jamaica or Haiti. From there, you should be able to make your way to the colonies."

"If you can assure my safety, I will be forever in your debt."

"I will protect you with my life, ma'am," Jack promised with a quick bow. "As I said, there is some semblance of honor among these men and I believe they will respect your well-being. They are not in the business of harming women, certainly none as beautiful as you. Might I ask your name?"

"I am Marion Charlotte Ashton, daughter of Lord and Lady Ashton." She extended her hand. "What may I call you, sir?"

"Jack….Jack Herbert at your service, ma'am."

Jack soon left Marion alone to gather her things while he went looking for William. He found William next door, still searching the quartermaster's cabin. Without a word, Jack pulled his friend into the captain's room. Marion stiffened with fear at the sight of the two men.

"It's all right, Miss Marion," Jack gave a little bow. "William here is my friend and you can trust him with your life. William, this is Marion Charlotte Ashton. She is on her way to Boston to marry a captain in the British army."

"Ma'am, I can't approve of your choice in men, but I can say that your presence here is certainly unexpected and may present a problem." William turned to Jack. "What are we going to do with her?"

"I have given her my word that we will protect her and see to it that she finds safe passage to America."

"And how do you propose we do that?"

"We must convince the captain to allow her aboard so that we might escort her safely to a port from which she can sail north."

"I'm not sure that the idea of a woman on board will go over with the crew," William said hesitantly.

"After that incident with Bellier, you are the one with the in-fluence," Jack reminded him. "I think you ought to talk to the captain."

"I can't make any promises." William looked from Marion to Jack and then back to Marion. "But if you are willing to take a message to our families, I will see what I can do."

"Yes, of course," Marion nodded. "I understand you are being held against your will."

"We are," William sighed. "It's been so long, I'm afraid our loved ones must think we are dead."

"Then I must correct their thinking." Marion smiled for the first time. "It's the least I can do for the men who have come to my rescue."

"My Fanny will be relieved to know I am alive." William smiled, too.

"And just who might be waiting for you back home?" Marion raised her eyebrows at Jack.

"Only my mother," Jack grinned with a wink.

"Then I will set her mind at ease once I have reached the safety of the colonies."

"My lady," Jack sighed. "From what we hear of the war between the Crown and the colonies, I'm not quite certain that you will be safe there either."

While Jack and Marion waited on the schooner, William sought out the *Blade*'s captain. Ever since his recent victory with Bellier, William carried far more weight aboard ship. Even so, it took some serious discussion with the captain to persuade him to allow Marion on the *Blade*. William argued that they could take the lady directly to Port Royal where they planned to sail anyway in order to trade their newest cache of weapons for gold and other provisions. The captain was hesitant, but agreed only if the other men concurred since they all had a say in the decisions made on their ship—especially one that would allow a woman on board, even for a few days. Female passengers, no matter the circumstances, were forbidden by the code. However, not one man wanted to break the rule which prohibited the harming of a woman.

Thus, it was with great reluctance that the captain surrendered his cabin to their newest passenger until they could see her safely to port. Hosting a woman on the *Blade* was certainly an unexpected turn of events, but William and Jack were impressed with the discretion the men showed Marion. They all felt that it was extremely bad luck to have her on their ship—all except for Jack, William, and Samuel, that is. During the few days it took to sail around Cuba and back through the Windward Passage to the east end of Jamaica, Marion Ashton found the reassuring company of the smitten Jack Herbert calming.

William had other plans for the lovely lady. He penned a letter to Fanny explaining their circumstances, with instructions for Marion on how to locate the Lovell and Campbell home. Jack then managed to slip the message into Marion's belongings without anyone being the wiser.

CHAPTER 5

Good News

Fanny was exhausted and sick with worry. It had been more than a year since she'd seen or heard from William Lovell. Even his parents believed he was dead, but Fanny refused to give in to such morbid, negative thoughts. She would know if William was no longer alive. She would feel such a great loss in her heart. Besides, Moll had told her that William would return one day and marry her. The fortune-teller's prediction was the one hope that Fanny clung to, since she knew Moll's incredible reputation for accuracy.

As Fanny struggled with her own troubles, civil unrest swirled all around her. The animosity between Great Britain and the colonies increased on a daily basis. Tension heightened even more during the summer of 1774 when, on July 2, the British passed The Quartering Act, which forced the colonists to provide English soldiers with housing whenever they demanded it. Now, it seemed that Americans were no longer entitled to privacy in their own homes.

The Sons of Liberty gathered more frequently at the old Tunnel Meeting House in Lynn. Henry Campbell and his fishing partner, William Lovell, attended each and every one of the meetings. Time after time, Fanny begged her father to take her along, but he always refused, saying such formidable talk of war was only meant for the ears of men. Desperate to take some form of action, Fanny slipped into young William's room to find clothing that would help disguise her as a member of the opposite sex and, at the very least, someone allowed to listen in on the discussions of war. She shortened William's trousers and rolled up his shirt sleeves. Dressed as a boy with her long hair tucked neatly under a black cap, she fooled even her father when she entered the meeting hall for the very first time. Her initial success at remaining undetected gave her confidence and she continued to attend the gatherings—always staying inconspicuously in the back of the room. She even came to like dressing as a man, feeling more and more comfortable in her male guise, but no matter how many meetings she attended, she never spoke out. Fanny always sat back and listened carefully to the men as they talked over current events. To her delight, no one paid any attention to an adolescent boy who had nothing to say.

Late one Friday evening in mid-July, 1774, Fanny was up to her elbows in fish scales. The catch had been good that week and more than the usual amount of fish were waiting to be cleaned and dried. Weary from the work, Fanny felt as if these creatures were multiplying just like they had in the Bible. Also exhausted, Agnes and Sarah prepared the fish for drying as Fanny cleaned them. None of the women complained, but Fanny secretly wished she had something far more exciting to do.

While the women worked, Henry and William sat near the unlit hearth. They talked quietly about their latest Sons of Liberty meeting. They'd had a long day of fishing and were glad to be home. Tomorrow morning they would be up before dawn and out to sea again. They had to take full advantage of the warmer months because during the winter season, there would be no sailing and no fish to sell. Besides, the political climate was worsening and who knew what might lay ahead in the coming months.

An unexpected knock on the front door interrupted the normalcy of the day.

"Who could that be at this hour?' Sarah glanced over at the men.

"I hope it's not bad news." William got up and opened the door.

"Good evening, sir." A petite girl with long blond hair and a British accent gave a slight bow. She wore a long blue dress and dainty blue shoes that were caked with mud. "Would this be the home of Miss Fanny Campbell?"

"I'm Fanny Campbell." Fanny dropped her knife on the table and wiped both hands on her soiled apron before she joined William, Sr. at the door. The smell of dead fish wafted after her.

"Forgive me for arriving at this late hour, Miss Campbell, but I came straight from Boston, and I'm afraid I didn't even take time to make myself presentable."

"Do I know you?" Fanny tilted her head to one side, confused.

"No ma'am, we've never met, but I feel as if I know you after everything William has told me."

"William?!" Fanny gasped. "You know my William?" She grabbed the girl's arm and pulled her inside. Henry bolted from his chair while Sarah and Agnes rushed in from the kitchen.

"You have news of my boy?!" The words flew from Sarah's mouth.

"I have better than news," the girl smiled. "I have a letter from William."

"Come and sit down, child." Agnes gestured toward the table that was still full of dead fish.

"If it's all the same to you, I'd rather not."

"Of course! Of course!" Henry offered his chair. "By all means, sit down. Rest your feet, but please tell us everything you know about William." But before the poor girl could speak, the Lovells and Campbells peppered her with questions.

"Where is he?"

"How is he?"

"Where has he been?"

"Why hasn't he written?"

"Is he well?"

"Is he safe?"

"Is he coming home?"

"I promise to answer all of your questions, but first let me explain how I came to find you. I am Lady Marion Ashton and a number of weeks ago, I sailed from England. I was coming to Boston to be married, but my ship was attacked by a band of pirates. I thought they would kill me, but three kind gentlemen saved my life and your William was one of them." Marion proceeded to tell the story of how she met Jack, William, and Samuel. Her audience was spellbound and listened in silence as she described just what had turned the three men into pirates. "They are all desperate to come home," Marion concluded her tale. "Jack is worried sick about his mother and Samuel misses Boston. William thinks only of you, Fanny...and his parents, of course...but he fears he may be too late and that you have given up and married someone else."

"I assure you, Miss Ashton," Fanny said through happy tears. "I have never once thought about another man!"

"Please, call me Marion."

"All right, Marion," Fanny wiped her eyes. "But did you say

you had a letter?"

"Yes." Marion reached into her pocket and held out a small envelope to Fanny. "It's addressed to you."

Fanny immediately recognized William's handwriting and tore the letter open.

Sarah took a deep breath. "Read it out loud."

Fanny's trembling hands could barely unfold the paper, but her voice was steady as she began:

My darling Fanny,

I hope this letter makes it from my hands to yours.

Not a day goes by that I don't think of you. I assure you that I am trying my hardest to come home and I pray that someday soon we can be together as we always planned.

I am being held on a pirate ship called the *Crimson Blade*. Please don't worry. I am safe even though I keep company with sea bandits. Jack Herbert and Samuel Breed are here too…you must help Marion get word to their families that they are alive and well.

We are planning to make our escape as soon as the ship gets close enough to Cuba that we might all three swim ashore to safety. We hope to find a frigate in Havana Harbor that will bring us back to Boston. In the meantime, please pray for us and be kind to Marion, as she has proven to be a good friend…especially to Jack. I believe he's smitten with her like a schoolboy.

Tell my parents, I am well and with God's grace, I
will see them and you soon.

As for you my dearest, please know that my love
has never wavered. The thought of you is what
keeps me going and gives me hope.

All my love,
William.

"He's alive!" cried Fanny, pressing the letter to her chest. "I
knew it! I knew it! My William is alive and he will come home to
me."

"And Jack will come home to me," Marion smiled. "Oh, Fanny, it will be a happy, happy day when our men return!"

Fanny threw her arms around Marion. "How can I ever thank
you for bringing such good news to me?!"

"I'm afraid I have many favors to ask you," Marion admitted.
"But perhaps we can talk outside where it doesn't smell of fish."

⚓

As it turned out, there were several things that Marion needed.
She wanted to locate Jack's mother, as well as the Breeds and
also find a place to stay. Fanny assured her that she was most
welcome at the Campbell/Lovell home indefinitely and that tomorrow morning she would accompany her new friend to Boston.
Together, they would locate Mrs. Herbert and Samuel's adoptive
parents. Fanny liked Marion and her genteel manner. Best of all,
the British girl made her feel just a bit closer to William.

When the sun rose the next morning, Fanny and Marion ventured into downtown Lynn. As they walked, Fanny confessed to

dressing in William's clothes and attending meetings of the Sons of Liberty.

"You must take me the next time you go!" Marion was intrigued. "I can dress like a boy, too!"

"Somehow, I feel free when I masquerade as a man," Fanny admitted. "It's like I can finally be a part of something important—not just an onlooker."

"I know exactly what you mean," Marion nodded. "I like being a girl, but why must we be content to cook and sew when there is so much of more importance going on in the world?"

"Sometimes, I want to pick up a pistol and shoot those Brits myself!" Fanny grinned and then checked herself. "I'm sorry, Marion. I forgot for a moment that you are from England. I would never shoot you."

"I certainly hope not," Marion laughed. "We must work together to bring our men home."

The girls bonded as they continued on to Boston by getting a ride with a local farmer, Josiah Pettibone, who was taking his goods to sell in the big city. As luck would have it, Pettibone knew Mrs. Herbert and agreed to drop them off at her home on his way to market. He even told Fanny and Marion to help themselves to his strawberries and raspberries if they were hungry.

When they finally arrived at the Herbert home, they thanked Farmer Pettibone profusely for his kindness. He insisted that he liked having the company. It made the time pass quicker and he offered to pick them up that evening for the return trip to Lynn. The girls would meet him at the Herbert home at six. In the meantime, they had much to do.

Jack's home was dark and despite the summer heat, the windows were closed. Marion knocked on the door and it opened, but no one was there.

"Mrs. Herbert?" Marion called. "Mrs. Herbert, are you home?

I'm here with Fanny Campbell. We have news of Jack."

No answer.

"Mrs. Herbert?" Fanny hesitantly stepped inside.

The house smelled musty from a lack of fresh air. A rustling sound came from the back bedroom and a bent figure dressed in dark nightclothes emerged leaning on a long wooden stick. "Who's there?"

"I'm Marion Ashton," Marion took the old lady's arm and gently eased her into one of two chairs by the fireplace. "And this is my friend, Fanny Campbell. Mr. Pettibone brought us here from Lynn."

"But why?"

"I've seen your son, Jack." Marion knelt in front of the woman. "He asked me to come and find you."

"My Jack?!" Tears welled up in her eyes. "He left months ago. I thought he'd be home by now, but I haven't heard a word from him and I miss him so much."

"And he misses you." Marion squeezed her hand. "That's why he sent me. I'm going to take care of you from now on. You don't have to worry about anything."

"But when will my Jack get here?"

"I promise, he'll be home as soon as he can, but for now you must come with us." Marion looked up at Fanny.

"That's right," Fanny agreed. "We'll take you to Lynn so you're not alone."

"It's what Jack wants," Marion lied. "He told me so himself."

"The neighbors check on me." Mrs. Herbert shrugged. "They make sure I eat and have what I need."

"And fine neighbors they must be." Marion patted the old

lady's thin arm. "But you see, I have no mother here...so I would be honored if you would come with me and be my mother now."

"But how will my Jack find me if I leave this house?"

"I promise you," Marion assured her. "Jack will find the both of us and he'll be pleased to know we're together."

Mrs. Herbert was too tired to protest. She simply gave in with a shrug. The girls searched the kitchen and found some crackers and cheese. They fed her and then gathered her few personal belongings.

"We'll be back here at six," Marion told the woman. "Mr. Pettibone will help us get you to Lynn where you'll have good food and be safe."

"And my Jack will come?"

"Yes, my dear," Marion nodded. "I promise our Jack will come."

⚓

Fanny and Marion left Mrs. Herbert sitting in her chair. Before they returned to Lynn, they needed to speak with the Breeds. The family was well-to-do and Samuel had provided an address to a large home in Boston's west end. It was mid-afternoon when they arrived at the brick mansion with the manicured lawn and blooming shrubs boasting brilliant red, yellow, and purple flowers. There was a stable out back with three sizable horses quietly grazing in a corral. Fanny strode up to the front door and knocked. No answer. She tried again, knocking a little harder this time. Still no answer came.

"Now what?" Marion turned to Fanny.

"Let's wait a bit." Fanny sat down on the front step. "Maybe they'll be back soon."

The Breeds, however, didn't return. Instead, an older Negro man came along after a while. Neatly dressed in servant's clothes, he had a slight build with a full head of wiry, white hair.

"You ladies looking for the mister and missus?" he asked as he approached the house carrying a large bag of feed.

"Yes, sir." Fanny stood up. "Do you know where they are?"

"I do," he nodded and then pointed to himself. "Old Zacariah takes care of this place and the folks that live here, but they left for Charleston a few weeks ago. They are in deep mourning, you see, and the missus wanted to be near her family."

"Mourning?" Marion repeated. "Who died?"

"They lost their only boy at sea." The man shook his head in sorrow and set down the bag. "Samuel, they called him. He wasn't their real son, but they loved him as if he were. No mother loved a child more than the missus loved that boy. We all loved him."

"But Zacariah, Samuel isn't dead." Marion stood next to Fanny. "That's why we're here....to tell them that Samuel is alive."

"It can't be!" The man was incredulous.

"I saw him myself!" Marion smiled and told Old Zacariah her story. So overcome, his legs gave out and he had to sit down.

"Can we get word to the Breeds?" Fanny asked him.

"If I could read and write, I'd send a letter," Old Zacariah said.

"We can write a letter," Fanny offered. "If you tell us where to send it."

"Come inside." The old man stood up and pulled a key from his pocket. He slowly opened the front door and held it for the ladies. "You'll find what you'll need on top of Mr. Breed's desk in the drawing room."

⚓

Late that night, Fanny, Marion and Mrs. Herbert arrived home in Lynn. Farmer Pettibone was kind enough to take them all the way to the Campbell/Lovell house. He even helped get Mrs. Herbert inside. Agnes and Sarah welcomed her, fed her, and put her to bed in William's room while Marion moved in with Fanny. As much as she enjoyed Fanny's company, Marion knew that she must find a place of her own. Her father, Lord Ashton, had provided for her through his bank, and she could easily afford a small cottage in Lynn.

The next morning, Marion brought the subject of housing up at the breakfast table. "I appreciate every kindness you've shown me," she began. "But I would like to move into my own home and take Jack's mother with me."

"There's a place near High Rock just past the Pitcher house," Henry mentioned as he buttered a freshly-baked biscuit. "I think it's been empty for a while."

"Is that where the Widow Edgefield lived?" Sarah asked.

"Yes," he nodded. "Now that she moved in with her son, he wants to sell the house, but he can't find anyone willing to buy it."

"That's because no one wants to live so close to Moll Pitcher." Agnes shook her head.

"Who is Moll Pitcher?" Marion asked. "And why doesn't anyone want to live near her?"

"That woman consorts with the devil," Agnes said, narrowing her eyes.

"She does no such thing," Fanny argued. "She has a gift to see the future, that's all. Why, she's the one who told me that William was alive when everyone else thought him dead."

"She sounds like a fine neighbor." Marion grinned and with that the matter was settled. Marion met with the Widow Edgefield's son a few days later. Funds were exchanged and Marion, along with Mrs. Herbert, soon moved into the cottage near High Rock where Moll Pitcher did indeed turn out to be a fine neighbor.

CHAPTER 6

A Sentence Worse than Piracy

It had been well over a year since William, Jack, and Samuel had left Boston Harbor on the *Kent*. The last several months aboard the *Blade* had yielded more than enough bloodshed and pirate life—none of which they had bargained for. They continued to plot their escape and as soon as the ship sailed close enough to Cuba they planned to make their move. The three men were convinced they'd find refuge on the island, as well as safe passage home, since they knew the Spaniards did not tolerate piracy. The thought of home and Fanny had made each day bearable for William. Jack was anxious about his mother and he secretly hoped that the lovely Miss Marion might have settled near Lynn—even if it was with her intended. Samuel missed the affluent home in which he was raised and the genteel ways of his adoptive parents. He even missed Old Zacariah who had always been so strict with him. If he ever got back to Boston in one piece, he would never, ever leave them again.

On one particularly warm night in mid-August, as the *Blade* cruised for ships to plunder off the northwest coast of Cuba, William and his companions decided to brave their watery flight for freedom. By now, the men had gained the trust of the pirates and often acted as lookouts during the mid-watch that lasted from midnight to four in the morning. As luck would have it on this fateful summer night, the moon was hidden by clouds and darkness prevailed. As the midnight hour neared, only a few men remained on deck and the three men prepared for their watch. The only regrets William had in leaving the *Blade*, were Josh and Levi, the boys he'd taken under his wing.

Patiently, the three friends from Massachusetts listened as the ship's bell rang every time the sand glass was turned, marking each 30-minute interval. By the fifth bell, or 2:30 in the morning, the *Blade* was becalmed a mere mile off the coast of Havana. While one deckhand dozed, William, Jack, and Samuel pistol-whipped the other two unconscious with quick, solid blows to the back of their heads. Once assured that there were no witnesses, the men quietly slipped down ropes along the ship's freeboard and dropped into the sea to start their long swim to shore and what they hoped would be freedom. As the time came for the sixth bell to ring at 3:00 a.m., no one noticed that the bell sat quiet and the *Blade* was missing three of its mates.

Before long, the escapees realized that they had grossly underestimated the northeastern equatorial currents around the island, which threatened to push them even further offshore and north into the abyss where the Atlantic Ocean met the Gulf Stream. With arms and legs aching from their fight to survive, they struggled toward shore urging each other on with shouts that eventually turned to hoarse whispers. Samuel was the weakest swimmer and, at one point, he went under.

"Leave me," Samuel gasped for breath. "Save yourselves."

"We came together," William reminded him as the salty water lapped around them. "We stay together."

"But I can't make it." Samuel shook his head fighting to stay afloat.

"Then we'll tow you." Jack grabbed the floundering man's right arm. "Just hold on."

William and Jack took turns dragging Samuel through the breaking waves that separated them from shore. He didn't have the energy to protest even though he knew he was holding them back. His companions never complained, but when they grew tired, they would tread water in an effort to catch their breath. It seemed like hours before they finally reached shallow water where their feet connected with terra firma once again. When they crawled ashore, they collapsed in the warm sand, relieved and feeling free for the first time in months. All three fell into an exhausted sleep and only awakened when the sun loomed high in the sky, baking their skin.

The beach area was deserted in those early morning hours. If they had calculated right, however, they were not far from Havana Harbor. All they had to do was walk the shoreline to find it. Once there, they would go to the authorities for help. Home seemed closer than it had in over a year as William, Jack, and Samuel headed west using the coastline to guide them.

⚓

Twelve years prior to the three colonists arrival there, England's King George III had declared war on Cuba. In 1762, five British warships carrying 4,000 soldiers attacked Havana, which was then under Spanish control. When the Spanish government surrendered, the British took over and established trade with North America, as well as several colonies in the Caribbean. Thousands of slaves were brought from Africa to work on the sugarcane plantations, which provided the island's main export—sugar and molasses. The British rule didn't last long, however. The following year the Treaty of Paris was signed by England, France, and Spain giving Cuba back to the Spanish in return for Florida, originally claimed for Spain by the conquistador, Ponce de Leon.

When William, Jack, and Samuel finally reached Havana Harbor, they were amazed to find the large shipyard abuzz with activity. Much like Boston Harbor, dockworkers were loading and unloading goods from ships of all types, rigs, and sizes. Merchants from town hawked their wares to sailors who had been at sea for weeks. Wives greeted their husbands while sad-eyed children begged for food and money. Frightened African men, women, and children chained together on a raised platform, trembled as potential buyers examined them to ensure their fitness. These dealers wanted only capable slaves on their sugarcane plantations and would pay top dollar for those they deemed worthwhile.

Unsure what to do, the three men just stood there taking in the sights and the sounds of the harbor. They were finally free from the *Crimson Blade*, but in a strange place where they could not even understand the language spoken. At a definite disadvantage, William approached a uniformed man who appeared to be a guard of some sort. The dark-haired man pulled a gun from his side and eyed the bedraggled William with a look of suspicion.

"My friends and I need help, sir," William hesitantly began. "We've just escaped from the *Crimson Blade*--"

"El pirata! El pirata!" The man screamed and pointed his gun at William's head.

"No, no, sir!" William stepped back. "We are not pirates! We were prisoners on board the *Crimson Blade*. We escaped last night and swam to shore just east of here."

"El pirata! El pirata!" he hollered louder not understanding what William was saying. In an instant, William, Jack, and Samuel were surrounded by a dozen men in uniform—all leveling their pistols directly at them.

"No, you don't understand," Samuel tried and, for his efforts, was pistol-whipped by one of the gun-toting guards. Horrified, William and Jack dropped to their knees to help their friend.

Their attempts were futile, however, as they were quickly hand-cuffed and dragged away.

Still protesting in English, the three Americans were locked in an underground dungeon in the fortress known as Fortaleza de San Carlos de la Cabana or La Cabana, for short. The massive structure was strategically located along the entrance of Havana Harbor for defense purposes and had been completed in 1764 after the British returned Cuba to Spain. Named after the Spanish king, Carlos III, it was the largest military fortification in the Americas. It was also one of the worst places a prisoner could find himself as the three colonists soon discovered.

Their hellacious prison cell was damp and dark with a dirt floor that smelled of must, urine, and rodent droppings. No fresh air or sunlight reached them in their underground dungeon. The only way they knew that another day had begun or ended was when the few guards changed shifts. To be sure, there were other prisoners, locked in their own cells, but there was no direct contact with any of them. They heard the sounds of merciless beatings, the guards talking in Spanish mostly among themselves, and the intermittent maniacal laughter of one man who must have taken too many blows to his head. All three wondered just what these other unfortunate men had done to be locked away in such a desolate, hopeless place.

Punched relentlessly by the prison guards, the three refugees remained shackled in irons most of the time, dashing any hope of escape. They were only free of chains when their jailers forced them, along with other prisoners, to break rocks for a new extension of the fortress, which was under construction. Always in leg irons, the grueling, backbreaking work in the tropical sun made the men miss their life aboard the *Crimson Blade*. In retrospect, the ruthless sea bandits suddenly appeared quite civil. Besides the fresh air, their only consolation was the temporary reprieve from the foul stench of their hell-hole.

The inmates were given contaminated water and fed stale

bread. All three men suffered from some degree of dysentery and the weight melted off of their frames like butter in the hot sun. Before long, the once-strong men were barely more than weakened skeletons. The language remained a barrier, allowing them to communicate only with each other. Many a day they despaired and wished that they had been felled upon their own decks by the swords of the pirates rather than to be held at La Cabana by the Spaniards.

⚓

Six months passed under these inhumane conditions while the three Americans remained locked away in La Cabana's dungeon. Emaciated and weak, they lost track of time, but still tried to encourage each other to stay strong. They clung to the hope that eventually they would be given a trial, where they would have a chance to explain themselves. Until then, they had to survive any way they could—no matter how long it took.

Just as the colonists started to think that there would be no trial, they were finally taken to the courthouse. The hearing proceeded quickly in Spanish and the men were not allowed to speak in their own defense. It really didn't matter anyway since none of the officials comprehended English. What was understood by all present was the serious charge of piracy. In the end, the court determined that there was no evidence against William, Jack, or Samuel, but also none that exonerated them. Since no one could speak on their behalf, they were simply remanded back to their prison cell where escape seemed impossible.

The days and weeks dragged on as their despair deepened. Samuel took to sharing his meager meals with the small grey mice that ran freely in and out of their cell. He claimed to find comfort in their steady company. Jack spent his days pining for Marion and writing poems in his head that he hoped to one day share with her—in this life or the next. William cursed himself for ever leaving Fanny. By now, she and his family must believe him dead and, worse yet, she might have allowed Captain Burnett to replace him. Even if by some miracle he made it home, Fanny could very well be Mrs. Burnett by now and already given birth to the British man's children. William couldn't blame her if she had given up on him, but the thought of Fanny sharing a bed with Burnett was more agonizing than life in La Cabana.

The dampness, the lack of good food, and their dirty surroundings were taking their toll—weakening their bodies and their souls. The island's water supply came from underground cisterns where rainwater was stored. Unfortunately, these cisterns also caught the dirty runoff from the city streets when tropical storms caused flooding, washing refuse and latrine waste into the water supply. William and Samuel were weak, but they weren't sickly. Jack, however, was different. They feared that he suffered from some sort of plague. When his dysentery grew even worse, his friends were certain that he would die. It wasn't until his fever spiked causing delirium that the prison guards took notice. They were finally concerned enough to transport the ailing man to the fortress infirmary where he was formally diagnosed with typhoid fever and treated with a regimen of unknown medicines and cooling baths.

For the first time in more than a year, Jack was no longer bound by shackles. Nearly unconscious from the incessant high temperature, he hallucinated and ranted about Marion and home until, after two full days in the infirmary, his fever finally broke.

"Amigo, it looks like you are going to live." The voice with a Spanish accent startled Jack awake. He hadn't heard a word of English, except from his friends, since they'd arrived in Havana Harbor.

"You speak English?" He tried to sit up, but his weakened state prevented him.

"Enough to get by," the man answered. He wore a long coat

and carried notepaper. A thin grey mustache that matched the color of his hair traced his upper lip.

"Are you a doctor?"

"Sí, I am your doctor and I thought for a while I might lose you."

"You should have let me die," Jack sighed. "I can't go back to that hellhole."

"Amigo, here in Havana, we do not care for el pirata."

"I am no pirate," Jack assured him and then spilled his story about how he and his friends were captured and forced to live on the *Crimson Blade*. "All we wanted in Havana was passage home," he ended with a plea. "Please, I beg of you, sir, is there something you can do for me and my friends?"

The doctor laid his paperwork on the small table next to Jack's bed and sat beside him. "There is nothing I can do for your friends." He leaned in with a sympathetic look and then whispered. "But if you should manage to escape from the hospital, there might be a frigate in the harbor that will take you to Boston."

"When does it sail?"

"Two days from now."

"I must be on it."

"I can bring you a soldier's uniform tomorrow night. You can slip out after midnight through the east gate, but if you get caught, I'll deny we ever spoke."

"Understood," Jack nodded. "But whatever happens, can you get word to my friends?"

"Sí." The doctor stood up gathering his notes.

"And if I should escape…" Jack pulled the doctor's coat. "Tell them I will come back for them."

"I'll tell them, but I think we both know your chances are slim."

As promised, the next evening the sympathetic doctor came carrying a small package and laid it discreetly under Jack's bed. He gave Jack a razor along with some soap and water to shave and bathe himself. He even took his patient into the hallway under the pretense of helping him exercise and walked him to the exit so Jack would know where to go. No words were exchanged, but there was a grateful understanding between them and, for the first time in a very long while, Jack Herbert felt hopeful.

CHAPTER 7

The Good Fight

T he first time Moll Pitcher met her new neighbor, Marion Ashton, the fortune-teller of Lynn knew it was fate that brought the young girl to the colonies. Marion's delicate looks belied her independent streak and her resilient nature, but Moll of course, saw through appearances. She saw a different Marion altogether and did not hold against her the fact that she was from England. On the contrary, Moll warmly welcomed the British maiden, along with Jack's mother, to High Rock. After all, Moll liked Fanny Campbell well enough and if Marion was a friend of Fanny's then Moll would look out for the girl, who had been brave enough to survive pirates and travel alone to the colonies. Besides, Marion validated Moll's visions about William. He was alive, but needed help. Moll foresaw from her prophecies that it wouldn't be long before the two young ladies would come under her tutelage for they had important work to do. The time, however, wasn't quite right for their lessons to begin and Moll knew how critical it was to be patient.

As for Marion, as soon as she was settled in, she wrote a long letter to her father explaining all that had happened. She told him that she could no longer marry the man her father intended and requested that he terminate their arrangement. She ended by writing that the only man for her was Jack Herbert. Marion sent the letter off hoping that her father would not be too disappointed in her decision.

⚓

Summer turned into fall and on the night of October 25, 1774, a wondrous event took place in the heavens. The aurora borealis, or the Northern Lights, streaked across the skies over Boston and its surrounding areas. The superstitious citizens found the colorful display breathtaking, as well as a bit unnerving. Could it be a sign of things to come?

Marion heard a commotion outside and saw from her front window, the entire Pitcher family gaping upward. She wrapped herself in a long woolen blanket and joined them. By now, Moll's first-born, Ruth, was eleven, followed by Rebecca who was nine. Lydia had just turned seven and was holding the hand of her little brother, six-year-old John. Their father, Robert, was pointing to the skies and telling his brood to be quiet, warning them not to wake up the neighbors.

"They didn't bother me. I was still up." Marion approached them with a smile. "What is all this?"

"A show of lights from Heaven," John answered with a serious face. "At least that's what Ma says."

"What does it mean, Moll?" Marion asked.

"I believe it's a warning," Moll answered. "The time is coming for bloodshed and bullets and we must prepare."

"Don't be frightening the children, Moll," Robert admonished his wife.

"I see what I see," she shrugged. "Our children will be safe, but many others will die for their freedom and the freedom of generations to come."

"I wish Jack were here." Marion pulled the blanket tighter as a chill went through her.

"Your Jack will be home before the summer solstice," Moll said continuing to stare at the sky. "But he won't arrive until after the first shot of war is fired. By then, we'll have a plan."

"A plan for what?"

"For you and Fanny, of course." Moll closed her eyes. "Have you ever carried a sword, Marion?"

"No," Marion shook her head. "Do I need one?"

"You need two." Moll turned toward her neighbor. "One for you and one for Fanny."

Tensions heightened even more that February when the British Parliament formally declared that the Province of Massachusetts Bay was in rebellion against the Crown. Statesman Patrick Henry's words spoken at St. John's Church in Richmond, Virginia with General Washington in attendance, 'Give me liberty, or give me death', echoed throughout the land, inspiring many to take up their arms as skirmishes ensued between British soldiers and Americans. Most were minor, but they served to amplify the bitterness between the two adversaries.

As the cold days of winter subsided and spring rains began in earnest, the good people of Lynn tried their best to plant their gardens and tend to their everyday chores. No matter what they did, however, they couldn't shake the threat of war that loomed over their daily lives. Fanny and Marion took to heart Moll's words and each purchased a sword that they kept well hidden. Moll arranged fencing lessons for them in the nearby woods and the girls practiced together as often as they could. They never questioned why—they just did what Moll instructed. In reality, they enjoyed the swordplay and thought that the weapons might come in handy in case they had to defend themselves against a bloodthirsty British lobsterback.

The English governor of Massachusetts, Thomas Gage, had been given orders directly from London to enforce the British laws and put an end to an impending rebellion by any means necessary. When he learned that the colonists were stockpiling weapons in the nearby city of Concord, he felt it was his duty to take action.

Early on April 19, 1775, an out-of-breath courier rode through Lynn on horseback. The minuteman stopped briefly at the old Tunnel Meeting House where several members of the Sons of Liberty had gathered for a morning session. Henry Campbell and William Lovell were absent that day. They were in the harbor replacing rotting lapstrake planks along the port side of their fishing vessel. Fanny, wearing William's clothes and Marion dressed in Jack's trousers and shirt, however, were present at that fateful moment when the courier arrived with his message.

"I'm sent by Paul Revere," the man announced. "There's fighting in Lexington and heading toward Concord! The time has come for all neighboring villages to gather arms and take action against the Crown!"

"How many troops?" one man asked.

"I don't know, but I can't stay to talk," the rider answered. "I have orders to go on to Danvers, Salem, and Marblehead. We need all the able-bodied men we can get. Arm yourselves and get to Lexington as quick as you can!"

With that, he whipped his horse and raced down the road leaving behind a cloud of dust and those within earshot dumbstruck. The colonists had known war would eventually erupt, but no one expected it that particular Wednesday morning. The citizens of

Lynn wasted no time spreading word throughout the town. Within two hours, more than 100 men had gathered in front of the meeting-house, including Henry Campbell and William Lovell. Most were ill-prepared to fight. A few owned muskets, while others carried bayonets, but several had nothing more than pitchforks and knives. Nonetheless, they marched off toward Lexington hoping to put the British in their place.

Fanny and Marion knew they couldn't join the men, but they did the next best thing. The girls ran all the way to Moll Pitcher's house. Maybe the good fortune-teller of Lynn might know how the battle would end, or at the very least, assure Fanny that her father and William's father would come back alive.

⚓

"Moll! Moll!" Fanny screamed as she and Marion neared her front door.

"What is it?" Moll stepped outside. "What's got you two so upset and why are you dressed like that?"

"We were at a meeting with the Sons of Liberty," Marion's breathless words tumbled out. "We have to dress like boys, or they won't let us in."

"You clever girls." Moll gave a broad smile and a wink. "You must have learned something quite important to have come here in such a hurry!"

"A messenger was sent by Paul Revere!" Fanny squeezed Moll's hand. "He says they're fighting in Lexington. My father and Mr. Lovell left with at least one hundred others to go and fight the British! I'm afraid they may not come back. Do you know anything, Moll? Can you see what will happen?"

"Come inside." Moll tugged at the girl's arm. "We can sit and talk."

As usual, Percy was there to greet Fanny, but the children were all in school. He sidled up to her leg and rubbed against it, but Fanny was too upset to take notice. The cat pawed at her knee before she finally reached down to scratch his head.

"Percy won't be ignored," Moll said as she made the tea. "You might as well pay him some attention. It will calm you."

"I'm sorry, Percy." Fanny stroked the cat as she and Marion sat down at Moll's Queen Ann-style mahogany table. The feel of his soft fur and his loud purr was indeed soothing as usual. "I'm just so frightened, Moll. With things so uncertain about William, I couldn't bear to lose my father, too. And if Williams's mother lost her husband, it would kill her."

"Don't let this nasty business scare you, child." Moll set out three porcelain cups. "I knew about the impending attack. A British marine officer by the name of John Pitcairn paid me a visit a few days ago. He wanted to know if he would be a famous soldier. I told him that with one shot from his rifle, he would spark a fire and from its flames deathless heroes would emerge along with the eternal fire of liberty."

"What did he say to that?" Marion asked as Moll poured.

"He called me a witch!" Moll grinned and sat down across from her. "And then he told me that his troops were ordered to set fire to the stores and supplies at Concord. They planned to shoot down any and all rebels who dared to defend them."

"What else did he say?" Fanny asked, fascinated.

"He said that the Yankees would pay for their insolence and their illegal tea parties this very week."

"Moll, did you tell anyone?" Marion leaned over the table.

"Of course! I went directly to my contact and warned him. I believe they are ready for a good fight. But there's more my child, if you care to hear it."

"Of course, we want to hear everything!" Fanny sat on the edge of her chair in anticipation. "Tell us, Moll!"

"I also traveled to Marblehead. That's where I'm from, you know. I wanted to warn the fishermen there not to keep anything of value in the Pirate's Glen, since the British are surely watching all of Saugus. They asked if they might send their cache of weapons and ammunition to me for safekeeping and I told them I could bury their guns in the woods where I keep my tea. No one will find them there."

"Can we help you, Moll?" Marion asked.

"Well…" Moll tilted her head to one side. "I hadn't thought of it before, but seeing you two dressed as boys, I think maybe you can. Would you be willing to wear your disguises and deliver messages for me?"

"You mean like a real spy?" Fanny was incredulous at the very thought of such a great adventure.

"You mustn't tell a soul."

"We won't," Marion and Fanny agreed in unison. "We promise."

"Our freedom comes first," Fanny nodded. "And we will do whatever needs to be done to ensure that."

"I believe you both," Moll smiled. "But I've had one more vision I must tell you about."

"What's that?"

Moll leaned in closer. "Soon the fighting will be worse on Breed's Hill than in Lexington and Concord today. Those slopes will be filled with blood and the lives of many will be lost there. I saw heaps of slain on that hill and the sight of it made me sick."

"Do you see any good things?" Fanny wanted to know.

"I saw one happy light concerning two young lovers... Dorothy Quincy and Mr. John Hancock who is wanted at the gallows."

"Does he escape, Moll?" Marion asked.

"Yes, and his name will live forever in America."

"And does America win in the end against the British?" Fanny was almost afraid to ask. "I mean, will all the bloodshed be worth it?"

"Yes....the hoofbeats of Paul Revere will be heard throughout the world and they will echo the drumbeat of a great nation where the unstoppable star of freedom shall rise and shine forevermore."

"Oh my goodness...I don't know what to think about all this....it's all happening so fast." Fanny finished her tea and set the cup down, her brow furrowed with concern. "But, tell me Moll, will my father and Mr. Lovell come home safe?"

Moll picked up Fanny's cup and grew quiet as she studied the tea leaves in the bottom. Fanny held her breath as Moll closed her eyes and rocked back and forth. Finally, Moll spoke.

"Four citizens of Lynn will perish in the battle."

"No!" Fanny let out a gasp before Moll could continue.

"Neither Henry Campbell nor William Lovell will be among the dead. They will return weary, but well."

"I hate to hear of any losses," Fanny sighed. "But I am relieved to know that they will be safe."

"War brings loss." Moll sipped the last of her tea. "No one likes it, but it can't be helped."

"What can we do, Moll?" Marion spoke up.

"Meet me here tonight when the moon is high and be sure to dress like boys. We have work to do."

⚓

Later that same night after Agnes and Sarah went to their rooms, Fanny once again donned William's clothes and quietly slipped out, making her way under the full moon to Moll's house, where she met Marion who was also in disguise. The women, accompanied by Moll's husband, Robert, called upon several neighbor boys and the group hitched a team of horses to an empty wagon. They traveled to Saugus and while it was still dark, they retrieved crates of munitions from the fishermen there. Then the group returned to the woods behind the Pitcher residence. There, on a pretty, wooded knoll, on an isolated island in Breed's Pond, they dropped three heavily laden chests into a deep wolf pit.

Next, Moll directed the boys to dig up another trunk she had previously buried nearby. From this chest she removed provisions—blankets, powdered wigs, men's clothes, a woman's white dress, a medicine chest, a sheet, and a bolt of muslin. Just then, the group heard voices coming from the woods. In the dim moonlight, they could barely make out a group of intoxicated British soldiers tramping loudly through the forest. One of the boys placed the blanket over his shoulders, while another covered himself with the sheet. A third boy put on the white dress and began making ghostly sounds. Moll stood by with pistols ready, but when the startled soldiers saw the unearthly specters, they stumbled backwards in fear. In a flash, the frightened redcoats ran off practically falling over each other in their attempt to flee the ghosts.

"They must have been looking for the pirate's treasure," chuckled Moll.

"Do you know where it's buried?" asked one of the boys.

"If I did," Moll winked. "I'd be digging it up, now, wouldn't I?"

"We sure gave those old Brits a scare," Robert hooted.

"I was afraid you would laugh and give us all away," Moll beamed at her husband. "I had a hard time not to laugh myself!"

Over the next few weeks, Moll and her group made several clandestine trips to Saugus and Fanny became her primary messenger. Always dressed in William's clothes and calling herself, Francis Houghton, she passed information to the Sons of Liberty detailing exactly where and what armaments were hidden in the backwoods of Lynn.

⚓

As Moll had predicted, Henry Campbell and William Lovell returned from Lexington unscathed. Four others, however, were not so fortunate. Lynn lost William Flint who left a widow, Sarah; Thomas Hadley who had been widowed himself four years before; Daniel Townsend, who had a wife and five young children; and the newly married Abednago Ramsdell who had two older brothers, Shadrach and Meschech. In addition, two were wounded, including Timothy Monroe who took a ball through his leg and 32 bullet holes in his clothes and his hat—keepsakes that he later liked to show off. Another was taken prisoner, but soon released. Families mourned, buried their dead, and braced themselves for an uncertain future. Most of all, they united in their quest for liberty.

In early May 1775, when the Second Continental Congress was forming, Fanny kept busy between her underground work with Moll and cleaning the fresh catch her father brought home. She was anxious to help the Patriots and honored to share important secrets with the great fortune-teller of Lynn.

CHAPTER 8

The Homecoming

J ack Herbert was torn as he layed in his hospital bed trying to formulate a plan. He knew he had no choice, but to try and escape from Cuba. Leaving his friends behind, however, was an agonizing decision. They had been through so much together and always remained united despite the most difficult of circumstances. None had been so hard as these last long months in La Cabana, but he would come back for them as soon as possible—somehow. He only prayed that he could return in time to save them.

Just before midnight, Jack donned the smuggled uniform and walked down the empty hallway toward the exit. He breathed a sigh of relief when he ambled outside where moonlight awaited him. Following the doctor's directions, he walked to the docks. The day's hustle and bustle was over and a calmness brought by the night pervaded the tropical air. Jack found the frigate with little trouble and then hid behind several oversized bundles that were waiting to be loaded onto the ship at daybreak. He managed to doze for a while, but he didn't rest easy. Every sound he heard made him jump, afraid of being apprehended and sent back to La Cabana. It wasn't until the sun rose and the harbor came to life that his soldier's uniform allowed him to blend in with his surroundings.

Picking up one medium-sized box, he simply carried it aboard the frigate and down into the vessel's hold. Once there he slipped behind the many barrels of molasses and waited for the ship to set sail. Several hours later, he heard the sails being unfurled, lines running through the blocks, and the sound of water rushing past the hull as the ship tacked its way from Havana Harbor and out to sea. It was only then that Jack Herbert closed his eyes and slept— the longest sleep he could remember. He was finally free.

Jack knew that he couldn't remain in the ship's hold for the entire passage, but he waited until they were far enough away from Cuba that returning would be impossible. He needed food and water so after two days, he stumbled out onto the sunlit deck. Even if these sailors put him in the brig until they reached Boston, it could be no worse than what he'd already endured. The ship's cell would feel like a palace compared to La Cabana. Two mates spotted him and immediately pulled their pistols shouting: "Stowaway on board! Stowaway!"

"Please—" Jack lifted his arms in a show of surrender. "I am only a colonist from Boston trying to get back home. My friends and I sailed away on the *Kent* more than a year ago."

"That was the ship that disappeared," one sailor noted as several more men surrounded him.

"Rumor has it that pirates were responsible and there were no survivors," another salt added.

"There were three survivors," Jack corrected them. "William Lovell, Samuel Breed and myself, Jack Herbert. We were all forced to live on the *Crimson Blade* for months. After we finally escaped from the pirates, we were arrested in Havana. I just managed to escape La Cabana."

There were gasps all around. "But no one has ever escaped from La Cabana," exclaimed one mate in awe.

"The doctor there helped me when I was in the infirmary recovering from typhoid."

The crew was impressed by this man who had not only survived pirates, but survived the notorious La Cabana.

"But I must go back for my friends or they'll die," Jack continued. "Once I get to Boston, I can plan their escape. I beg you gentlemen to at least listen to what I have to say."

"Tell us your story, man," one crew member put away his gun and the others followed suit. Jack told them everything. In the end, he offered to work for his passage. The sailors brought him to their captain who was touched by the man's plight and agreed to take him to Boston. In return, Jack worked as a deckhand, swabbing floorboards, polishing brass fittings, and sanding rails since he was far too weak to work the lines and ropes, or climb to the crow's nest. Impatient to get home, Jack knew that his stay in Boston would be short as his thoughts remained with Samuel and William. Nothing would be right until his friends were safe and back on American soil.

After two weeks of uneventful sailing, Boston Harbor appeared on the horizon. "Land ho!" The man in the crow's nest called out.

Jack stopped rubbing the side rails and looked up. The sight of the waterfront caused him to fall to his knees and weep. He had made it. Jack Herbert was not just free, he was home.

⚓

Boston Harbor was much like he remembered—bustling with activity and filled with people. It was there on the docks that Jack first heard about the battle at Lexington and Concord. He was especially saddened to hear that Abendigo Ramsdell was among the victims from Lynn. They had been friends in what seemed a lifetime ago. He would have to call on his widow, Hannah, and express his sympathy. In addition, Jack learned that a call for American soldiers had recently been made and the homegrown forces had overtaken Fort Ticonderoga in New York. The ammunition seized there was on its way to Boston now.

The Second Continental Congress led by John Hancock had just met in Philadelphia and declared that the colonies were officially in a state of defense against the oppressions of the Crown. Jack would have liked to join the Continental army, but he knew he was in no condition to fight. Besides, his friends were desperate and needed him. Maybe all three of them could one day join up together and serve their country. But that thought would have to wait for another day.

At the moment, his immediate concern was finding his mother so he rushed to their small stone house not far from the docks. As he knocked on the front door, it opened slightly. Jack stepped inside to find that no one was home and it appeared that the house had been left empty for quite some time. There was no food in the pantry and all of his mother's personal items were gone. Overcome by despair and assuming his mother had passed away, he collapsed into the oversized armchair that had been abandoned near the fireplace. He closed his eyes remembering how his father had once sat in this very spot—this particular chair being his favorite. No one had used it after Mr. Herbert died—his mother wouldn't allow it and now she, too, was gone. She had died not knowing what had befallen her son. Even worse, she may have died alone. He should have done more to get home sooner. Jack took a few moments to mourn his loss and then with a last look around, he left the house. He had to find Fanny.

It was a ten mile walk to Lynn, but that gave Jack plenty of time to think about what he might say to William's girl. He arrived at the Lovell/Campbell home as dusk was settling in and the two families were just sitting down to dinner.

Fanny answered his knock. "May I help you?"

"Miss Fanny," Jack began. "I bring you news about William Lovell." A plate fell from Sarah Lovell's hand when she heard her son's name.

"You know my William?" Fanny was breathless.

"Yes, ma'am. You probably don't remember me, but my name is Jack Herbert. William and I sailed off together aboard the *Kent* close to two years ago."

"Oh my God, Jack!" Fanny screamed. "I didn't recognize you, you're so thin."

"Is my son alive?" Sarah stepped into the doorway, her face colorless.

"Yes, ma'am, at least he was when I left him."

"Come in Mr. Herbert." Henry beckoned from the kitchen. "Sit down. Eat with us and tell us everything you know."

The fresh fish stew and boiled potatoes seemed like a feast to Jack. Even the green beans made his mouth water. He breathed in the warmth of the freshly baked bread as he happily filled his plate with the first home-cooked meal he'd had in ages. All the while, he tried his best to answer each question that the Lovells and Campbells peppered him with.

Until Marion Ashton's arrival last summer, William's family had long mourned him as lost. She had given them and Fanny hope that William would one day return. Now, Jack Herbert described how the men survived the pirate attack on the *Kent* and how they had lived on the *Crimson Blade*. He told of their daring escape and how they ended up in La Cabana where William and Samuel remained. Forgetting to eat, Fanny hung on every word this young man had to say.

"Tell me Jack....has William suffered much in prison?" She knew the answer before it was spoken.

"Yes ma'am...it's as horrible as one could ever imagine. I'm sorry to say that the conditions there are miserable and we were lucky to get enough food to survive. We spent most of our days in shackles or doing hard labor."

"Oh, my poor boy!" Sarah gasped at the news of her son's treatment. "God help him!"

"But is he well considering the circumstances?" Fanny was almost afraid to ask.

"As well as can be hoped, Miss Fanny."

"Then everything Marion said was true," she sighed.

"Marion?" Jack's ear perked up and he dropped his fork. "Marion Ashton?"

"Yes, Marion Ashton," Fanny smiled. "I believe she's an acquaintance of yours."

"You've seen her?"

"Yes, she arrived in Boston months ago. She brought me a letter from William and came to tell us that he was on the pirate ship. We tried to find the *Blade*, but had no luck."

"So, Miss Ashton made it safely to America." Jack smiled broadly. "I'm so relieved. I have thought of her a great deal since we put her on a ship in Port Royal, but I would imagine by now she is happily married to her English captain."

"On the contrary, my dear Jack." It was Fanny's turn to deliver good news. "It seems that you made quite an impression on her. She broke her engagement because she said she could never be happy with another man. It seems that her thoughts were still aboard a certain pirate ship where she longed for the brave man who saved her life."

"Is it possible she is still in Boston?"

"Not in Boston," Fanny shook her head. "She has a small cottage here in Lynn and prays daily for your safe return."

"I must go to her!" Jack jumped from the table upsetting the platters.

"First, you must tell me how we can save William and Samuel...then you must make yourself presentable before you call on Miss Ashton."

"Of course," choked Jack, so giddy that he could hardly stand still.

"Now tell me about the fort....and Havana Harbor," Fanny urged him on, desperate for information that might help save William.

He then described how the fort was land-locked—guarded by Morro Castle, which wasn't always manned. He further explained that although the harbor was large, not more than one ship at a time could sail in or out of the entrance. As for the actual prison, it was only guarded by one jailer—a rough, grey, old Spaniard—and a handful of soldiers posted at different walls. Jack's dire description made Fanny realize that time was of the essence. Neither William nor Samuel could survive indefinitely under such brutal circumstances. At least with the pirates, they had the freedom to live. Now their very existence was nothing more than that of common murderers. How ironic that their only real crime was to escape a life with criminals, to end up chained and shackled like convicts.

"Jack...would you join an expedition to release William and Samuel?"

"Yes ma'am...I swore I would return and risk my own life to free them."

"Then I will put you in touch with someone who may be able to help us," Fanny replied. "But you must not speak of this to anyone."

"Fanny!' Agnes frowned. "What fool thing are you planning now?"

"I will see to it that William comes home," she announced with such firmness that no one—not even Agnes—questioned her further. She then turned back to Jack who had just finished his bowl of fish stew. "Now, Mr. Herbert, I think you should stay the night. In the morning, you can wash up and change into some clean clothes. I believe we have some here that might fit you. Then you must go and see your Maid Marion. She has been waiting for a very long time." Jack smile liking the sound of a reunion with his beautiful Miss Ashton.

Jack was given William's room, but he could hardly sleep. At first light, he politely declined Agnes's offer of breakfast. He washed, shaved, changed into a shirt and pants that once belonged to William and then, with directions from Fanny, was off to find Marion.

The day was overcast as he walked along the road that led to High Rock. He was excited yet nervous to see the beautiful Miss Ashton after so much time had passed. He had lost a lot of weight while in prison and feared that she might not recognize him. He also worried that she was far too sophisticated for a simple boy like him. How could she give up a captain in the king's army for a commoner born in the colonies? The fact that she was a British subject was also troubling. Where would her sympathies lie— with the Crown or the colonies? Would she still feel the same about him as she had aboard the *Blade*, or had she simply felt indebted to him because he had once saved her?

As Jack made his way up the path, and as he passed Moll Pitcher's house, he wondered if she was still in the business of telling fortunes. Maybe he should pay the lady a visit and ask her about Marion. He quickly changed his mind when, just past the Pitcher residence, a small stone cottage came into view. Wash hung on a line that was stretched across the front yard. A few raindrops fell and just as Jack quickened his step, Marion leapt from the front door in an attempt to retrieve her clean, dry clothes.

"Marion!" Jack called as the rain began in earnest.

Marion squinted, looking at the man coming down the path. "Jack?!" she hollered at the sight of him. "Jack, is it really you?"

"It's me!" he called back and any doubts he had quickly vanished as she threw herself into his open arms.

Without thinking, Jack kissed her again and again as the rain beat down around them and she responded in kind. Marion Charlotte Ashton was even more beautiful than he remembered despite the rain that bedraggled her hair and clothes. To Jack, she looked like a welcoming angel.

"Jack, you must come in out of the rain." She pulled him toward the cottage door.

"But your clothes," he hesitated.

"My clothes be damned!" she smiled. "I just want you to kiss me again!"

"If that would not compromise your reputation, I would love to."

Marion threw back her head with a hearty laugh. "Well since I spent several days at the mercy of a band of cut-throat pirates, I doubt very much if my reputation is still intact." She took his hand and led him into the cottage, closing the door behind him.

"I've missed you so!" She threw her arms around him once again and kissed him with a passion he'd only dreamt about. Thank goodness, he'd wasted no time at Moll Pitcher's place.

"Marion!" a feeble voice called from a room in the back of the house. "Do we have company?"

"Yes!" she answered as she tugged Jack along. "There's someone here to see you!"

As Jack entered the tiny bedroom, he saw a diminutive figure lying in a bed. She had covers up to her neck. Only her wrinkled face and wiry grey hair were visible.

"Mother?!"

"My boy?" gasped the old woman.

"Yes, mother, it's me, Jack!" He scooped her frail body into his arms and lifted her against him.

"My Jack!" she cried, running her crooked fingers over his face. "Oh, dear God, my Jack! You're really here! I thought I would die and never see you again."

"I looked for you, mother!" He cradled her close to his chest. "Our house was empty. I thought you were gone."

"I'm still here thanks to Marion's good cooking and her kind care."

"After I called off the wedding, I wrote my father and explained what had happened," Marion offered. "I told him how I would probably be dead if it weren't for you. He bought me this place so I could have somewhere safe to wait for your return."

"But how did my mother get here?"

"After all you did for me, Jack Herbert, taking your mother in was the least I could do for you."

"You really are an angel." Jack's eyes brimmed with tears as he laid his mother gently back in the bed.

"Nonsense." Marion shook her head. "I just knew how worried you were about her so I found her and moved her in here with me and fine company she's been."

"Trouble is all I've been," Mrs. Herbert sighed. "But now I can die happy knowing you're safe, my boy."

"There'll be no dying in this house today," Marion admonished her with a smile. "Today we celebrate!"

"I don't know how to thank you, Marion." Jack's voice shook with emotion.

"Exactly how I felt when you saved me from the pirates," Marion ran her hand along his side. "But you're so thin, I can feel your ribs. I guess I will just have to fatten you up. Good thing I have a hearty soup on the fire."

"Whatever you're cooking, it smells like a meal fit for a king, and an immense improvement over the slop from prison."

"Come help me set the table," Marion beckoned.

Jack gave his mother a quick kiss on the forehead and left her to rest. Once in the kitchen, he could no longer stand the distance between them. He placed his hand on Marion's waist as she stirred the pot of soup. She paused for a second and he wondered if he had overstepped his boundary, until she turned to face him. Jack could no longer resist her. He leaned down and kissed her softly on the lips as Marion let out a sigh and drew herself in to rest against his full frame. Jack held her and kissed her as if he thought he would never see her again. And he wondered—was it possible that two people from such different backgrounds might find happiness together? At that moment with Marion returning his kiss, he was certain it was.

CHAPTER 9

A Strained Friendship

Captain Burnett arrived at Fanny's home the evening after Jack's return. She told him of William's capture and imprisonment in Cuba following his escape from the pirates. Burnett had always respected Fanny's feelings for William and had never spoken ill of him, until now.

"Fanny dear, I know how you feel about William, but even you must admit that after all the time he spent living with pirates, he is no longer the innocent boy you remember."

"What exactly are you saying, captain?" Fanny bristled.

"I'm saying that pirates are a bad lot...they plunder, they kill, and they strike fear in the hearts of any worthy seafarer."

"And?"

"And William was one of them. Why else would he be locked up in a Cuban prison?"

"My William is an honorable man," Fanny seethed through clenched teeth. "He was given no choice, but to go along with the unsavory men who forced him off the *Kent*. He had to do what he did in order to survive."

"But Fanny, surely you can see that your William has turned into a criminal of the worst sort."

"You will not speak of him like that under his own roof," she fumed. "He is not here to defend himself. And if you really think about it, what would you have done in his place?"

"I would never have left you to begin with, Fanny."

"I think it would be wise if you left me now," Fanny commanded, her voice harsh and unforgiving. "I have plans to make and very little time to make them. I won't have you distracting me with your stories of dishonor. And to be perfectly clear, you are no longer welcome here."

"But Fanny--"

"--go!" She abruptly cut him off with a wave of her hand. "You do not compare with brave men like William and you never will."

Now it was Burnett who bristled with jealousy, as he stomped away from Fanny's home. What was it that Lovell had over him? After all, he was a king's captain while Lovell was merely a poor colonist and a common sailor—and now, of all things, a pirate. Surely, it wouldn't be long before Fanny came to her senses and realized how much more he had to offer her. Perhaps he would have to confront William Lovell, once and for all, in order to prove to Fanny that he, Burnett, was indeed the better man. He could only hope his chance would come soon—if the rogue were still alive, that is. A dead William Lovell would be the best option by far. Fanny would then be forced to get over him, or live a lonely life as a spinster.

Shortly after Burnett's upsetting visit, Fanny found herself at

Moll Pitcher's doorstep, overwhelmed with worry. In order to help William, she needed help herself and Moll was the only person she could think of who might provide some insight and assistance and, perhaps, some comfort. Lynn's famous fortune-teller knew that Fanny was coming and opened her front door before the girl could even knock.

"You've got to help me, Moll!" Fanny blurted out, frantic with fear. "It's William! You said I would be the one to save him, but he's being held prisoner in Cuba. What should I do...how can I help him when he is so far away?!"

"First, you must calm yourself." Moll pulled her into the house. "I have a plan, but I have been waiting for the right time to share it. You must be ready and brave enough to fulfill your destiny, or you and William will both perish."

"If my destiny means saving William, I'm ready...no matter what the risk or cost. I've been so lonely, Moll, I ache for him more and more every day. I would rather give my life than spend my days without him!"

"There'll be no dying as long you keep your wits about you, my child." Moll pushed Fanny toward her table and pulled out a chair. "Let me make you a cup of tea to help you relax then we can talk about this sensibly. There's much you need to do and my visions have gotten stronger. I believe that it's now or never."

Percy came from the back room and cocked his head to get a better look at Fanny. "Come here, Percy," she called to the black cat, who quickly sidled up to her. She picked him up, cradling him like a baby and scratched his head, desperate for the affection he offered. She watched as Moll scooped a ladleful of boiling water from the black kettle that hung in the hearth and poured it into a small, brown cup. Moll picked a jar from one of her many shelves and opened it. She pulled out several dried, green leaves, which she then crumbled into the cup. After giving the mixture a quick stir, she set the steaming brew in front of Fanny. It smelled of mint.

"Drink up, my girl." Moll sat down at the opposite side of the table. "This will calm your nerves."

"But William--"

"--what William needs now is for you to think clearly if my plan is to work."

"I'm sorry." Fanny picked up the cup, still holding Percy and sucked in a deep, calming breath along with a sip of tea.

"It's clear to me how that cat loves you. I can't even hold him that way," Moll chuckled.

Fanny smiled and settled the cat in her lap. "I just can't bear the thought of William suffering."

"Yes, I know, dear, but the sooner you turn your worry into strength, the quicker you will be holding Mr. Lovell in your arms again."

"Please....just tell me what I need to do."

"I think you'll find that these past months of studying the sea, as well as your recent swordplay, will be most beneficial." Moll pushed her chair from the table and walked across the room to an old, wooden hutch. She opened the top drawer and took out a large pair of shears.

"What are those for?!" Fanny sat back in her chair, alarmed at the sight of Moll coming towards her with what looked like a weapon.

"This long hair won't do for a naval officer sailing on a merchant ship, now would it?" She waved the scissors in the air. "Turn around, girl, and let me get to work if you want to bring your William home."

Confused at first, Fanny never protested as she began to catch onto her mentor's plan. She even smiled at Moll who gathered her voluminous locks and lopped them off just below the ear. By the time Moll was finished snipping away, Fanny looked more like a handsome boy than a pretty girl. Then Moll turned back to her shelves and selected a bottle filled with a strange, clear liquid. Using a small sponge, she applied the fluid to Fanny's hands. Surprisingly, it had no odor, but Fanny blinked in disbelief as her skin turned from pale white to a deep sea-faring tan—reminiscent of a seasoned, West Indian sailor.

"What are you putting on me?"

"Silver nitrate....it tans the skin and will help you pass as Bartholomew Channing, a young, but weathered and experienced ship's officer from the West Indies. I have paperwork to identify you as the son of a British officer and a wealthy Barbadian heiress. With the right clothes, the right letters of recommendation, and the right accent, your masquerade aboard-ship as Officer Channing will be convincing."

"What ship?"

"The *Constance*. According to an officer I know in the king's navy, she sails to the West Indies in two weeks carrying a shipment of fabric. I can arrange your position as third officer, but you must know that the crew isn't happy. With a little clever cunning, I believe you can instigate a mutiny, take control of the ship, and sail it to Cuba if you are willing to risk your own neck."

"You know I am willing," Fanny nodded. "But don't you think your plan is a bit far-fetched? Do you think anyone will believe I'm a man?"

"You pass as a man when you attend the Sons of Liberty meetings and there you're among people who know you. On board the *Constance*, you will be a stranger to the crew. They'll have no reason to be suspicious unless you give them one, but there is one more thing you should know."

"What's that?"

"I have it on good authority that the captain plans to seize the crew and take them to England. There, he will sell them off as slaves to the highest bidder. They will be indebted to you, Fanny, if you save them from such a terrible fate."

Fanny bit her lip in hesitation, but just for a moment. "I'll do it, Moll!" she declared. "If it means saving my William, as well as the men, I'll cause a mutiny and take charge of the ship. I'll sail her to Cuba and back. I'll even fight pirates and go after the entire British navy myself if I have to!"

"That's what I want to hear." Moll smiled, pleased at Fanny's enthusiasm. "Now, you'll need these." She handed Fanny a brown, leather purse containing documents that identified her as Bartholomew Channing—a man. While Fanny perused the paperwork, Moll opened an old chest that sat in a corner near the hearth. She pulled out a striking sailor's guise including a black cavalier hat, complete with a gold buckle and white feather.

Fanny smiled, placed the hat atop her newly shorn curls and held the uniform against her. "What do you think?"

"Not bad." Moll frowned as she looked down at Fanny's ample chest. "But we have to find a way to disguise those."

Fanny watched Moll as she once again rummaged through the trunk. "Ah, here it is." Moll smiled as she pulled out the bolt of muslin they had retrieved from the woods. "We'll bind you in this and that should do the trick."

"You've thought of everything, Moll." Fanny couldn't hide her amazement. "But what about money? The crew will have to be paid and paid well, not to mention provisions for the ship."

"The finances are taken care of," Moll explained. "I've spoken to Old Zachariah and the Breeds are desperate to bring their Samuel home so they have agreed to fund our little expedition. The gold will be here before you set sail. Enough money to pay a crew of thirty double wages....in case they need convincing."

"Moll, you really are a magician!"

"No my dear. I'm a witch," smiled Moll as she unfolded the

bolt of fabric.

⚓

Fanny had a lot of thinking to do as she walked home from Moll's house dressed in her new blue sailor's pants and pea coat that fell half way to the knee. Her newly cropped hair was carefully hidden by the plumed cavalier hat. The outfit gave her a look of authority—like a navy man. The costume felt awkward at first—especially the small boots that Mr. Pitcher had fashioned for her and she had to keep reminding herself not to touch her right cheek where Moll had painted a long, thin scar. Most uncomfortable of all was the muslin wrap that bound her breasts. It was not only tight, but also very itchy.

Masquerading as a man, however, meant more than just donning a pair of pants, a long coat, and a short haircut. She would have to embrace a male demeanor, develop a confident swagger, and leave all traces of her femininity behind. Fanny also practiced Channing's Barbadian lilt—a lyrical form of the King's English. At first, she found the syllables tricky, but soon she surprised herself at how well she mastered it. Acquaintances passed by and nodded at her/him as if she were a stranger, which buoyed her spirits. Fanny's hesitant steps then quickly turned into self-assured strides. As her confidence grew, she even uttered a few words of greeting to passers-by and her voice sounded like a stranger speaking inside her head, but it was not enough to simply act like a man. For the plan to work, it must be more than a masquerade. She had to become Bartholomew Channing, a sailor from Barbados and leave behind her real identity as Lynn's own Fanny Campbell. Her very life, as well as William's, depended on the success of her charade.

The closer she got to her house, the more she worried about her parents and the Lovells. She had to find a way to explain to

Henry and Agnes, as well as William and Sarah, just why her hair was cut short and why she was dressed as a man. She certainly did not want to tell them about the planned rescue mission, but there was no getting around it. Aside from raising their hopes, she was sure that they would all fear for her life and try to dissuade her from going. But nothing anyone could say, or do, would ever change her mind. As she had told Moll, she would save William or die trying.

No matter how hard it might be to explain the plan, Fanny knew that she couldn't just disappear. She had to tell her family the truth. They may not like the risk she was taking, but she hoped they would go along with her once they realized her mind was made up. She wouldn't ask their permission—only their blessing. After all, she told herself, she was Fanny Campbell and both the Lovells and the Campbells knew full well how stubborn she could be. Posing as a man, however, was another matter entirely. This alone would make Agnes crazy, but there was no other way. Fanny knew that if she could fool the Campbells and the Lovells, she just might be good enough to fool a crew of hardened sailors she had never met.

Thank goodness Jack had promised to help her. He was determined to return to Cuba and release his friends from that hellhole as he called it, and his impatience grew with every passing day. The longer they waited, the more hardships William and Samuel would endure. Occasionally, Jack let his fears get the best of him and voiced the worst of his concerns. What if they arrived too late and found the men dead? When he talked that way, Fanny would take charge, silencing him with a sharp reprimand each time he expressed his doubts. She refused to hear such talk and clung to the fact that Moll insisted William and Samuel were still alive. It was all she had.

Steeling herself, Fanny knocked on her own front door and waited. After a moment, Agnes appeared, wiping her hands on her apron. "Yes…may I help you, sir?"

"Is this the home of William Lovell, ma'am?" The accent seemed to suddenly come easy.

"Why yes, yes it is, but I am sad to say he is not here. He's been gone a very long time. Are you a friend of his.... do you have news of him?" she asked hopefully.

"Why no, ma'am. I have been employed by a Miss Fanny Campbell to go on a mission and bring Mr. Lovell home from Cuba. He is believed to be in Cuba, right?"

"Oh my, yes....please....do come in." Agnes stepped aside and then shouted, "Henry! Come quick! There is a man here who says he is going to help us bring William home! Call the Lovells!" She grabbed Channing's hand, ushered him into the kitchen and offered him a seat at the table where she had already laid out the dinner plates. "I'm expecting my daughter anytime now and then we'll have supper. Would you care to share a meal with us... Mr...?"

"Channing, ma'am, Bartholomew Channing," Fanny removed her hat and gave a slight bow as the others entered the room.

"Where are you from, Mr. Channing?" Henry inquired.

"I hail from Barbados, an island in the West Indies, but I completed my maritime studies in England, Sir."

"And our Fanny hired you to bring my William back?" Sarah was almost afraid to hope for such a miracle.

"I don't know where our Fanny is." Henry held out his hand to the stranger. "She should be home by now."

"That's quite all right." Fanny firmly shook Henry's hand. "Your daughter has given me permission to share the plan with you."

Henry gestured toward the table. "Please...Mr. Channing, sit and tell us everything."

For the next hour, dinner was forgotten as "Bartholomew

Channing" explained how he intended to soon leave on the *Constance*. Jack Herbert was to join him on his mission and together they would sail to Cuba, free William and Samuel from La Cabana, and then they would all come home. The Lovells and the Campbells hung on Channing's every word, enthralled by his intricate plan, none suspecting that Channing was not who he claimed to be. As his tale ended, Agnes had grown more agitated and was now quite concerned about her daughter's whereabouts. She paced back and forth from the table to the stove, pretending to check on dinner.

"If Fanny knew you were coming, Mr. Channing, she would have been here. I apologize for my daughter's absence, but I can't imagine what's keeping her. It's not like her to be so late and frankly, I'm worried about her."

"But I am Fanny, mother," Fanny announced in her own voice with no trace of an accent. "And I am going to save William dressed in this disguise." She stood up as both sets of speechless parents looked at the man who now spoke with Fanny's voice.

"How is this possible?" Henry demanded. "Our daughter does not have such weathered skin."

"Of course you're not my Fanny," Agnes agreed with her husband, but stared a little more closely at this stranger. "I'd know my own daughter...I think."

With that, Fanny removed her hat and then walked to the wash-basin where she scrubbed her hands and face clean, washing away most of the silver nitrate, as well as the scar. When she turned and held up her hands they all gasped. Fanny, her hair cut short with her now fair skin, stood before them dressed in men's clothing.

"I guess I am a better thespian than I thought," Fanny grinned. "Maybe I should have been on the stage instead of drying fish."

"On the blessed Virgin, I did not know my own daughter!" Agnes fell into one of the chairs next to the table, fanning herself with her apron.

"How is this possible?" William Lovell circled Fanny to get a better look.

"As I live and breathe," Sarah gasped in disbelief. "How can you be our Fanny?"

"It's amazing!" Henry shook his head. "But, Fanny, tell us how you did it! Who helped you with this charade...this disguise?"

"Moll Pitcher."

"No!" Agnes threw her head back in a faint. "Saints save us! My daughter is consorting with a woman from the devil."

"Hush, Agnes!' Sarah admonished her friend. "Moll is no more a woman of the devil than we are. She's kind and smart and a true patriot, who nurses the sick and gives what little she has to the poor. And if she can help bring my William home then I will be indebted to her for the rest of my life."

"I'll not have any daughter of mine sailing on a ship across the ocean with only strange men to keep her company!" Henry shouted.

"But, I'm not going alone!" Fanny raised her voice. "Jack Herbert is going with me and I believe that Marion will come, too, if we can find someone to take care of Jack's mother."

"No!" Agnes stood up. "I'll not hear this kind of talk."

"But if it were your son who was missing all these months, you would want someone to find him, wouldn't you, Agnes?" Sarah's was the voice of reason.

"But why Fanny?"

"Why not Fanny?" Sarah pointed to the girl. "She loves William and always has. Who better to go after him and bring him back to Lynn?"

"But she's only a girl," Henry spoke up. "Sailing and rescuing are jobs for men."

"Then I will be a man from this day forward until I return to Lynn with William at my side!" Fanny vowed. "And there's nothing any of you can say to stop me. I've been studying the seas for nigh on two years and I think I know my way around a ship. I will go to Cuba and find William if it's the last thing I do!"

"Is that what Moll Pitcher says?" Agnes narrowed her eyes. "That it will be the last thing you do?!"

"Moll says we will return to Lynn and get married. She sees a happy home with lots of children in our future."

"Grandchildren!" Sarah smiled. "I'd given up on that dream."

"Do you hear yourself, woman?" Agnes raised her voice. "My daughter is planning to risk her very life and you stand here talking about grandchildren?"

"And grandchildren you'll all have once I bring William home," Fanny promised. "And to make things perfectly clear, I'd rather be lost at sea than spend another month without the man I love. He has been gone much too long, so talk all you want. Threaten me with any punishment you can think of, but rest assured, I will sail on the *Constance* in a fortnight and I will find William."

CHAPTER 10

A Secret Mission

The very next day under the disapproving eye of her mother, Fanny donned her new outfit, stained her skin, and then drew a scar along the curve of her cheek. Satisfied with her male persona, she once again practiced her Barbadian accent before heading to the Lynn docks where she was to meet Moll. There, Moll planned to formally introduce Fanny to Beauregard Brownless, the ill-mannered captain of the *Constance*.

The sun shone brightly reflecting on the water, causing Fanny to squint as she approached the pier. It took a moment for her to spot Moll who stood clutching her grandfather's curlew-peewit whistle—an item that she cherished as it was something that Captain Edward Dimond, the Wizard of Marblehead, always carried with him. Many a sailor claimed to have heard the sound of that whistle as it led them to safety through the mightiest of storms.

"Do you think you're ready?" Moll asked as Fanny approached.

"Yes," the young girl nodded. "If I don't do this now, I'm afraid I'll be too late."

Moll blew the whistle signaling the *Constance* to send the ship's tender ashore, which would then ferry them out to the brig.

Every seafaring man in the harbor recognized that shrill blast as a signal from Captain Dimond's famous granddaughter—friend and seer to all sailors of Lynn and the world. Every tar in the harbor who heard it removed his cap in respect. All motion seemed to cease as Moll and Fanny climbed aboard the tender under the watchful eyes of the seamen and made their way toward the *Constance*.

The *Constance* was a 400-ton brig—a beautiful example of naval architecture. She was bound for Barbados in the West Indies and well-armed with a long-tom amidships and a dozen six-pounders that could easily take on any enemies of England or other seafaring foe that might threaten her well-being. A crew of 26 men toiled before the mast of the strong-armed trader that carried 'Letters of Marque'—a government license allowing her to attack and capture enemy vessels and ultimately bring them before the Admiralty Courts. Despite the ship's good reputation, Captain Brownless was not a well-liked man. He was a tyrant who fancied spirituous liquors on a regular basis. The first mate, George Bunning, was a young, inexperienced imbecile who only held his position because his father was a principal shareholder. If Brownless agreed, Channing would be named the third officer in charge of the ship.

Once aboard the brig, Captain Brownless eyed the well-dressed Channing as if surveying the horizon for possible storms.

"I can vouch for this one," Moll spoke up. "Bartholomew Channing is a fine sailor if there ever was one."

"Channing" handed his leather credential purse to Brownless and then Fanny held her breath, fully expecting the captain to see right through the forgeries as well as her disguise. The stooped, grey-haired man, however, just scanned the documents with a loud grunt before shoving the paperwork back at her. "I guess you'll have to do, fancy dress or no," he grumbled. "Can't be too choosy when a man's short-handed. At least you have some experience and Mrs. Pitcher's word means a lot around here." He then turned toward his first mate. "Mr. Bunning! Show Mr. Fancy Pants here to his cabin and find me another two foredeck hands. This ship goes nowhere if we remain short handed!"

Fanny breathed a sigh of relief once Brownless walked away. Moll gave her a reassuring smile, knowing that Fanny would raise no eyebrows regarding her sex. It seemed she had quickly mastered thinking and acting like a man—a refined one albeit, but a man nonetheless who would easily earn the respect of the sailors aboard.

When the tender returned them both to shore, Fanny accompanied Moll to High Rock and thanked her for her help. The two women parted company at Moll's house, with Fanny walking on to Marion's cottage. It was time to share her rescue plan with her two closest confidantes. If she could make them believe that she was indeed Bartholomew Channing, third officer of the *Constance*, it would give her self-assurance an even greater boost.

A few moments later, Fanny stood outside Marion's cottage. "Good day," Fanny greeted her friends who were on their knees working in the garden. Her Barbadian accent now coming naturally.

"And you would be?" Jack stood tall, wiping his hands on an old rag.

"I would be Bartholomew Channing. I've been commissioned by Miss Fanny Campbell to complete a rescue mission for your comrades in Cuba. She said you might be interested in joining me —that is, if the names William Lovell and Samuel Breed mean anything to you."

"Yes, of course!" Jack held out his hand and Fanny accepted with a firm shake. "I insist on it. But why didn't Fanny come with you?"

"She is busy taking care of details."

"Sounds like Fanny." Marion pulled one more weed before

standing next to Jack. "But did she also tell you that I'll be join-ing the expedition?"

"She did," Fanny nodded.

"And you don't take issue with that?" Marion brushed the dirt from her hands.

"On the contrary," Fanny shook her head. "I welcome help from all sources...man or woman...it makes no difference to me."

"I have tried to dissuade her," Jack explained. "It won't be safe, but she will not have it any other way."

"Now that we are married, I will not let my husband out of my sight again." Marion's voice grew stern.

"Married?!" The news caught Fanny by surprise and she al-most forgot about her accent.

"That's right," Marion nodded. "We were married two days ago by Reverend Treadwell at the First Congregational Church and, now as Mrs. Herbert, my mind is made up. I go where Jack goes. There will be no further discussion about it."

"I see." Fanny nodded, trying to conceal a grin. "Perhaps we should go inside and talk."

Jack, Marion, and Fanny gathered at the small kitchen table, where they discussed their plan to board and overtake the *Constance*.

"It seems wrong to be making such detailed arrangements without Fanny," Marion frowned.

"I assure you that Miss Fanny is aware of every word I speak," Fanny smiled.

"But I feel like we are talking behind her back," Jack said. "And that isn't right."

"Let me put you at ease, then," Fanny removed her hat and with the back of her hand wiped away her scar. The sudden transformation into their friend, Fanny Campbell, left Jack and Marion dumbfounded. Twice now, Fanny's disguise had been tested with those who knew her best and twice she had triumphed. The thought of it made her giddy with confidence. As long as she never let her guard down, she just might pull off this ruse.

"I can't believe it!" Jack hooted.

"How did I not know it was you, Fanny?" Marion laughed delighted by her friend's deception.

"Maybe you were too preoccupied with your new marital status," Fanny offered with a grin. "I can't believe you up and got married without telling me."

"My father wrote and gave me his blessing so we just went ahead and did it," Marion smiled.

"That's right," Jack explained. "Once I found Marion, I didn't want to leave her again so in order to keep the neighbors from talking, I married her."

"And one day soon, you'll be marrying William," Marion assured her friend.

"I pray you're right," Fanny sighed. "And I hope our plan works."

The plan was relatively simple. Marion Charlotte Ashton would travel aboard the *Constance* as a wealthy, young maiden with several trunks, each filled with personal possessions as befitted a fine lady from England. Instead of clothes, toiletries, and family heirlooms, however, these trunks would carry some of the very weapons that Moll had hidden in the woods. In addition, one trunk would hold the gold from Samuel's family, which was intended to finance the rescue. When the time was right, "Channing" and company would take over the ship and offer the crew double wages to sail with them to Cuba.

As for the newlyweds, their only remaining concern was old Mrs. Herbert. She was too ill and weak to stay alone. Fanny agreed to talk to her parents and the Lovells about looking after the elderly woman while they were gone. She would somehow convince them to do it. With that settled, Fanny had one last thing to discuss. "We need another recruit in order to work the brig before the Constance can sail. Do either of you know of someone we might trust enough to take with us?"

"What about Terrance Mooney?" Jack suggested. "Do you know him?"

"Terrance Mooney?" Fanny repeated. "The name is familiar, but I'm not sure I've met him. Is he a friend of yours, Jack?"

"Aye, a friend of mine and Bill's," Jack nodded. "Terrance Mooney is a fine Irishman. He lives with his mother in a shanty near the shoreline not far from High Rock. Poor as dirt they are, but he can be trusted. Problem is he may not be able to leave the old lady. I hear from Moll that she is nearing the end."

"Do you think he might agree to go with us?" Marion asked.

"He may, depending on his mother's health," Jack shrugged. "Moll has been tending to her and trying to keep her comfortable. She says that Mrs. Mooney has only days left to live. Once she's gone, Terrance would probably be glad to get away on an adventure and make a few quid to boot."

"Bartholomew Channing will pay Mr. Mooney a visit then." Fanny spoke in her newly acquired accent. "And convince him to join us."

On her way home, Fanny once again walked past Moll's place. This time, she noticed a finely dressed, young British officer waiting on the Pitcher's doorstep. The lobsterback must be seeking Moll's counsel, Fanny thought, smiling to herself. He had no idea that the famed fortune-teller of Lynn would most likely lead him into a conversation about upcoming battles or impending British attacks. It was Moll's custom to find out any secrets she could and then pass along whatever she learned to the Sons of Liberty.

⚓

That evening, Fanny, dressed as Channing, made her way to the small shanty near Lynn harbor where Terrance Mooney lived with his mother. She was touched by the unkempt structure, which didn't look fit for animals to live in, let alone people. Many of the windows were broken and stuffed with wads of paper and rags. A garden had been planted nearby, but was now overgrown with weeds and dotted with trash. And the desolate place was surrounded by an aura of sorrow.

Fanny knocked, but received no answer, so she pushed the door open and entered the house. It was dark inside and the odor of death lingered in the air. She heard a woman moaning from the back room and moved toward the sound. She soon discovered a young red-haired man seated next to the old dying woman, who lay upon a modest bed of straw. She was so thin that Fanny could almost count her bones and her scalp was visible through her sparse white hair. A grey pallor was cast across her face and her breathing was labored as if each rasping breath might be her last. The poor fellow tightly held her hand as if by doing so he could keep her alive. Fanny was touched by the poverty before her and felt grateful for the nice home she lived in. Then she thought of William and the suffering he must be going through at that very moment.

"Mr. Mooney?" she began in Channing's accent.

"Yes?" The man looked up for the first time, surprised to find someone there.

"I'm sorry to disturb you, sir," Fanny began. "I am Bartholomew Channing and a friend of Jack Herbert's. He sent me here to see you. Is there something I might do for your mother? Does she need a doctor?"

"We have no money to pay a doctor." Terrance Mooney gently pushed a few strands of hair from his mother's face.

"I can pay if you think it will help," Fanny offered.

"We'll not take charity." Terrance shook his head. "Besides Mrs. Pitcher comes daily. She doesn't think it will be much longer now. My mother's been ailing for weeks and she took to her bed seven days ago. I'm not even sure she knows who I am, or that I am even here at this point."

"She knows." Fanny stepped closer to get a better look at the woman. "And I'm sure you have been a fine son and a great comfort to her."

"I'm afraid you are wrong about that." Terrance's grey eyes brimmed with tears. "I am a terrible son. I don't even have enough money to give her a proper burial and a saint she was in this life, with never a selfish thought in her head."

"I will see to it that your mother has a fine funeral befitting a saint, in a church with flowers."

"But why would you do that?" Terrance asked. "I can't pay you. I haven't a dime to my name."

"But I think you can help me."

"How could I possibly help you? I don't even know you."

"Come outside for a minute so we can talk. I promise not to keep you long."

With an anxious look at his mother, Terrance stood and followed Fanny to the front yard, which overlooked the harbor in Lynn.

"Have you ever heard of a merchant ship called the *Constance*?" Fanny asked.

"I have." He pointed toward the brig still moored in Lynn harbor. "I believe that's the ship you speak of."

"It is," Fanny nodded. "And I am an officer aboard that ship. She is scheduled to leave Lynn in one week. Jack Herbert has signed on, but we need one more hand in order to make sail. The position offers good wages and proper treatment. Will you come aboard?"

"If you make arrangements for my mother's funeral then I am indebted to you, Mr. Channing. You wouldn't even have to pay me."

"Nonsense. I wouldn't expect anyone to sail for free, but there's one thing you should know before you sign on," Fanny continued. "This is not just a normal voyage. Though the crew has not been told yet, it is our ultimate goal to rescue William Lovell and Samuel Breed from their prison in Cuba. Knowing that, if you want to change your mind about joining us, I understand."

"If the *Constance* is bound for Buccaneer latitudes she'll need a good stout crew and sufficient weaponry. That doesn't worry me, but I hear she has a cursed bad captain….worse than King George himself."

"No need to worry about Captain Brownless. As third officer, I will ensure that you and all the men aboard are treated fairly and paid well."

"Then I'll do it!" Terrance smiled for the first time. "Especially if it means helping Bill. Poor chap….I believe he'd do the same for me."

"Thank you," Fanny shook his hand. "I will talk to the captain and add your name to the ship's crew roster, but for now you mustn't discuss our plans to sail to Cuba with anyone."

"I understand." Terrance forced a smile. "Your real mission's a secret and that's as it should be."

⚓

Terrance's mother died peacefully three hours later with her son by her side. The very next day, Mrs. Colleen Mooney had a magnificent funeral that was talked about for weeks in the small town of Lynn. Attended by town officials and a choir that sounded like heavenly angels, she was surrounded by the grandest of flowers as her horse-drawn hearse carried her to the Old Western Burial Ground. There, after more prayers and songs, she was interred in a plot marked with a small marble stone that read:

"Here Lies

Colleen Mooney

A Saint if There Ever Was One"

Terrance Mooney cried like a baby as his mother was laid to rest.

CHAPTER 11

Breed's Hill

❝ Talk some sense into this man, will you, Fanny?" Marion sputtered as she dragged a large wooden trunk across the kitchen floor.

"Now, ladies, we won't be sailing until next week." Jack set a second oversized trunk next to the first one. "There is no harm in Terrance and me helping with the fortifications until then."

"But you know what Moll saw," Fanny reminded him as she inspected their muskets and pistols. "She said there would be bloodshed on Breed's Hill and you can't afford to be hurt....not with William and Samuel depending on you for their lives."

"We won't be hurt," Jack insisted. "The fortifications are to be built on Bunker Hill...not Breed's...so we will be safe."

"No one is safe these days," Marion snapped.

"Sorry, my dear," Jack shrugged. "I know you are English, but the redcoats have taken over Boston and it's high time that they are put in their place."

"Not by you or Terrance." Marion frowned and set her folded clothes inside one of the trunks. "If one of you gets hurt, you could jeopardize our mission."

"It's no use." Jack began packing the weaponry that passed Fanny's inspection in between Marion's dresses and shoes. "Terrance and I have already talked to Colonel Mansfield and we will join his troop until the *Constance* leaves the harbor. There will be no more discussion about it."

Fanny and Marion continued packing in an icy silence and their disapproving glances let Jack know he was not forgiven. Concentrating on the task at hand, it seemed they had everything they needed except the gold that the Breeds were supplying. Moll had assured them that Old Zachariah would soon come with the necessary bullion.

What they hadn't anticipated was the tension that now enveloped Boston. After the fighting at Lexington and Concord, the number of British troops occupying the city swelled to 6,000 under the command of General Thomas Gage who was ordered to prepare for war. With their harbor and waterways controlled by the English, the redcoats dominated Boston. It was a city under siege. Residents who lived within the city limits were forced to turn in their weapons and open their homes to the English soldiers.

On May 10, 1775, the Second Continental Congress met in Philadelphia and elected John Hancock as their president. Five days later, the colonies were officially placed in a state of defense and volunteer troops throughout America organized into a makeshift army. Skirmishes on Grape Island, in Boston's outer harbor, and on Chelsea Creek only served to heighten the already-strained situation. On edge, the people of Lynn formed a safety committee and three nightly watches were quickly established—one at Sagamore Hill, the second at the end of Shepard Street, and the third at Newhall's Landing along the Saugus River. In addition, these law-abiding citizens living outside of Boston proper now carried arms to church. Even the good Reverend Treadwell stood in the pulpit with a box of cartridges in one hand and his sermon in the other, always keeping his loaded musket within reach.

As May turned into June, the wet spring weather dried up and the summer sun seemed to dominate the days. Gardens were once again planted, horses were still fed, and mundane chores were completed, but the threat of war dangled over the land. On June 15, 1775, two events of note occurred. British Major Pitcairn paid a second visit to Moll Pitcher asking how he would fare in future battles. Moll had already foreseen the blood bath that would soon occur on Breed's Hill, but she read his tea leaves anyway. They warned of Pitcairn's imminent death, but she kept that to herself. Instead, she assured him that he would soon be hailed a hero. She just didn't tell him by whom and she certainly didn't give him the details.

That same day as Pitcairn was drinking tea with Moll, the Second Continental Congress unanimously named George Washington the General and Commander-In-Chief of the newly formed continental army. Moll rejoiced when she heard this news for she had already predicted that General Washington would remain an important figure in America for generations to come. Unlike Pitcairn, Washington's name would live on in history, never to be forgotten.

The very next day, in an attempt to deter the British troops, 1,200 colonists led by William Prescott came together. Jack Herbert and Terrance Mooney had been originally ordered to erect defenses on Bunker Hill. Instead, however, they were told to fortify Breed's Hill, which was closer to the harbor. The men worked hard, toiling under the hot summer sun building fortifications in an attempt to stave off the British.

In the early hours of June 17, 1775, the English launched their initial attack from Boston Harbor. The exhausted colonists lacked arms and ammunition, but fought back as best they could, fending off the first two assaults. During the third and final attack, Major John Pitcairn arrived with a large troop of Royal Marines. His son, William, also an officer, was at his side. As he led his men up Breed's Hill, a musket ball struck him in the chest and he fell into William's arms—his distraught son screaming for help.

Realizing that their beloved leader had been gravely wounded, his loyal men wept as they carried him back to Boston. As Moll had foreseen, Major Pitcairn died several hours later and was buried at the Old North Church by his men who deemed him a hero.

That third assault was not only deadly for Pitcairn, but proved too much for the ragtag continental army. With little ammunition, Prescott had no choice but to retreat. The British won the battle, but at an extremely high price with 226 dead and 828 wounded compared to the American loss of 115 lives and 305 injured. Broken bodies were strewn across the hill and the once-green grass was now soaked red in British and American blood—just as Moll had described it weeks earlier.

As it turned out Fanny and Marion needn't have worried. The men of Lynn under the leadership of Colonel Mansfield, never reached Breed's Hill in time to fight—something for which the colonel was taken to task. He was ultimately court-martialed for his tardiness and relieved of his duty, much to the chagrin of his outraged troop. Unlike the men, however, Fanny and Marion were secretly relieved that Jack and Terrance never saw battle, leaving their own mission intact. Although the actual fighting occurred on Breed's Hill, the incident was forever known as The Battle of Bunker Hill.

Three days later, Fanny ate a final dinner with the Campbells and the Lovells, before donning her pants and coat. An excited energy flowed through her as she darkened her skin. If all went as planned, she would be with William soon. Her parents still disapproved of this escapade, but they had long since given up trying to dissuade her. Fanny was determined and they knew that when she set her mind to something, there was no stopping her.

"Fanny, I know you don't want to hear it," Agnes said, shaking her head, watching her daughter carefully paint a scar along her cheek, "but if anything happens to you, I blame that devil-woman, Moll Pitcher, for putting ideas in your head."

"You know I have to save William," Fanny insisted. "There's no other way."

"But sailing as an officer aboard a ship like the *Constance* is a man's job," Henry reminded his daughter.

"And that's exactly why I will be a man," Fanny announced in her new accent.

"Why can't Jack do it?" Agnes asked.

"Because he's not an experienced sailor like I am," Fanny sighed, back to using her own voice.

"So your father is to blame, now, eh?" Agnes blinked. "For taking you to sea when you should have been home cleaning fish instead of catching them."

"If Fanny can bring my William home," Sarah interrupted before Henry could speak in his own defense. "Then I will be forever indebted to her."

"I will bring William home." Fanny took the woman's hand. "I promise you. I will not come back without him."

"Then Godspeed, my child." Sarah's eyes brimmed. "We will pray for your safe return...and for William's."

Henry and William dabbed at their eyes as they said their good-byes, while Agnes handed her only child a small Bible. "May God carry you safely back to me and in one piece."

It was dark when Fanny Campbell put on her feathered hat and left home to board the *Constance*. As third officer, Bartholomew Channing was expected to sleep on board ship the night before departing, in case the captain needed him. Jack, Marion, and Terrance would arrive early the next morning, well before they were due to set sail.

When Fanny reached the brig that evening, she went straight to her quarters where she left her fancy chapeau, believing that the captain might think Channing too girlish if she kept it on. She then met with Captain Brownless on the ship's bridge.

"Well Mr. Channing." Captain Brownless looked up from the charts he was studying. "Will the men you engaged make it aboard in time for our voyage?"

"Aye, captain, they will be onboard by sunrise. Mr. Herbert will be bringing Terrance Mooney, a fine Irishman if there ever was one."

"As long as you can keep him in line…those Irish can be unruly if they get too much drink in 'em."

"I can assure you, sir, Mr. Mooney is not a drinking man. A nip or two on special occasions, but he's not one to over-indulge. He's just spent the last year taking care of his sick mum. God rest her soul. He's a good, God-fearing man, I hear."

"I could care less about his fear of the Lord…he just best fear me and good old Mother Nature!"

"You will be pleased with him, I'm sure."

"As long as he works hard, I'll have no complaints."

"That he will."

"I just hope you're right when you say he's not the drinking sort…leaves more for me." Brownless threw back his head and bellowed with laughter.

"There's one more thing, captain," Fanny began. "I've found a paying guest who seeks passage with us."

"A paying guest is always welcome aboard the *Constance*." The captain formed a smug grin.

"Our guest is a lady."

"A lady?!" His grin turned into shock.

"A British lady who needs to join her father in the Caribbean."

"A British lady?! Oh no, Channing. There's no place for a woman aboard my ship. Where will we put her?"

"The owner's quarters are empty and I think she'll be comfortable there. She won't be any trouble, I assure you. And she will pay well as she tells me that she is very grateful for the safe passage."

"Paying well you say?" Brownless reconsidered. "Very good then, but if she causes any problems with my crew, she will be confined to the brig and you can tell her that from me."

"You can tell her yourself, sir. Miss Marion Ashton has asked to meet you personally when she boards tomorrow morning."

Brownless just grunted before returning to his cabin and his rum. Fanny watched him with a certain satisfaction as she realized just how easy it was going to be to overpower a man under the spirituous influence of the devil's brew, or perhaps an island elixir was more like it, since rum was the man's drink of choice.

Jack Herbert and Terrance Mooney arrived at the harbor the next morning just as the sun rose in the east. Once aboard, they were shown to their quarters and quickly assigned their duties. Fanny did not speak to either man, as she did not want to show them too much familiarity. One hour later, the beautiful Marion Ashton appeared wearing a light green dress with matching shoes and parasol. Her blond hair was swept up in a bun and she brought three large and very heavy trunks along with her. The crew stopped their work at the sight of her and one man let out a long whistle, which drew a sideways glance from Jack.

"Enough of that there mate....we'll show respect to our passenger, do you hear?!" Fanny pointed at Terrance. "And you there, get Miss Ashton's trunks. See to it they are put in the owner's quarters and do it now in case the lady needs something before we set sail."

"Aye, sir," Terrance nodded and set out to the docks with another man to retrieve Marion's belongings.

"Miss Ashton." Fanny turned to Marion and gallantly kissed her hand with a sly wink. "Welcome aboard the *Constance*. I do hope you will be comfortable here. We have reserved the owner's quarters for you. Should anyone offend you, please inform me immediately and I will see to it they will not have a second chance to upset you."

"I'm certain I will be fine, Mr. Channing," Marion smiled with a quick glance at the men as they reluctantly returned to their jobs. "But I asked that I might meet the captain to properly thank him. Is he here?"

"Aye, ma'am." Captain Brownless appeared on the deck in his finest uniform and swept off his hat. "Officer Channing neglected to tell me about the extent of your beauty." He frowned at Fanny, while extending his hand to Marion. "May I show you around my ship, ma'am?"

"Yes, of course." Marion smiled before giving a quick curtsy and taking his hand. "I just hope you don't mind the inconvenience of traveling with a woman."

"A lady as striking as you is no inconvenience," Brownless leered. "As long as you agree to join me for dinner every evening."

"Of course," she said with an eye toward Jack who bristled even though it had been previously agreed between them that Marion might be very helpful when it came time to ensure that Brownless would be heavily inebriated on the evening of their planned mutiny. "I would be honored."

CHAPTER 12

The Taking of the *Constance*

The *Constance* hoisted anchor with the morning tide and spread her sails. She set out to sea, carrying Third Officer Bartholomew Channing, Jack Herbert, and Terrance Mooney amongst the newly signed crew. The ship carried only one paying passenger, Marion Charlotte Ashton. They sailed past the billowing red and white ensigns that waved from the tall masts of 12 ominous British ships anchored in Lynn harbor. Known as men-of-war, their very presence reminded all aboard the *Constance* that their beloved Boston remained a city under siege. Fanny, Jack, Marion, and Terrance couldn't help but wonder what their future held, concerned for their family—both at sea and at home as they headed southeast toward the horse latitudes.

Once the *Constance* was fully under sail, Captain Brownless summoned the crew aft. "You will all do well to remember just who is in charge aboard this brig," he bellowed, pacing back and forth in front of the men, but refusing to make eye contact. "As your captain, what I say goes and I expect no man to challenge me or my orders. Do as you are told and you will have nothing to fear, but cross me and I will feed you to the sharks....piece by piece." Brownless finally turned to face them. "Are we clear?"

"Aye, sir," many of the salts mumbled, but it was obvious to Fanny, as she heard them muttering under their breath, just how much they really hated the man. Within minutes the captain disappeared below deck and within the hour he became so intoxicated that he forgot all about dining with the lovely Lady Marion. Bunning, the incompetent first mate, also took cover below deck, pretending to attend to other duties. That left the sailing of the brig entirely up to "Channing"—the third man in charge.

Hesitant at first, Fanny's voice was shaky, but soon the sailors found the rhythmic lilt of her accent endearing. Over the next week, with a course set to port and a stiffening wind, they recognized her as a knowledgeable and seasoned sailor, who was well at home on the sea. They soon grew to trust and respect her because she treated them kindly—unlike Captain Brownless who, usually inebriated, resorted to physical blows and vulgar language when he was displeased with a man's work.

With most of the daily duties left up to Fanny, she quickly became acquainted with each and every man, uniting the crew and aligning their loyalty with her. In turn, the men wanted to please him and gladly took direction under her watch. Of course, Jack Herbert and Terrance Mooney made it their business to ensure that even the most skeptical man in the crew thought Bartholomew Channing was a fine leader. In addition, Jack and Terrance discreetly planted the seeds of mutiny amongst the crew, then watched as the insidious idea of rebellion sprouted its roots throughout the ship.

Terrance especially had become somewhat of a leader amongst the crew since he was gifted with the 'gab' and possessed a jolly nature. He always stood up for Channing and never held back his high opinions of the third officer.

"I've sailed upon the sea before, but I never would have thought a man as young as Channing would have such fine experience," Terrance lifted his rum-filled flask in a toast. "God bless him!"

The other men raised their own flasks in agreement.

"So Mooney, seems you've yet to spin a yarn since we've been at sea these many days," piped one of the mates.

"Well my men....I will not bore you with a story, but I will tell you of what happened to me not so long ago."

"Does it involve Mr. Channing?" an old tar asked.

"That it does," Terrance replied, piquing the men's interest. He proceeded to relay the story of Channing's kindness to his poor dying mother with genuine emotion. Those old sea dogs barely had a dry eye amongst them as they thought of their own dear mothers. Terrance's words stirred their loyalty as they all agreed that Channing was a good man who cared for each and every one of them.

"That was a fine tale, my mate," the oldest tar, known as Findley, spoke as he rolled a generous quid of tobacco about his mouth. He plugged it inside his cheek before settling down to spin a yarn about his own adventures in the northern latitudes.

⚓

On their eighth day at sea, Bunning uncharacteristically appeared on deck in the early hours of the morning. Clasping his hands behind his back, he barked orders at the men. "Shake out that reef from the fore and main topsails and do it now!"

"But sir," one shocked sailor protested. "That will be far too much sail to carry us in this wind."

"I didn't ask for a weather report," Bunning growled. "Now do as I say or the lot of you will be reported to the captain for insubordination to an officer."

The men looked to Fanny as Channing, who remained silent at

the helm.

"I am the superior officer here, not this man," Bunning bellowed. "Now get to work on those sails, or you'll find yourselves in the brig."

Despite their doubts, the men obeyed Bunning's order and within minutes the *Constance* was leaping over the waves like a racehorse and burying her nose deep into the troughs between the waves.

Fanny, concerned over the turnout of the extra canvas, could no longer contain herself and said, "Mr. Bunning...do you really think it's safe to make that sail in this tropical depression? I realize that this is an unusual wind for this time of the year, but we are not in a race to Barbados as far as I'm aware. The ship is straining under this much sail and I fear Miss Ashton may fall ill from the motion. I am sure she doesn't have sea legs like the rest of us."

"Miss Ashton is no concern of mine, sir!" Bunning shouted just before he nearly lost his own footing as the ship slammed hard into a wave trough. The hard jolt caused Findley to tumble head first from the rigging. Several crewmen rushed to help him as he sat up in a daze, blood dripping down the side of his head. Now embarrassed by his foolish order, Bunning begrudgingly turned to his third officer. "Mr. Channing, put the rig under whatever canvas you like. I have more pressing matters to attend to." With that, Bunning slunk away knowing full well that the men disliked him just as much as they hated the captain.

Fanny simply nodded and gave a wave to the crew and within minutes, the canvas was reefed and shortened, allowing the ship to continue gracefully on its southeastern course. Fanny then tended to the injured man.

"That's a nasty gash there, Findley." Fanny helped the grey-haired man to the ship's medic.

"I'll be all right, sir."

"I insist you stay below and take it easy until you're feeling right again."

"Yes sir, but first I would like a word with you."

"Of course," Fanny nodded. "What's on your mind?"

"There's talk among the men of mutiny," Findley confided. "The captain and his first mate are not liked. We feel that Brownless is selfish and prefers his bottle over the *Constance*. His indifference to our needs is apparent and as for Bunning, he is totally incapable of running this brig. If you should decide to take over, the men want you to know that we are all behind you, sir."

"Mutiny is a serious deed," Fanny sighed. "We mustn't take it lightly, but I will keep what you said in mind and in the strictest of confidence, of course."

"Thank you, sir...none of us feel safe under Brownless's watch." Findley rubbed his forehead. "We all want to get home safely to our loved ones."

"Understood." Channing nodded, knowing full well that the entire crew of the *Constance*, except for the captain, first mate, and the cook were colonists. She could easily persuade the men to turn this British mercantile ship into an American man-of-war. After all, most had families and fully expected, when they left Boston Harbor, to return home in a few months. Little did they know that Brownless and Bunning had other plans for them.

⚓

For the most part, Marion stayed below, in the owner's cabin, but she would take a brief morning and afternoon stroll on the aft deck where Jack Herbert worked beside Fanny. Marion and Jack were careful not to make their relationship obvious, but they managed to spend time chatting as if they had only recently met.

To their delight, they found that they enjoyed their ruse, since such niceties had evaded them when they first became acquainted. They kept up their charade with quiet enthusiasm.

On the evening of Findley's unfortunate fall, Marion arrived on deck for a clandestine visit with Jack, who was alone, since Fanny had left the helm to her trusted friend. It not only gave Jack and Marion a moment of privacy, but also afforded Fanny the opportunity to rest and reflect upon their future fate.

The moon shone on the ocean off the ship's beam like a giant white orb rising out of the ocean. The heavens had strewn an endless blanket of stars across the sky, which blended with their reflection upon the water. The romantic setting was not lost on them, but the reality of what they were about to do hung over the newlyweds.

"I'm growing anxious, Jack." Marion clutched her husband's arm.

"We are all anxious." Jack stood at the wheel and covered her hand with his. "My biggest fear is that we will arrive too late to save William and Samuel. No one can live indefinitely in such horrible conditions."

"Perhaps we shouldn't dwell on the negatives." Marion moved even closer. "Perhaps, we should just think that what we are about to do will matter greatly to the men on this ship and to our friends."

"It's hard to think at all when you are so near and smelling like roses." Jack kissed the top of her head taking in the heady aroma of her flowery perfume. "I miss waking up next to you."

"Once the mutiny is over, maybe we can arrange to be together…secretly, of course."

"Until then," Jack smiled. "It seems that I must be content with a stolen kiss or two."

"There's too much at stake to take such risks," Marion agreed.

"This is the way it has to be...for now."

While Jack and Marion talked under the stars, sleep eluded Fanny as she lay in her bunk contemplating the present situation, as well as what was in store. Worry over William's rescue and the heavy burden of responsibility concerning the crew's welfare kept her awake.

The North American colonies were at war with their mother country and they were sailing on a British brig with a mostly American crew. Fanny, an avid supporter of the American cause, was greatly disturbed that twenty of her fellow countrymen were about to be betrayed into the hands of the enemy by their very own captain, who planned to take the ship to England with the men aboard—unbeknownst to them. This alone justified the mutiny regardless of the ultimate goal to rescue William.

Still, she was troubled. Piracy and mutiny were the two most serious sins of the sea and both transgressions now stared her full in the face. She had long ago decided to gain possession of the vessel without knowledge or help from the others, in order to pro-tect them from any conspiracy charges that might result. She would take full responsibility if her plan backfired. She refused to let her crew or her friends be arrested for mutiny, but if she was successful, every man aboard would be given a choice: stay with double pay until the ship returned to the colonies, or disembark at the next port, no questions asked.

And as if that weren't enough, the agonizing thoughts of William, still languishing in that Cuban prison tore at Fanny's heart. Hopefully, they would not be too late.

As the northern chill warmed to the sunny breezes of the West Indies, they found themselves only a day's sail from the Mona

Passage, where they would enter the Caribbean Sea to head south to Barbados. Fanny knew that it was time for the Constance to become an American brig and strike down the British colonial red ensign that the men referred to as the 'meteor' flag. She had to take action before they sailed past their ultimate destination, Cuba.

Just before sunrise the next morning, Fanny entered the captain's cabin, where Brownless slept in the throes of an alcoholic stupor, totally unaware of the other man's presence. Fanny quietly removed a cutlass from the wall before pulling her pistols from their sheathes.

"Captain Brownless, as of this moment you are my prisoner," Fanny asserted with a bold, commanding voice.

Still half asleep, the groggy captain looked up from his bunk, confused. "What did you say?" he mumbled, hung-over.

Fanny pointed her pistol directly at the captain's chest. "I said, you're a dead man, sir, if you leave your cabin or try to resist. Remain here peacefully and you will not be harmed. I am taking over this ship and if you refuse to cooperate, you will be flung overboard into eternity with only your sins to keep you company."

"Why this is mutiny!" Brownless sat up, suddenly sober.

"Call it what you will, but as a captain, you are incompetent." Fanny shrugged. "As of this moment, I am the captain of this brig and you, sir, are my prisoner."

Without another word, she stepped outside and locked the captain in his quarters.

"You can't get away with this!" Brownless pounded on the door. "I'll have you hanged and quartered!"

"I suggest you accept your fate a little more quietly," Fanny told him. "Because if I have to come back in there, I will silence you permanently." She stood there for a moment and listened, satisfied when Brownless did not reply.

Next, she secured the first mate, who was terrified and surrendered without incident. "Please, Mr. Channing, I will do whatever you say. I won't cause a minute's trouble if you just spare my life."

"Show your obedience by being quiet, Mr. Bunning" ordered Fanny. "You and the captain are under arrest. We will bring you food and water, but as of right now, you must stay in your cabin or go to the cell below decks. It's your choice."

Before Bunning could answer, Fanny locked him in. She waited a moment and when no sounds of protest came from inside, she turned to go.

Back on deck, Fanny found Jack Herbert at the helm. "It is done, Jack. I've secured Brownless and Bunning in their quarters."

"So you are now our captain?" Jack smiled.

"Yes, for better or worse, I am in charge of the Constance. Or, shall I say we are in charge here since you are now my first mate."

"We should let the men know," Jack offered quietly.

"Yes, yes, of course," Fanny agreed. "Go call everyone on deck."

As soon as the men were gathered, Fanny wasted no time. "I have news," she began with a ring of authority in her voice. "Captain Brownless and Mr. Bunning have been disarmed and are now locked in their cabins as my prisoners. Some of you may call it mutiny, but I have taken possession of this British brig for your own safety." Her words were greeted with stunned faces and mostly silence, although a few men sighed in relief. "I alone am responsible for what has happened on board this ship today, but there are things you don't know so if you'll allow me, I'll explain further unless there are objections."

"Go on, sir," Findley spoke up first.

"Yes, sir," another called out. "You've always treated us fairly and we owe you the courtesy of listening to your story."

"Thank you," Fanny nodded touched by the crew's sincerity. "I believe most of you signed up for a short time. You planned to be back in the colonies with your families in a few weeks. Is that right?"

A chorus of 'Ayes' went up in reply.

"My good men, I want you to know that Captain Brownless had other plans and his treachery threatened each and every one of you. He intended to take this brig to England and you along with it. He was going to press you all into service for several years...whether you agreed or not."

A collective gasp greeted this bit of information.

"Are you sure about this, sir?" Findley asked quietly, knowing the answer.

"I am sorry to say I am," said Fanny. "This, in part, is why I have taken over the Constance and it's my intention, as your captain, to pay every man aboard a double wage--"

The men interrupted him with a loud cheer—all except the rotund cook who was the only other Englishman aboard. He remained quiet and withdrawn, glaring at Fanny who duly noted the man's sullen expression, but did not make mention of it.

"I will treat all of you fairly, but if any of you so choose." Fanny looked squarely at the kitchen master, "we will drop you at the next port and pay your passage home, no questions asked. But now, I need to know just how many of you are willing to stay on board with me?"

"ALL!" was the response from every quarter except the cook, who scowled.

"Thank you, my men," continued Fanny keeping a suspicious

eye on the Englishman. "Your support is essential in our imminent quest, which I will try to explain. From now on, Mr. Herbert will be my second in command. You will obey him as you would me. I shall alter our course to Port-au-Prince on Hispaniola where we will rid ourselves of Captain Brownless and Mr. Bunning, along with anyone else who wishes to forego our new mission and leave the *Constance*."

"And good riddance to 'em!" one man chortled.

Now Fanny spoke directly to the man from the kitchen. "When we get there, if any of you change your mind about staying, you will be free to leave…as I said, no questions asked…and your passage home will be paid. As for me and this brig, we are bound on an expedition to free two noble Americans wrongly held in a Cuban prison. After that we will determine what comes next…together."

The crew of the Constance then joined in with a unanimous "Hurrah! Hurrah!" while the cook folded his arms in a show of even greater displeasure.

"In the meantime, you can be sure that I have the comfort and well-being of every one of you at heart for as long as we sail," Fanny promised with a smile. "And one last thing, mates…since you are nearly all Americans, it is my intention to make this an American ship. As such, we might possibly be of service to the colonies in their struggle against the king."

"Three cheers for Captain Channing!" shouted the men while the cook stomped back to the kitchen without a uttering a word.

"Enough!" Fanny raised her hand. "It's time to get back to work and take your enthusiasm with you. This ship can't sail herself!"

⚓

It was several day's sail to the Port-au-Prince side of the island of Hispaniola—a place Fanny chose due to its well-known tolerance of piracy. The other half of Hispaniola, known as the Dominican Republic, was a mixture of Spanish and French rule. These citizens did not take as kindly a view of piracy as their Port-au-Prince counterparts. Jack Herbert knew of a small cove along the coast where they could row the men ashore and be well on their way before Bunning or Brownless could walk to the nearest town where they might report the crew of the Constance as renegade pirates. Hopefully, they would not encounter the real pirates of the *Crimson Blade*.

The men appeared to be happy under their new captain. They worked hard and had no complaints, especially about their pay increase. The cook, however, remained moody and angry, but he kept to himself, preparing food and serving meals as usual. If Fanny had any suspicions as to the man's loyalty she said nothing, but kept her guard up at all times. For the most part, Marion remained in her cabin, but now with Fanny in charge, she welcomed Jack to her bed after his watch in the wee hours of the morning, when most were asleep.

On the fourth night under Fanny's authority, Jack Herbert was on watch at the helm, while the new captain was asleep in her cabin. The cook quietly left his hammock carrying two swords and crept to the captain's cabin where Brownless was still being held. He released the prisoner, handed him a weapon and the two men snuck out to find Fanny. They were pleasantly surprised to see that her door was ajar and the light extinguished. They entered the room full of confidence, groping their way through the dark cabin. Just as the two reached the cot where Fanny lay, she suddenly jumped from her bed, sword in hand. The fat cook and the alcohol-ridden Brownless were no match for the agile Fanny who was quick with her long saber. As the three men battled, the ruckus they made was heard by the night crew and within seconds several men, led by Terrance Mooney, arrived carrying lanterns.

They were too late to help, however. Instead, they found the former captain along with the cook lying on the floor soaked in their own blood—three swords lay next to them. Fanny stood in the doorway with a pistol cocked in each hand.

"Get them out of here," she ordered with a slight catch in her voice. "Consign them to the deep once they've taken their last breaths!"

"Aye, aye, sir" Terrance nodded his approval. "Let them be the devil's problem from now on."

It wasn't long before the two men expired and were cheerfully interred in Davey Jones's locker. The crew however, voiced their suspicions of Bunning who was still locked in his room. It was obvious he could not be trusted, but Fanny forbade any further bloodshed. Her stern countenance kept the men from killing the former first mate, but it wasn't until the next day, when they finally anchored off the deserted bay near Port-au-Prince and Jack rowed the man ashore with all of his belongings, that Fanny breathed a sigh of relief.

As she watched Bunning depart, Fanny nodded with satisfaction. There was no question—she was truly the master of the *Constance*, where now only loyal Americans remained aboard. As they set sail for Havana, Fanny prayed they would find William Lovell alive.

CHAPTER 13

Liberty and Union

Shortly after Fanny took control of the *Constance*, the lookout stationed atop the mast shouted, "Sail ho! A large one, Sir! Two degrees forward of the starboard beam, captain!"

Fanny, who was headed north through the Windward Passage on a port-reach searched the horizon with her spyglass. There, just as the lookout had described, was a great ship making her way south through the passage. It appeared to be a large English barque of about 500 tons, which soon could be seen in its entirety by all hands on the deck of the *Constance*. The men were in awe of her three graceful square-rigged masts forward, with the sternmost, fore and aft rigged. Her masts were so tall that her skysail appeared like a bird in flight. She was stunning and would no doubt be a fine prize if the *Constance* could outrun and out-gun her.

Unable to determine what kind of weaponry the ship held, Fanny ordered Jack up the ratlines to the crow's nest where he might assess the stranger's munitions. Jack strained as he peered through the spyglass trying to make out her guns.

"Can you see anything?" Fanny shouted up to her first mate.

"Seems she has five or six cannonades on deck, but nothing of a heavy caliber so far as I can tell," Jack called down. "But she carries the flag of the British East India Company and should be a rich prize, captain."

Fanny hesitated. Taking the risk of attack might deter them from their real mission. As captain, however, she knew that the barque might attack first and, being the aggressor, would give them the upper hand.

"Very good, Mr. Herbert," Fanny made her decision. "That's all we need to know. Let's see how well our little brig can hold up against such a heavy lady."

Jack shimmied down the lines. "Should we run up the flag of Taunton to let them know we are colonists?" he asked Fanny.

"I believe so," Fanny concurred. "You can be sure that our flag has never been seen in these latitudes. It's probably the first time it has flown anywhere near the West Indies and I think it's about time we announce ourselves as American Patriots." Fanny paused for a moment, deep in thought. "Perhaps we should wait until we attack. If they continue to believe we are a British merchant ship then we will take them by surprise."

"Very good, sir" Jack gave a quick bow before he left the helm and made his way to Marion's cabin. There, he warned his wife to stay below-decks and far away from any stray bullets that might find their way to the Constance.

"But Jack," she protested with a frown. "You are putting yourself in harm's way."

"We all knew the risks we might have to take on this journey," he assured her with a quick kiss. "But you shouldn't worry...I'll be fine."

"Then why did you come down here if you weren't worried?"

"I need the flag that Moll made us bring."

"The Taunton flag?"

"Yes, do you have it?"

Marion opened one of her large trunks and pulled out a folded red banner, which she handed to Jack. "Godspeed, my love," she whispered. "I will be praying for you."

"Pray for all of us." He held her close and felt her tremble. "And as soon as it is safe, I'll come to you."

"Promise me, Jack," she whispered.

"I swear on all that is good, I'll hold you in my arms again soon."

When Jack returned on deck, he carried a bright red flag bearing a Union Jack in the upper left-hand corner. Emblazoned in large white letters across the lower half of the flag were the words 'Liberty and Union'. Commonly referred to as the Taunton flag, the banner was first raised in October of 1774 by the Sons of Liberty in Taunton, Massachusetts, in defiance of the British, after the colonists ran the Loyalists out of their town. Many Americans had since adopted the flag as a symbol of their revolt.

Fanny then gave the order to fire one shot across the other ship's bow, announcing the presence of the newly ordained 'American' brig.

"Run up the flag, Mr. Herbert," Fanny called out. "And do it quickly so there is no question about our identity. We are proud Americans! Isn't that right, men?"

The crew cheered in response as they watched Jack hoist the flag up the aft halyard in an act of rebellion. When it reached the peak of the gaff about two-thirds of the way up, Jack stopped pulling the ropes. This position announced their hailing port to the barque.

Fanny knew that the *Constance* did not appear well-armed, especially from a distance. With her ports closed, she hid her armament well and this deception gave them an advantage. Even their long-tom gun amidships on her starboard was covered with line and disguised as ship's gear. The English barque's captain returned fire long before he was within range, believing he could make easy prey of the *Constance*.

"Clear the long-tom," ordered Fanny. "Let's play a game with our long barrel, Mr. Herbert! That just might do it if they lack arms as you say."

"I'm convinced of it, sir," Jack grinned. "Otherwise, he wouldn't be using such small shot at this distance."

"Then step lively and don't waste one shot from that gun, sir."

Jack aimed the weapon directly at the English ship, but his inexperience with heavy weaponry affected his accuracy. That first shot sunk halfway between the two vessels. His second shot hit the water a quarter mile in front of the barque and the third followed as far astern.

"It appears you have the elevation right, Mr. Herbert," Fanny pointed toward the barque. "Now aim the shot right between the last two and I think you've got it."

"Aye aye, sir!" Jack fired the gun once more and a massive amount of splinters flew from the deck of the English ship.

"Well done, Mr. Herbert!" smiled Fanny as the crew cheered. "Now don't let that gun cool! Keep firing!"

It was a one-sided battle with the crew of the barque. Their short-range weaponry made it impossible for them to return the volley with any real damage to the *Constance*. Fanny wisely kept her distance and within a short time, the *Constance* shredded the barque's rigging and deck, killing a number of her crew. She quickly took on water due to the holes in her freeboard and waterlines.

The British captain soon realized that it was time to lower his flag, or his ship would surely sink where she lay. The crew of the *Constance* cheered as they watched the British flag fall to their Taunton flag of the American colonies, a flag the British captain had never seen before.

As far as Fanny knew, this may have been an American ship's very first capture on the high seas. More glory and power might follow, but for now, Fanny was relieved that they had triumphed in their first encounter with the enemy.

⚓

Once the *Constance* was close enough, grappling hooks were hurled to tether the English vessel to her own bow. Several members of Fanny's crew cautiously climbed onto the *St. George of Bristol* intending to overtake it. Once aboard, they found several bloodied bodies scattered upon the deck and the barque's captain, with his white-powdered wig slightly askew—a puzzled look etched across his face.

"What kind of flag are you sailing under, captain?" he demanded of Fanny who was just climbing over the ship's rail.

"The flag of the colonies," Fanny replied with a slight bow.

"The colonies?!" The man sputtered obviously unprepared to face a political enemy of the Crown. "I assumed you were buccaneers...another pirate ship on the prowl for booty!"

"Hardly buccaneers, sir!" Fanny drew her sword. "We are American Patriots!"

"Is there a difference?!" the British man growled, clearly agitated since he and everyone else knew that the colonists did not have a navy, let alone any real ships. "I should have sunk her where she lay!" he raged on. "Or better yet, have her taken by real pirates!!!"

"It makes no difference," Fanny shrugged. "You were beaten by a superior foe. That is all there is to it."

"I lowered my flag to a REBEL!" he screamed. "My superiors will have me hanged and quartered for this!"

"Your superiors will soon realize that we Americans are a mighty foe," Fanny raised her sword for emphasis. "As mighty as any pirates who sail these waters."

"The devil you say!" The captain spat on the deck near Fanny's feet. "What do you Americans plan to do with my ship and crew? Hang us all from the yardarm?"

"Sir, I give you my word that you all will be treated justly as 'prisoners of war' should be."

"Pardon me, Captain Channing?" Terrance Mooney interrupted the two men. "I know a good Irishman on board this ship, sir. He's volunteered to join our side and be part of our crew.

"An Irishman, like you?" asked Fanny.

"Aye, aye, sir, he's Irish to his backbone…his name's O'Hara. My sainted mother taught him to read and write when he was just a wee lad. We used to hunt in the woods for leprechauns in between lessons."

"Well then, Mr. Mooney, we could use another man like yourself. If you will take responsibility for his good behavior, he will be paid double wages along with the rest of the men. And if we should run into any leprechauns, I trust the two of you will know what to do."

"That we would, sir!" Terrance smiled and motioned for O'Hara to join him. The lanky, red-haired man looked weathered, but his green eyes held a glint of mischief, which made Fanny smile.

"Now, Mr. Herbert, let's see if there are any other sailors aboard who would like to double their pay," Fanny said, turning to Jack.

"Aye, aye, sir!"

As it turned out, the *St. George of Bristol* proved to be a rich prize indeed. The ship was ultimately bound for Boston, carrying a large load of gold and silver coin along with tea and other provisions fitting for any army. She also held a stable of small arms and munitions, which would soon prove handy to the crew of the *Constance*. The prize also brought with it three British officers and 14 crew. Two claimed to be Americans and volunteered to join the *Constance*, along with the Irishman, Tom O'Hara.

Having learned his lesson with the immoral *Brownless*, Fanny ordered half of the remaining men to board her ship and kept the other half on board the barque. All were detained under close confinement. She then divided her own crew between the two ships putting Jack Herbert, with a crew of six from the *Constance*, in command of the *George*. As repairs were made to the damaged ship, Fanny and Jack agreed to remain within hailing distance of each other should they need to communicate.

Back in the colonies, Boston remained a city under siege and in desperate need of munitions, as well as provisions. General George Washington had arrived in Cambridge and, brandishing a sword, formally took charge of the Continental army. He set up his headquarters in the Benjamin Wadsworth House on the campus of Harvard College, but soon found the place too small to suit his growing staff, so he moved into a larger place located on Brattle Street. This mansion had been built in 1759 by a Loyalist named John Vassall who, like other Loyalists in the area, had fled and abandoned their homes once the conflict started. At the time of General Washington's occupation, the house was being used as a hospital for those soldiers wounded at Lexington and Concord.

As Washington settled in, the Second Continental Congress was hard at work putting together 'The Olive Branch Petition' in one more effort to make peace with King George III and avoid war. In their document, they pledged loyalty to the Crown and at the same time asked that their rights as British citizens be upheld. Patriot John Adams had his doubts about the whole matter, however. He believed there would be no sympathy from England and that war was inevitable.

The Second Continental Congress also wrote another document, which they called the 'Declaration of the Causes & Necessity of Taking up Arms'. This paper outlined exactly why they had resorted to violence against the British army in the first place. It further stated that they held no ill will toward the king, but strongly felt that they were being mistreated by his representatives and would resort to violence if their voices were not peacefully heard.

All the while privateers like the *Constance*, manned by young patriotic sailors who felt passionate about their cause, continued capturing stores and munitions on the high seas, and delivering them to the colonial army back home to aid in the war effort. It was their fervent hope to help General Washington and his army, no matter how small their contribution.

Moll Pitcher continued to secretly receive the arms and bury them deep in the wolf pits behind her home in Lynn. If her recent visions were accurate, the time would soon come when the Continental army would need her cache of weaponry and she would be ready.

In the meantime, "Bartholomew Channing", totally unaware of events back home, felt fully justified in capturing the *St. George of Bristol*. Now the enemy had one less ship with which to wage war upon the colonists, or provide the British with much-needed stores.

CHAPTER 14

Dead Reckoning in Havana

Both ships remained within sight of each other as they
sailed on towards Havana. They stayed within sight of the
Cuban coastline even after they reached the eastern end of
the island in the Windward Passage. At dawn, they rounded the
island's northeastern side, and headed towards the Straits of Florida, keeping well offshore to avoid the keen eyes of the natives.
Fanny stood on deck and breathed in the pleasing scents that
graced the air with a feel of perpetual summer. That fresh aura
was in deep contrast with the steep and rugged shoreline that
foretold of immediate danger. Soon, they would be ashore and
their real mission only beginning, thought Fanny as she closed
her eyes in an effort to dispel the foreboding feeling that gripped
her stomach.

For the most part, however, Fanny was pleased with her
choices so far. Jack made a fine captain on board the barque, as
well as a faithful confidante who never failed to bolster Fanny's
spirits when her fears surfaced. Other than a morning and afternoon walk, Marion stayed inside her cabin. Her outings were
strategically timed so that she and Jack could glimpse each other
from the foredeck without raising any eyebrows. Terrance, who
had taken Jack's spot as first mate, was happy to have his boy-

hood friend, Tom O'Hara, nearby. The two reminisced about their past and O'Hara was genuinely saddened to hear of Colleen Mooney's demise.

"When me own mother died." O'Hara wiped away a tear "It was your mother, Terrance, who taught me right from wrong. I never forgot her and I never will. I often tell me wife and children about how kind she was to a lad who was lost."

"You're married?" Terrance was surprised and delighted.

"Nigh on three years now," O'Hara nodded. "With two fine sons to show for it."

"Where is home now, Tom?"

"Marblehead and when I get back there, I'm going to join General Washington's ranks. I hear he is in need of good men and I don't want my boys growing up under a king's rule."

"So how did you end up on that British barque?" Terrance asked.

"We needed the money and all I'm really good at is sailing. So when the job was offered, I took it, but now with the extra money from Channing, I can provide for me family and fight for me country all at the same time."

"My sainted mother would be proud of you," Terrance smiled, but his eyes held a certain sadness.

"She would be proud of both of us," O'Hara corrected his friend. "We are on a risky mission....one that she would surely approve of if she were still with us."

"Do you really think so?" Terrance asked.

"I do," O'Hara nodded. "But what are your plans when we get back home?"

"Maybe I'll go with you," Terrance smiled. "It would be fitting to fight together."

"Maybe it was your mother that brought us together again," O'Hara mused. "Did you ever think of that?"

"Maybe," Terrance nodded.

"Either way, Washington will have two good men to fight for him!"

"And under the sainted Colleen Mooney's heavenly watch," Terrance grinned.

⚓

Fanny routinely monitored the stars with her sextant to determine their position, since she was unfamiliar with the local waters of the Greater Antilles, as well as their hidden shoals and reefs. Luckily, there were several among the crew who had sailed the West Indian trade route for years—these men possessed an unparalleled wealth of knowledge concerning their course, its waters, and, most importantly, its hazards. Fanny, being a shrewd captain, put these more experienced sailors in charge of navigation for the two vessels making sure that the most efficient and safest course was plotted. It was imperative that no more time be wasted in reaching their ultimate destination.

During daylight hours, Fanny as Channing maintained her authority and her camaraderie with the men. The crew liked her sense of fairness, as well as her quick wit. They were also grateful to her for saving their hides from British captivity and openly swore their allegiance to her. At night, when Fanny was alone in her cabin, she allowed her real self to surface with all of her frustration and fears. What if they were too late to save William and Samuel? What if this whole ruse was for naught? What if she had committed mutiny and killed two men for nothing? What if William had somehow escaped and found another lover on a neighboring island? Worst of all, what if Captain Burnett was right? What if William had become a hardened criminal? In her heart she knew that wasn't possible, but what if?

Due to the fact that the *Constance* had to slow her speed in order to keep the barque within hailing distance, Fanny calculated it would take nearly six more days to reach the coast of Havana, which was troubling. Maybe she had made a mistake capturing the *George* since it would add more time to their dead reckoning course to Havana. As unsettling as they were, Fanny refused to let her doubts dominate her head for long. She still clung to Moll Pitcher's prediction—she and William would soon return to Lynn, where they would marry and raise their children. Of course, once they got home there was a revolution to deal with and God only knew what trying times that might bring. She wondered what the current state of affairs were back home and hoped that their families were safe. Most nights, Fanny slept well knowing she was doing all she could to save the man she loved and, now with the barque in tow, to also help the cause of the colonies.

Although she slept in Channing's uniform in case of emergencies, each morning Fanny washed herself and would once again bind her breasts with the muslin before donning the rest of her disguise. She would then carefully re-tint her skin, repaint the scar on her cheek and then run her fingers through her bobbed hair. Something about the disguise gave her comfort. Pretending to be someone else forced her to concentrate on the matters at hand, instead of an uncertain future. Somehow dressing as a man gave her greater confidence and more courage than Fanny would have ever found as a woman.

Three days after the taking of the *George*, Fanny stood at the aft-rail watching the barque as it followed in the *Constance's* wake. He made sure the taffrail log was secure as it dragged

along behind them, gauging the ship's speed. Fanny leaned over
the stern to get a closer look at the mechanism, but a commotion
on the deck of the *George* caught her eye as the ship turned into
irons. Within seconds, she gave the order to strike the topsails
and likewise heave-to in irons in wait of the barque. Then, she
ordered a tender to be lowered and Fanny, along with Terrance
Mooney, who carried enough pistols for both of them, descended
into the boat. They quickly rowed over to the *George* and as they
grew closer, they could hear shouting and the sounds of scuffling.

Fanny and Terrance ascended the side of the ship and climbed
over the railing before the crew of the *George* even noticed their
presence. To Fanny's horror, she found Jack Herbert bound and
bleeding from a wound to the shoulder as well as a gash above
his right eye. Two of Jack's crew stood guard over him, but no
one tried to help him, or tend to his injuries. Fanny leapt upon the
deck with a pistol in each hand, two in her waist, and a murderous look in her eyes. Terrance stood next to her ready to fire his
own weapon if needed.

"Untie that man!" Fanny pointed her pistols at the scoundrel
who seemed to have led the attempted mutiny. The crew gathered
forward of the mast grumbling under their breath, but no one
stepped up to release Jack from his restraints. Before Fanny could
utter another word, one man bounded aft to cut the tiller line that
held the ship in irons. He grasped the rope in one hand and his
blade in the other. "According to my reckoning," he screamed at
Fanny. "You ain't old enough to command two vessels!"

"You cut that rope and you sever your own life!" Fanny's calm
voice belied her anger as she pointed both pistols directly at the
renegade.

The man paused for just a moment before defiantly slicing the
rope, allowing the ship to fall off the wind. In the blink of an eye,
Fanny fired a ball straight through the man's heart. With a loud,
agonizing scream, the man was blown straight into the sea—a
corpse before he ever hit the water.

"Now then," Fanny said, maintaining a low, lyrical tone. "Might there be any more of you who wish to share that man's fate?" She looked over the men keeping her fingers perched on the triggers of her two Flintlocks.

"No, sir," mumbled several of the mutinous men, who had somehow managed to escape their confines.

"That Turner made us do it," one long-haired tar spoke up. "He was a bad apple, sir, and I assure you, we are not like him."

"Give us another chance, sir, and we'll prove our loyalty," a second man added in a shaky voice. "It won't happen again and we'll even sail for you if you are still offering up those double wages."

"From now on, we'll follow your orders to the letter," a third joined in as their late comrade-in-arms floated face down alongside the hull. "You seem a fair sort. If only you might find it in your heart to forgive us."

"My forgiveness depends upon your future conduct." Fanny frowned at the men. "And be assured, I will be watching each and every one of you, closer than your mother did. And, I can promise you this…there will be no more chances under my command or you will join your mate in Davy Jones's locker. Is that understood?"

"Aye, sir," they all nodded meekly.

"Then untie Captain Herbert and tend to his wounds. NOW!"

Once Jack was on his feet, the mutineers were taken aboard the *Constance* and exchanged for the same number of that ship's original crew. Fanny could then see for herself whether these men really had had a change of heart, or if they were indeed a threat to her crew and their mission.

Fanny remained aboard the *George* long enough to see that Jack's wounds were only superficial.

"Are you well enough to keep charge here?"

"I am," Jack nodded. "But thank God you came when you did, or I might not be here at all."

"We are all here to take care of each other," Fanny smiled. "You would have done the same for me."

"Please let Marion know that I'm all right," Jack whispered. "She'll be worried."

"That I can do," Fanny nodded. "But everything else aside, we must remember why we are really here."

Jack nodded his agreement. "We have to get to Havana before it's too late."

That night, the sun set rapidly and Fanny put her most trusted man, Terrance Mooney, on mid-watch, between midnight and 4 a.m. It had been a trying day and if she didn't get some rest, she would be useless if another uprising occurred, even though the mutinous men now seemed contrite and regretted their deceitful conduct. They had noted how she'd kept her temper during the entire skirmish, exerting an amazing amount of self-control. Even the shooting of Turner garnered their respect. "Channing" may have been a young captain, but at the same time, he was strong and decisive—traits of a good leader. Of course, the double wages helped.

While Fanny rested, Terrance stood watch. It was a quiet night with calm seas and bright moonlight that danced off the water. Something about the endless blanket of stars made Terrance think of his mother. He said a quiet prayer for the redemption of her soul, even though it most likely didn't need redeeming. If the sainted Colleen Mooney hadn't passed through those pearly gates then there was no hope left for the rest of them.

⚓

Luckily the next three days were uneventful because the excitement of seeing William again was almost more than Fanny could contain. She still desperately feared for his life and well-being. What if he hadn't made it? The thought crept into the back of her mind over and over again. Life without William was inconceivable and, as the days dragged by, she tried to shake off that morbid feeling by concerning herself with the situation at hand. Despite the danger that surrounded them, it was imperative that they anchor off the coast in a place where they would not be noticed or raise suspicion. There, they could wait until dark before attempting the rescue. Fanny would use the time to collect her thoughts and step up to her ultimate job, not just as the captain of two vessels, but also the savior of the man she loved.

Fanny chose a spot off-shore to lay anchor, in a remote and unpopulated area of the Cuban coastline where hills shrouded the ships from the harbor, yet close enough to row their tender into Havana harbor. As the moon rose over the water, she called a meeting with Jack, Terrance, and Marion. By now, Terrance knew mostly everything including the fact that Jack and Marion were married. He was not aware, however, of "Captain Channing's" real identity. Not that he couldn't be trusted, but the fewer who knew their secret, the better.

As they huddled together on the bridge of the *Constance*, they fine-tuned their plan. It was mutually agreed that they should not be brazen and enter Havana harbor with their ships. Instead, they would wait until the next evening and, with a few chosen crew, pilot the small tender directly into port. Fanny and Jack would then go on to rescue William and Samuel, before the two ships lying at anchor well outside the breakwater raised any questions from the local authorities.

Fanny consulted a small, hand-drawn map of the harbor that Jack had prepared from his memory of the prison.

"Are you sure that this map is accurate?" Fanny questioned

Jack one last time.

"Every inch of it, sir. You have my word. That hell-hole will be ingrained in my memory forever."

"And the exact location of the jailer's ward?"

"At the entrance of the underground prison, port-side...right where I marked it." He pointed to a spot near the middle of the paper.

"Then we proceed as planned," announced Fanny with an air of confidence.

"Aye aye, sir," Jack nodded. "We will take a boat with six well-armed men. Once we reach La Cabana, we must subdue the sentinels that guard the turrets."

"And you're sure there is only one guard stationed at each turret?" Terrance asked.

"I'm positive," Jack nodded. "One of them also covers the entrance to the prison. And we have the element of surprise on our side. These cursed Spanish sentries sleep at their posts half the time....so if we're lucky, we will find them napping."

"When is the guard changed?" Terrance wanted to know.

"Eight, twelve, and four," Jack answered. "So it's imperative that we arrive at one. By then, the midnight guard will be settled in for his watch."

"And we must, at all costs, maintain complete silence," Fanny spoke up. "We can't risk rousing the entire barracks. Are we all in agreement here?"

Terrance and Jack concurred.

"Good," Fanny smiled. "Come aboard the brig at half past nine this evening. Be well armed. I will select the rest of the men and I will leave a trustworthy force in charge of our ships."

"Can I come with you?" Marion spoke up for the first time.

"Absolutely not." Jack shook his head. "La Cabana is no place for a lady."

"But Fanny--?" -she cut herself short.

"--Fanny will be grateful to see William come home," Fanny raised an eyebrow. "And she will be grateful to all of you who played a part in saving him."

"I just want to do more," Marion sighed. "And I want to be with Jack, in case--"

"--In case I find an attractive Spanish woman?" Jack grinned at his wife. "I don't recall meeting any senoritas the last time I was there."

"It's not funny, Jack." Marion narrowed her eyes. "I've simply come all this way and I want to be part of the mission."

"You have been an immense help to us," Fanny assured her. "We never would have gotten this far without you. Besides, we need someone we can trust to keep an eye on the ships while we're ashore. You can brandish a sword, or a pistol if you need to."

"I don't like being left behind," Marion frowned. "If you don't hurry back, I'm not sure how long I'll be able to wait before I take a tender to shore myself."

Thus, Fanny, Jack, Terrance and a disappointed Marion went their separate ways planning to meet again at the appointed hour.

⚓

As the sun dipped below the horizon and evening stretched across the water, the two vessels sat side by side just beyond the island. The minutes dragged and the hours seemed endless as Fanny picked at her dinner, impatient for their mission to begin.

Doubts plagued her once again as she paced up and down the main deck, hands clasped behind her back.

Finally....it was time for them to go ashore and launch this long-awaited rescue. The tender, loaded with Jack, Terrance, and their chosen men, tied up alongside the *Constance*. Fanny appeared, wearing dark pants and a dark jacket. A heavy silk sash, which held a pair of boarding pistols, was tied tightly around her waist along with a light cutlass that hung at her side. Before descending into the stern of the tender, she passed down an extra brace of pistols and another cutlass. "Our friends may require arms once they are liberated," she explained as she settled into the boat. "Is all in order here?"

"Aye aye, sir," Jack replied. "All is according to plan." He called up to Marion, "Remember...if we are not back by dawn the ships must weigh anchor and sail without us."

"You must be here," insisted Marion. "I cannot live with any other outcome."

The men waved to Marion as she stood alone, bent over the railing on the deck. She blew a kiss for good luck and stood there shivering, despite the warm air, until the tender was lost from her view.

The new moon and silent oars guided the boat with speed and stealth. There was just enough light to make out the rocky shoreline. It was a long way to the harbor entrance, but eventually they slipped past the enormous Moro Castle. They kept close to shore and soon reached the chosen spot where they had agreed to disembark.

CHAPTER 15

The Rescue

Leaving one man in charge of the tender, Fanny and the others crept quietly toward the fort's prison. Fanny's heartbeat quickened and her hands were sweaty in anticipation of this long-awaited moment. She prayed that they weren't too late. Would they find William and Samuel alive? If so, what condition would they be in after all these months of captivity and suffering? Either way, it wouldn't be much longer before Fanny had her questions answered, assuming they weren't caught and imprisoned themselves.

The natural rock that the fort was built upon allowed them to climb the upper wall and get close enough to the gun turrets, so they could throw a rope over the barrel of the mounted cannon. Pulling themselves up, they were easily able to scale the steep walls of La Cabana. As Fanny and company reached the top, the sharp voice of the sentinel guarding the western, starboard wall rang out. "Quien va alla? Muéstrate!"

Jack put a finger to his lips indicating silence and then motioned for the rest to keep close. He led the group, crawling on his hands and knees and then snuck up on the first guard before the man was able to utter another word. Jack pounced upon the soldier from the rear, covering his mouth and hitting him behind the knees, quickly taking him to the ground. Jack then shoved the sentinel's own neck-cloth down his throat to keep him quiet. The others secured the struggling man with several ropes and then tied him to the guard-rail.

They quietly moved forward following Jack toward the staircase that led down to the courtyard and the underground prison entrance. Jack and Terrance easily overpowered out the next sentinel at the end of the bridge. The group then crept to the top of the stairs and peered over the edge. There stood another guard directly in front of the prison entrance. He seemed unaware of the recent scuffle. He was a muscular man and no matter how difficult, it was imperative that they seize and silence him before he could alert the fourth sentinel on duty.

Terrance stood over the man's head ready to pounce, while Jack and the others prepared their advance. Upon a signal from Jack, the others rushed down the staircase while Terrance leapt from the landing above, coming down squarely onto the back of the stunned guard. Within seconds, Terrance and Jack found themselves in a violent skirmish with the large man who called out for help. Before they could subdue the guard, the fourth sentinel appeared at the top of the stairs and drew his sword. He raced down the steps to help his comrade, but instead, found himself face-to-face with "Captain Channing", also brandishing a sword.

The others aided Jack and Terrance in capturing and binding the man on the ground as Fanny fended off their latest attacker with the handy swordplay that Moll had insisted she learn. Fanny did not wish to kill the man, only to subdue him. Rather than forcing the man back up the stairs, Fanny maneuvered him down to the courtyard below where she would be on level ground and closer to her companions. As the sentry lunged aggressively Fanny moved swiftly, but she stumbled backwards over iron shackles that were built into the stone floor and landed on her back. Fanny's weapon flew from her hand and slid away.

Realizing that Fanny was now prone and unarmed, the guard saw his chance to run her through and bounded over the chains with his sword in the air ready to finish her with one easy stroke. Out of breath and chest heaving, Fanny waited for the feel of cold steel slicing through her, but instead, the man fell forward and his weapon clattered on the stone floor. Fanny looked up to find Terrance Mooney standing over her holding a large wooden stake. Terrance had struck the guard in the back of his head and Jack had tackled him to the ground. Fanny scurried sideways like a crab, grabbed her own sword then leapt to her feet, as Terrance and Jack together bound the fourth guard. Within seconds, the angry guard was tied and gagged like the others.

Fanny bent over, placed her hands on her knees and took a deep breath. "Thank you, Terrance. I was about to become a skewered hog on the spit. I owe you my life."

"No thanks necessary...I owe you for the kindness you showed my sainted mother."

"Then perhaps we are now even," Fanny smiled.

"Perhaps," Terrance shrugged. "But I must ask, where did you learn how to handle a sword like that?"

"I had an excellent mentor." Fanny looked to Jack who now stood over the roped guard. "But that's a story for another day. Now, we must concentrate on the rest of our mission."

The guards-turned-prisoners were all moved to the same cell in the courtyard, and were left under the watchful Irish eyes of Terrance Mooney and Tom O'Hara. Only then did Fanny finally breathe a sigh of relief. So far, everything had gone somewhat according to plan.

Now, Fanny was anxious to find William. It was imperative that they be back on the ship and under sail before the changing of the guard at sunrise, when the jailbreak would be discovered. Jack leaned over the helpless sentry who had been stationed at the prison entrance and silently unclipped the ring of keys from his belt. Then he strode to the wrought iron gate leading into that horrific tomb, from which he'd escaped months before. It all came back to him in a surge of emotion—the stench, the hunger, the suffering.

Overcome by his own memories, Jack hesitated a moment before turning the key into the locked gate.

"Are you all right, Jack?" Fanny whispered.

"I will be." He steeled himself before entering that dark, narrow passageway. Fanny followed closely while the others, according to plan, stood guard outside. Only one more obstacle stood between them and their goal.

Jack guided Fanny to the old jailer's quarters, where they found the elderly man asleep in his bed. He started at the sound of their footsteps and sat straight up, his gray hair tousled.

"Give us your keys, old man," Jack demanded.

"No English, sénior," the toothless man muttered. "No English."

"Key!" Jack repeated and with his hand made a motion of opening a lock.

"I've got them!" Fanny strode into the bedroom and held up an old iron ring with several keys dangling from it. "They were hanging over the doorway. We walked right past them."

"Misericordia! Misericordia!" the terrified jailer repeated. "Misericodia!"

"Tie him up, but not too tightly," Fanny ordered, feeling a twinge of sympathy. "Just make sure he doesn't escape. We are so close now, we don't want anyone making trouble...not even a harmless old man."

"He's hardly harmless," Jack frowned. "I recall being beaten within an inch of my life by this harmless old man and his wooden club."

"Take care of him accordingly then," Fanny suppressed a shudder. "We've wasted enough time here."

After trussing up the jailer, Jack once again took the lead, rushing down two long, dark hallways and then descending what seemed like an endless set of winding stairs. They passed several dirty cells—some with occupants, some empty. The dank air and stench that seemed to emanate from the ground overwhelmed them and it was all Fanny could do to keep breathing. How could anyone survive this appalling place? Jack was right when he called it a 'hell-hole.' The thought of William being here for a day let alone over a year was more than Fanny could bear.

With each step forward, Fanny's tension grew until Jack stopped abruptly in front of a cell.

"William?" She peered inside. "Samuel?"

Two emaciated men stirred from the spot where they lay, but didn't answer.

"Open the door." Fanny's voice rang with impatience. "Hurry!"

Jack tried the first key, but it didn't work. Nor did the second one. Fanny strained to see past him into the darkened cell, but could barely make out the two figures inside. "Come on, Jack!" Fanny could no longer contain herself. "We've got to get them out of there, now!"

As Jack inserted the fifth key, a loud click echoed in the silence and the cell door opened.

The two men inside remained silent, but watched as Jack and Fanny rushed inside.

"Bill!" Jack fell to his knees next to one of the skeleton-like men. "Are you all right?"

"Jack?!" The weakened man tried to sit up. "Jack Herbert, is it really you?"

"It's me, my friend. I've come back for you just like I promised."

The two bearded men grew more alert as they recognized Jack, who could hardly believe the miserable condition he'd found them in. Both were gaunt with stringy long hair and knotted beards. Badly bruised, Samuel had lost several teeth while William suffered open wounds on his arms and legs. Jack felt bile rising up in his throat, but he tried not to gag. It was worse than he had ever imagined.

"Bill." He reached out a hand to his friend. "Thank God you're alive."

"Jack, we knew you escaped," William choked, overcome with feeling, as the two friends embraced. "The doctor came here to tell us. He said you'd be back, but I feared once you made it home you might be afraid to return."

"You should have known me better than that. I could never have just left you here to die."

"If you can get us out of here...." Samuel finally spoke. "We will be forever in your debt.

"This is not the time for talk." Fanny made an effort to suppress her own emotions.

"Who is this?" William asked Jack, motioning toward "Channing".

"This is Captain Bartholomew Channing, the man your dear Fanny hired to orchestrate this rescue. I'm afraid you owe everything to him since I would never have been able to come here on my own."

"I'm glad we made it here in time." Fanny choked on her words as her eyes brimmed with unwanted tears.

"Captain Channing." Jack emphasized the name in an effort to remind Fanny of her position. "This is William Lovell, the man that Miss Campbell hired you to save....and our good friend, Samuel Breed, whose only sin was setting sail with us."

"Gentlemen." Fanny trembled ever so slightly as she took a deep breath. "I'm afraid we must do away with these niceties for the time being. We have to leave here at once! All can be explained once we are safely away from this awful place. Are you men able to walk?"

"I will run if I have to," Samuel said. "I would rather die trying to escape than spend one more hour here."

"Then let's go." Fanny turned, not just to lead the way, but to hide the tears that still threatened to spill out. "There's no time to waste."

With their two liberated men in tow, the rescue party collected the men who were left standing guard and hastened out of La Cabana, scrambled down the wall, and rushed to their tender. As they all climbed into the small boat, they heard the first of many drumbeats sounding the alarm back at the fort.

"One of those bastards must have gotten loose," Jack noted.

Luckily, the darkness shrouded their tiny vessel as they quickly rowed across the harbor and around the point to where both the *Constance* and the *George* awaited them. It was a long row, with the threat of capture in their wake, but finally they could make out the two ships, where they sat offshore.

As they neared the *Constance*, a lone figure could be seen peering over the rail.

"Marion!" Jack waved. "Marion! We made it!"

"Jack! Jack! I've been so worried!" she shouted back. "Did you find William and Samuel? Are they alive?"

"They're here with us!" Jack told her. "But we need help bringing them aboard. Get some men...and hurry!"

A relieved Marion dashed from the rail and returned moments

later with several crew members who helped, with a boatswain's chair attached to a halyard, to lift the weakened men from the tender up to the deck. The moment Jack's feet touched the deck, Marion rushed into his arms. After a quick embrace, he turned his attention back to his newly freed friends.

"Easy there, Bill." He steadied his friend as he stood, while Fanny let Samuel lean on her as they guided the two shaky men from the rail.

"William!" Marion gasped at the sight of this man who had once protected her from the crew of the *Blade*. He was a ghost of his former self—thin, frail, and filthy. Samuel was not much better.

"These men need food and water," Fanny ordered. "They need baths, a shave, clean clothes, and a good night's sleep."

"I'll make sure they have what they need," Terrance volunteered and then sent four mates scurrying in different directions.

"O'Hara!" Fanny went on. "Hoist the anchor! Take charge of the helm! We must set sail immediately. There's no time to waste! We will surely be caught if we remain here until daylight."

"Aye, captain!" O'Hara bowed then turned to the men. "Shake out her sail now. Anchor's aweigh!"

"Very good," Fanny nodded. "I will be in my cabin if you need me."

Within minutes the two ships' anchors were touching the hawse-pipe and the canvas was shaken out—they fell off the wind at once—hoisting full sail away from Cuban waters.

Jack led William and Samuel below decks while Marion went to check on Fanny. She knocked lightly on his door so she wouldn't wake her in case she was already asleep.

"Who's there?" Fanny's accent chimed out.

"It's Marion."

A moment later, the door opened and a bedraggled Fanny stood before her. Marion entered the room and quickly closed the door behind her. "Fanny, are you all right?"

"Hardly." Fanny, gulping for air, spoke in her normal voice. "Did you see them? Did you see how terrible they looked? Like living corpses waiting to die."

"It's all right, Fanny." Marion put her arms around her friend. "You did it! You saved them. They are going to be fine."

"We took too long." Fanny broke down, sobbing.

"But we freed them and it's all over," Marion tried to soothe her. "From now on, they are safe thanks to you. Now you have to tell William the truth."

"I can't look at him without my stomach turning," Fanny cried. "In my worst imaginings, I never dreamed it would be that bad. Oh, God, Marion, it was a hundred times worse than Jack described. The filth! The stench! The suffering! It's all too much!"

The two women crumpled to the floor—Fanny, exhausted and hysterical, with Marion who tried, but could do so little to comfort her.

"You've been brave for so long," Marion whispered. "But even heroes grow weary."

"I am weary," Fanny choked. "I am so tired, I can't even think."

"You don't have to." Marion squeezed her hand. "Get some rest. The ships are in good hands and William is out of harm's way. That's all that matters right now."

"I can't keep up this charade," Fanny confessed. "I can't let him know who I really am. I'm not sure how to face him without falling apart. What if he no longer wants me? Look at me…I look like a man. What am I going to do, Marion?"

"Give William a little time," Marion suggested. "Let him regain his strength before you tell him."

"But when shall I tell him? How shall I tell him?"

"You'll know when the time is right, dear Fanny."

"And in the meantime?"

"Continue to be the captain of the *Constance* and the *George*," Marion smiled. "Gain William's trust just like you have the rest of the men and it will all come together."

"Go take care of them, Marion." Fanny calmed herself. "Please….go do what I can't."

⚓

William was given Captain Brownless's former quarters while Samuel was assigned Bunning's berth, but they seemed most comfortable together. After all the time they were imprisoned in the same cell, it was hard for them to be separated now. For the time being, they chose to stay in Brownless's cabin where Marion brought each a tray of food and clean clothes. Jack supplied soap, water, razors, and shears.

"I still can't believe you came back for us!" William told his friend in between bites of fresh fruit.

"I can't believe you brought Marion here," Samuel added, as he too chewed on an orange that Marion had already peeled.

"She was an important part of the plan," Jack said.

"And I wasn't about to let my husband sail through the horse latitudes again without me!" Marion grinned.

"Husband?!" William echoed. "You two are married?!"

"Legally and officially!" Jack grinned and put an arm around his wife. "And when we get home, you and Fanny will do the same!"

"If my Fanny hasn't found someone else by now." William looked glum for the first time since he'd come aboard.

"You needn't worry about Fanny," Marion assured him. "I can promise you that. She is anxiously awaiting your return."

"I still don't understand how you did it," Samuel sighed. "But we are so very grateful you did."

"Your family offered the financial assistance required for the mission to work, Samuel, and they are anxious for your safe return. I know you both have many questions, but Captain Channing will explain everything in due time," Jack promised. "For now, we must clean you up and make you strong again."

"I want to talk to this mysterious Captain Channing," William mused. "I must properly thank him and I'd like to know just how he and Fanny met."

"I can assure you," Marion smiled. "It's a story you will find hard to believe."

"For now, you have nothing to worry about," Jack added. "You only need to rest and concentrate on regaining your strength so you can help us sail these two fine ships home."

"And that's another thing...just how did you come to procure two first-rate ships?"

"It seems we learned some valuable skills during our time spent as pirates," Jack smiled. "In addition to our taste for fine rum."

"Rum," Samuel repeated. "We haven't had a good drink in ages."

"How about if you each go to your own cabins and I'll bring you your very own bottle?" Marion offered with a grin.

And so for the first time in many months, William Lovell and Samuel Breed took leave of each other and slept in separate rooms—after partaking in a good, stiff drink of the finest island rum.

CHAPTER 16
Pirate Watch

The *Constance* and the *George* set a northeasterly course via the Windward Passage to the Atlantic, avoiding the Straits of Florida, since Florida, as well as the Bahamas, was still under British rule. When Spain gave Florida back to the British, it caused an exodus of the Spanish population to Cuba, leaving mostly British Loyalists to inhabit the large peninsula. As a result, Florida declined to send a delegate to the Continental Congress, thereby, taking a stand and remaining loyal to Britain. Fanny's men informed her that the British navy had a strong presence in that area, so she chose to risk a possible encounter with pirates along the northern coast of Haiti, rather than face a military battle with the redcoats. Besides, traveling near the Dominican Republic and around the Turks and Caicos, a tiny group of French-held islands, would also set them on a better point of sail to North America.

Jack Herbert informed Fanny that the Turks and Caicos were primarily populated by salt-merchants from Bermuda, not by British Loyalists. Therefore, it seemed more likely that they might encounter commercial ships owned by the British in those waters instead of the English navy. Goods on board a mercantile vessel might very well prove valuable to the American cause, as long as the threat of pirates remained at bay.

Jack was particularly worried about meeting up with the *Crimson Blade*. Those buccaneers might still be patrolling nearby waters in search of new prey. The Turks and Caicos, along with Tortuga, remained favorite enclaves for pirate ships to lay in wait for unsuspecting victims as William, Jack, and Samuel knew all too well. That great vantage point allowed the buccaneers, who were in a better position for maneuvering, to pick off the wealthy merchant ships that sailed through the Windward Passage. The wind was light in the lee of Cuba and the *Constance* was barely making five knots—the *George* even slower. With the island measuring more than 750 miles long, it would take days to escape from Cuban waters, so the ship's watch was not only on the lookout for pirates, but for official Cuban boats as well. Luckily, it seemed the Cubans weren't all that concerned about two escaped convicts who had never actually been proven to be pirates.

William and Samuel were given all the comforts they needed to recover from their long and grueling ordeal at La Cabana. Within two days, good food, warm beds, much-needed shaves, haircuts, baths, and clean clothes produced changed men on deck. Although they were still weak and very thin, their spirits were high and their newfound freedom boosted their energy. Once back on the water, William's sailor instincts had returned as sharp as ever along with a heightened awareness concerning the threat of attack. He was determined to offer up his assistance to "Captain Channing" if only he could be found. For reasons he couldn't fathom, William felt as if Channing were avoiding him, since the captain seemed confined to his cabin below deck.

⚓

Even though the colonists aboard the *Constance* and the *George* didn't know it yet, General Washington was busy gathering his army and appointing officers from his headquarters in Cambridge. A celebration marking the official founding of the Continental army was held on a Sunday afternoon in early July. Washington, in full military dress, made a regal appearance astride his horse on that bright, sweltering, summer day. Moll Pitcher was there by invitation from John Glover, an old childhood friend who had also grown up in Marblehead.

At first, Moll had declined the man's invitation. She had been preoccupied for weeks over Fanny Campbell and her expedition to save William Lovell. Moll's visions assured her that their success was imminent, but still she worried. Especially whenever she ran into Agnes Lovell who could be counted on to narrow her eyes and glower in disapproval. It was Moll's husband, Robert, who convinced her to accompany Glover, now a high-ranking officer under Washington, to Cambridge. He thought she needed the distraction and promised to take good care of the children with the help of twelve-year-old Ruth.

Glover knew full well of Moll's powers and hoped that she might have a vision or two during the festivities. As soon as they arrived, he presented her to General Washington as the 'daughter' of his Marblehead regiment. Wearing a long-waisted, black lace dress, Moll sported a dark blue bonnet and a matching lace scarf. Her elegant dress garnered respect from the crowd, as her reputation and that of her family's preceded her, but the newly named military leader just smiled kindly at this mysterious woman.

Moll gave a little curtsy as Glover spoke. "General, Mrs. Pitcher is the famous seer of Lynn. My family has had the pleasure of knowing her family in Marblehead for years...including her grandfather, The Wizard. She predicted the carnage at Breed's Hill and before that she tipped off the Sons of Liberty about the attack at Lexington and Concord."

"Then, Mrs. Pitcher," the general took her hand. "You are a true Patriot and your predictions have been more than valuable to our cause. It seems we have adopted a sibyl and a saint, and it is an honor to have you present here today."

"I assure you, sir, the honor is all mine." She gave another little curtsy before Glover escorted her to her seat behind Washington.

As the military music began, Moll had the first of her visions that day. She described a great white cloud in the sky that formed into a capital 'A'. "I see victory for America, but not before a long and hard battle," she whispered. "We must be prepared, for the worst is yet to come, but God is on our side and he will send his angels to help defend us."

"What else do you see, Moll?" Glover asked.

"I see a great land emerge." She spoke in a dream-like state. "One of the greatest lands that the world will ever see. I see that a noble friendship between Britain and this country will eventually unfold, but not in this century."

When Glover repeated Moll's predictions to the Washingtons, the general dismissed them with a smile. Not so with Lady Washington who was intrigued by Moll's words and wanted to hear more. Martha Washington had no time that afternoon to entertain the psychic, but she was determined to speak with the seer of Lynn soon. The general, who was glad that his wife had found someone to amuse her, had no objection when she invited Moll to tea two weeks later.

"Do you have any predictions for us today, Moll?" Mrs. Washington asked her honored guest as the tea was poured.

"My lady," Moll smiled. "My visions come and go. I have no control over them. I see what I see and that is all."

"So you have nothing for me today." The lady was obviously disappointed.

"I can tell you this." Moll leaned in closer to her hostess. "Let your husband know that I have arms and goods the army might use buried deep in the wolf pits of Lynn."

"But how is that possible?" Lady Washington gasped.

"The privateers and I have an understanding," Moll winked. "They obtain the merchandise and I understand what to do with it. When the army is in need, and I assure you, they will be in need, come directly to me."

"I'll tell the general of your offer." Lady Washington sipped her tea. "He will be pleased I'm sure."

"And once he gets word to me, I will hang a red tablecloth on my line to signal that the supplies are ready to be picked up. The Sons of Liberty can relay the message and no one will be the wiser."

"You are a clever woman, Moll Pitcher," Mrs. Washington smiled. "Tell me something. Is it true that you were aware of the fighting at Lexington and Concord before it actually happened?"

"I'm afraid I can't attribute my psychic abilities to that," Moll admitted with a grin. "You see, I often get visitors....British visitors....who come into my home asking me to tell their fortunes. The redcoats sometimes talk more than they should and tell me things they wouldn't normally say. And I listen....all while reading their tea leaves."

"I understand the value of your line of work to the Patriots, my dear," said Martha. "Would you do me the honor of reading my tea leaves?"

"I will try." Moll took her teacup and studied its contents in silence.

"Well?" Mrs. Washington was curious.

"My lady," Moll began. "You and the general will be forever known in this great country. Not only will he lead these colonists in battle, but once the war is over, he will lead our new nation. He will finish what the hoofbeats of Paul Revere began. The name of George Washington will be known to every man, woman, and child for generations to come...perhaps for eternity...and you are the woman who must inspire, encourage, and support all that he does."

And the first thing Martha Washington did to help her husband was to tell him about the fortune teller of Lynn and the goods she kept buried deep in the wolf pits not far from her home.

⚓

As dawn broke on their third full day at sea since leaving Cuba, William insisted that Jack arrange a meeting between himself and the elusive Captain Channing. Early that morning, William joined a reluctant Fanny on deck at the helm. Deep inside, Fanny's heart leapt to see the man she loved outlined by the rising sun as he approached her. After all of the pain and heartache caused by William's absence, she finally knew that Moll had been right all along. They would be together, but first she had to wait until the time was right before revealing her secret to him. Although it was painful to keep her distance, she managed to restrain herself and continue in her role as captain— avoiding William at all costs. It had to be this way, since Fanny feared that William might recognize her and inadvertently expose the truth. What would happen if the crew discovered they had committed mutiny under a woman's command, instead of their beloved Captain Bartholomew Channing?

As William stood next to her, Fanny took a deep breath and reminded herself that she was Captain Bartholomew Channing— an officer from Barbados. "Mr. Lovell," Fanny said as she kept her eyes focused straight out to sea. "I trust you have found your accommodations comfortable."

"Very comfortable, sir," William nodded. "But I have been wondering how I have offended you."

"I assure you," Fanny's heart skipped a beat. "You have done no such thing."

"But I feel as though you are avoiding me, captain."

"I have been busy." Fanny caught her breath. "With two ships under my command, there's much to do....especially here in pirate territory."

"That is why I am here, sir." William stood as tall as he could. "I realize how hard it is to lead one ship let alone two and so I am here to offer my services. I am an experienced sailor and I know my way around the sea."

"So Jack Herbert has told me," Fanny said.

"Has he also told you that the pirate ship, on which we were prisoners, hunts these waters and uses the Island of Tortuga as a hidden vantage point to spot prey?"

"Aye, that he did."

"Then you should also know that the *Crimson Blade*, as the ship is known, may very well think that we are a wealthy cargo ship. They just might try to dispatch us to Davy Jones's locker and confiscate our stores and provisions."

"Yes...Captain Herbert has warned me about the *Crimson Blade*. I am prepared for such an encounter if we should be unlucky enough to run into those buccaneers." Fanny hesitated a moment before continuing. "Are you concerned about what they might do to the three of you if they capture us?"

"I am sure they wouldn't allow us to live a second time."

"What if I told you that we had the advantage and could defeat them?"

"Nothing would please me more and I know that Jack and Samuel feel the same, but these delinquents are cut-throats and murderers, and far more experienced at sea battle."

"They don't scare me, Mr. Lovell," Fanny looked him in the

eye for the first time. "I will not run from the men who enslaved you for so many months. We will face them and fight. My mission is to deliver you safely back to Lynn and I intend to do just that. If the *Crimson Blade* shows her colors, they will be sorry that they ever heard the name Bartholomew Channing."

"I believe you, sir," William said, with new-found respect for the captain's bravery.

"And do you still want to offer your services?" Fanny asked.

"More than ever, sir," William nodded. "Just give me your orders."

"I would like to appoint you as my first mate."

"It would be my honor to serve you." William bowed.

"Good," Fanny smiled. "Now that we've established your rank aboard this ship, I want you to share all that you know about the *Crimson Blade*....their strategy and habits...their customs and tactics. We must know everything in case we are faced with the unpleasant task of battling them upon the open sea. We must have the upper hand at all costs."

William nodded thoughtfully and rubbed his freshly shaven chin before speaking. "Well then, sir, since the *Constance* appears to be the faster ship and can sail closer to the wind than most gaff brigs, I would suggest that if we meet them, we lure the *Blade* into the Windward Passage. But...only if we are able to gain the advantage by taking her to weather. Should we get under her lee, we will risk her fateful blows. If we can hold her at distance since she cannot sail as high, we can beat her with our long-tom. It appears to be a heavier weapon than theirs and will throw a greater fetch."

"That is exactly how we took the *George*, Mr. Lovell," Fanny said. "I believe we think alike."

"The *George* wouldn't fare well against the *Blade* so we must bait them away from her."

"I agree with everything you've said. Should we find ourselves in the position of defending the ship against them, then you will be in charge of navigation and strategy, since you did the same for them and know their inner workings."

"As honored as I am by your faith in me, I hope it's an opportunity that doesn't arise."

"I can only hope for the same," Fanny agreed. "But we must be prepared at all costs."

"Not to change the subject." William shifted from one foot to the other. "But may I ask how you came to know my Fanny?"

"I....uh....um," Fanny was caught off guard. "I met Miss Campbell through a friend of yours by the name of Moll Pitcher."

"Good old, Moll," William smiled. "Is she still having visions?"

"She is one of the finest ladies I've ever had the pleasure to know." Fanny quickly wiped away an unexpected tear hoping that William hadn't noticed.

"Fanny and I must pay a visit to Moll as soon as I return to Lynn. Maybe you could come, too, and we could tell Moll all about our adventures."

"If she doesn't know about them already," Fanny chuckled "And if it's questions we're asking...there's something I've been wondering about."

"What's that?"

"If you don't mind me asking....how did you and Mr. Breed manage to survive in the bowels of La Cabana for as long as you did?"

"It was the good doctor," William replied. "When Jack escaped, he was aided by a doctor. That doctor paid us a visit not long after Jack left. He told us that Jack promised to come back for us and that he would do what he could for us in the meantime.

He came almost every week, sneaked in medication and food. If it hadn't been for him, Samuel and I would have never made it."

"Thank God for him," Fanny murmured under her breath.

"What did you say?" William stepped closer in an attempt to hear better.

"I said, thank God someone looked after you, Mr. Lovell." Fanny felt the warmth of his breath against her cheek. He was much too close and it was all she could do to keep from taking him in her arms.

"He was very kind." William looked at her curiously. "Are you all right, Captain Channing?"

"Yes, yes, of course." Fanny caught herself. "I'm fine, but I need you well rested. Please go below now and take some more time to recover. I assure you that you will be notified immediately if our watch spots any suspicious vessels."

"I should stay on deck--"

"--that's an order Mr. Lovell." Fanny didn't trust herself. She needed him to go.

"Of course, captain, as you wish." As William turned to leave, Fanny smiled in relief. He had not an inkling who Channing really was. She had passed the most important test—Fanny had managed to fool the one man who loved her most.

CHAPTER 17

Justice

By the end of the forenoon watch, William emerged back on deck. He looked more rested, so Fanny felt secure that, between William and Terrance Mooney, the ship would be in good hands if she went below to have a meal and get some much needed rest. As a result of the overwhelming excitement that had occurred during the last twenty-four hours, she was feeling a bit under the weather. She was physically exhausted from the daring rescue and William's presence now took such an emotional toll that Fanny needed a break.

After joining Terrance at the helm, William searched the horizon with the spyglass. The *Constance* had shortened sail to allow the *George* to stay within hailing distance of their port aft quarter. William spotted Jack at the *George*'s helm and shouted to the foredeck crew that he would like a word with Captain Herbert. Within a few minutes, Jack had reached the bow so that he might converse with his friend.

"You're looking well, Bill," Jack smiled.

"Thanks to you," William grinned.

"How is Samuel?"

"Still resting," William answered. "He fared much worse than I did, I'm afraid, and remains weak, but getting stronger every day. Your Marion has made it her mission to nurse him back to health. She hovers over him like a mother would."

"Then he should be up and around in no time," Jack said. "She has a knack for care-giving. She was taking care of my mother when I got back home."

"Home," William repeated. "It seems so far away and so much has happened."

"Something on your mind, Bill?"

"There is." William leaned over the railing. "I've had a talk with Captain Channing about the *Blade*."

"Are you worried we might run into her?"

"Aren't you?'

"It's crossed my mind," Jack admitted. He, too, leaned in a little closer. "You know those buccaneers will kill us if they catch us again."

"Then we can't let them catch us," William said. "We have to stay alert and spot them before they spot us."

"We'll not fall victims to the *Blade* a second time," Jack agreed. "We'll be on the lookout and if we see them, we will be ready."

He then explained the plan he'd made with Fanny to lure the *Blade* away from the *George*.

⚓

Over the next several days, the two ships sailed in calm lee of Cuba with no threats to report. The men knew better than to let their guard down, however, and were always on the lookout for any signs of storms or impending danger unrelated to the weather. The waters near the Turks and Caicos were tranquil, but as they passed under the island known as Iguana, things took a sudden turn when the watch in the crow's nest of the *Constance* shouted, "SHIP AHOY! SCHOONER! OFF THE STARBOARD BOW!"

Both William and Fanny were on deck. Samuel, now feeling much stronger thanks to Marion, had also joined them hoping to take in the healing rays of the warm sun. At the sound of the warning, William snatched up the spyglass to check the horizon. His heart sank and his stomach turned as he focused on the unmistakable profile, rig, and canvas. He lowered the glass and the look on his face told Fanny that this ship was indeed the *Crimson Blade*.

Fanny ordered Samuel below decks where he was to warn Marion that trouble was afoot. They were to stay in her cabin until the all clear was given, while the *Constance* and the *George* took their predetermined positions. Fanny then signaled Jack aboard the *George*, but he had already seen the cursed schooner. All the while, William kept a close eye on the enemy ship, as well. The pirates had waited until the *Constance* was nearly into the Windward Passage.

Exactly as planned, the *George* made a quick jibe to the north and sneaked under the lee of Iguana as the *Constance* baited the *Blade* by heading straight for her. As the two ships grew closer, they remained on a collision course. Now within hailing distance, the *Crimson Blade* fired a warning shot across the bow of the *Constance* before running up its skull and crossbones.

William, at the helm of the *Constance*, was giving navigational instructions to Fanny who held firm to the course. Just as the *Blade* was almost close enough to ram the *Constance*, William shouted, "NOW!"

Fanny turned hard to weather to a beat—about 33 degrees off

the wind—leaving the *Blade's* crew scrambling to make a slow jibe around and give chase. At the same time, the *Constance* positioned her long-tom to fire upon the buccaneers. Within a minute, the first shot hit the *Blade* broadside, just at the waterline. The second took out much of the rigging, causing the foremast to plunge onto the deck below, crushing many of her crew.

Screams and shouts were heard over the wind in the sails of the *Constance* in between shots. The *Blade* attempted to return fire, but her metal was too short and the shot landed more than 100 yards away from the brig before falling harmlessly into the sea. A few more shots and the *Blade* started taking on enough water to doom her. Soon she would sink to the bottom of the very channel from which she had attacked many innocent merchant ships that had been unlucky enough to cross her path.

The men on board the *Constance* and the *George* watched as the able-bodied Pirate crew abandoned their schooner and jumped into the sea, attempting to swim to shore. Moments later and with water rushing into the gaping holes in her hull, the *Crimson Blade* made her final death roll. Many of the men in the water were caught up in her rigging or swept away by the strong current that raced through the passage. As the *Constance* tacked to come around and fall off the wind to witness her spoils, William spotted Josh and Levi, the two young boys indentured by the pirates, clinging to a wooden rail. William immediately gave the order to harden up into irons, so that he could rescue his young friends under Fanny's watchful eye. He had often thought about the boys he had mentored while he was in La Cabana, and always felt guilty about leaving them behind.

Once aboard the *Constance*, the two boys threw their arms around William as they recognized the man who had shown them such kindness. "Mr. Lovell, Mr. Lovell!" the boys cried, thrilled to see their trusted friend. "It's you!"

"Yes, it's me! I have worried about you and I had hoped you two had found a way to escape those buccaneers."

"We tried," Levi answered. "But there was just no way out."

"Let me look at you for a moment." William took a step back. "You've grown and become men since I saw you last."

"We speak better English now, thanks to you," Josh sighed. "But like it or not, the *Blade* was our home and now we have nowhere to go."

"You can come home with me," William smiled. "As a matter of fact, I insist you do. You can go to school in Lynn and learn a trade."

"You mean we'd be free?" Levi asked.

"To do whatever you want," William assured them. "And I will be there to help you."

Fanny smiled, touched by the closeness she saw between William and the boys, but the moment was short-lived. The sounds of a man floundering in the water below caught their attention.

"Help! Help!" the *Blade's* captain screamed as he thrashed about while his precious ship and many of his men went under. William blanched and caught his breath at the sight of Pierre Boudreau.

"Are you all right, Mr. Lovell?" Fanny noticed how the color had drained from William's face.

"I will be," William answered without taking his eyes off of Captain Boudreau.

"Do you recognize that man?" Fanny asked.

"I do." William's tone remained cool. "Captain Channing, may I request that we pick up this buccaneer, the captain of the *Crimson Blade*? He and I have a score to settle."

"Tell me about it," Fanny prodded.

"Not now." William continued staring straight at Captain

Boudreau, who still managed to keep his head above water. "Right now, I would get a great deal of satisfaction and justice if we put him ashore on a deserted island. He doesn't deserve the honor of going down with his ship."

"I think we can oblige you, Mr. Lovell," Fanny agreed, giving the signal to sail toward the struggling man.

As they neared the pirate captain, a net was cast over him, entangling him in the mesh. Several men from the *Constance* plucked him from the water like the day's catch, as he yelled and cursed at them. Once the man was dropped on deck and cleared his way out of the net, he jumped to his feet, still swearing. He stopped short and was quickly silenced at the sight of William Lovell and the cold smile that slowly spread across his face.

"Welcome aboard the *Constance*, Captain Boudreau," William gloated. "So sorry about your ship and crew, but we just couldn't let you continue preying on any more innocent victims unfortunate enough to sail through these waters."

"I should've killed you on the *Kent* when I had the chance." Boudreau spat on the deck. "Instead of trusting you to join us!"

"Your mistake, sir." William stepped closer to the bedraggled man. "You see, we were never ruthless murderers like the rest of your crew, but when we left your ship, we were arrested for the very thing we thought we had escaped from…piracy!"

"You're a free man now."

"That's right," William nodded. "But not before spending months in La Cabana because of our forced association with the likes of you."

"So what are your plans for me? Are you sending me to La Cabana, or wherever the hell you came from?"

"La Cabana is too good for the likes of you," William answered. "Instead, we're going to drop you on Little Iguana Island. Alone. "

"I am an honorable captain, sir! You should have let me drown with my men!"

"Oh, no….that would have been too easy." William shook his head. "This way you can go out like the true pirate you are. All alone on a desert isle with just a jug of water, a smoke, and a pistol loaded with only one bullet for when you can no longer stand it."

Fanny ordered several of the men to bind Boudreau, while William looked on. "Take this man to the brig and make sure he is well secured down there. We'll leave him to his destiny first thing in the morning….let him contemplate his lot overnight."

"Too bad Jack and Samuel are not here to see this." William checked the ropes to make sure they were fastened tightly. "But we'll make sure to tell them all about it when we see them."

"You'll be sorry for this!" Boudreau bellowed as he was led away. "Sorrier than you can ever imagine."

William simply smiled at Boudreau, who scowled back.

"I will get you for this!" He threatened William one final time.

William didn't even bother to respond, but only nodded toward Fanny before walking away. A feeling of satisfaction washed over him. Finally, justice would be served and these waters would be safer for other unwitting sailors.

⚓

It took the *Constance* a while to sail back to the Isle of Iguana, where the *George* now lay at anchor. Fanny and William decided to also set their anchor for a night of celebration after defeating the men that had caused so much pain and suffering for so very long. Jack and Samuel were relieved to see the two young boys safely aboard the *Constance* and they welcomed them as new crew.

Rum was passed around and the men imbibed with gusto. They knew they were heading home where most had a wife or sweetheart awaiting their return. They had earned a good wage on this trip, but the risks had been great. Finally, the worst was behind them and the feeling of relief, mixed with triumph, gave them cause to be merry. Watching the revelry from a distance, Fanny contemplated confessing her secret to William. She felt a little more comfortable knowing that he believed she was quite capable of taking charge.

Fanny saw a new maturity in the man she loved, especially in his kindness to Josh and Levi. She watched his boyish side shine through as he talked with his young students. However, his skill and confidence against Boudreau and the *Blade* was definitely not that of a boy, but of a hero who had faced the worst kind of adversity and won. She was proud of him, but still, she thought better of disclosing her true identity too soon. Perhaps it would be better to wait until they were long at sea. She couldn't risk it should the crew discover her secret by some unfortunate event; it might not settle well with them. Knowing that they had been sailing under the direction of a woman all these weeks, albeit a capable one, might even spark a mutiny. It was a chance she couldn't take—at least not yet.

Fanny bade them all good night and retired to her cabin leaving William in charge of the *Constance*. The truth would have to wait a while longer. That night, sleep eluded Fanny even though she was pleased with the way things had turned out. Still, she ached for William's arms and wanted so badly to unburden herself of the secrets she kept, but she knew in her heart it just wasn't time.

"You've got to keep up the charade for a little while longer. William will find out soon enough," Fanny told herself. But would William be overjoyed by her news or would he be angry that she kept something so important from him for so long? Her predicament kept her awake as she tossed and turned in her bunk debating in her own head just how and when to tell him.

Shortly before the two ships set sail the next morning, the three colonists, William, Jack, and Samuel, rowed the tender ashore with Captain Pierre Boudreau, bound in the bow, while the crews of the *Constance* and the *George* looked on. They were generous enough to leave him not only a keg of water, but one of rum as well. In addition, William decided to give the man a week's worth of provisions to help extend his suffering. Lastly, Jack tossed a pistol loaded with one bullet far into the scrub as William and Samuel untied the pirate and set him ashore.

The three friends climbed back into the tender and as they rowed to the *Constance*, they watched Boudreau who stood alone on the beach glowering at them. "You'll pay for this!" He shook his fists in the air. "I swear, you'll pay dearly!"

"This is a good day." Samuel smiled at the other two men. "The sun is shining and the devil is getting his due."

"And the *Blade* is no longer a threat," Jack added as they watched Boudreau stomping around in a fit of rage.

"The worst is behind us now," William sighed "And we can look forward to the future...unlike that evil beast we just dropped off."

And so it was with great satisfaction that William Lovell, Jack Herbert, and Samuel Breed boarded the *Constance* and the *George* to set sail for home.

CHAPTER 18

The Reunion

That morning, the two ships weighed anchor for Boston. After all of the excitement surrounding the dangerous rescue at La Cabana and the deadly battle with the *Blade*, it was a welcome, uneventful sail that took the brig and the barque serenely around the Turks and Caicos northward into the Atlantic. No one complained about the good weather and, to a man, each was thankful to be heading back—anxious to return to the colonies and the safety of his own family circle. Of course, the siege of Boston and the redcoats were a main topic among the crew, but they had no idea what was really happening back on the mainland.

⚓

One particularly quiet afternoon, the *Constance* and the *George* both sat becalmed in the horse latitudes, around 32 degrees north. William took advantage of the still waters and rowed over to the *George* to have a word with Jack Herbert.

"William!" Jack greeted his friend with a smile and a friendly pat on the back. "Glad you're here!"

"Not half as glad as I am." William grinned, still not taking his freedom for granted.

"What brings you to the George?" Jack asked. "Did Marion send you to check on me?"

"Oh, no," William laughed. "If your Marion wanted to check on you, I have no doubt she would have rowed over here herself."

"I believe she would." Jack smiled at the thought of his pretty and independent wife. "But something must be on your mind. What is it, Bill?"

William hesitated for a moment before he answered. "I feel as if I haven't properly thanked you for coming back for Samuel and me. Knowing what fate awaited you if you failed, it was really quite a brave thing you did."

"I couldn't have lived with myself if I hadn't tried, mate…that was some hellhole we were living in. Innocent or guilty, no one deserves to be in a place like that."

"I owe you my life, Jack," William said. "I could never repay you for the risks you took."

"Just be happy with Fanny…like Marion and me. If one good thing came of all this, it's Marion. I would have never found her if I hadn't sailed away from Boston."

"She's a fine girl," William nodded. "And you're a lucky man, but Fanny, well, who knows? It's been a long time and some handsome sailor like Captain Channing or Captain Burnett may have swept her off her feet by now."

"No….not your Fanny, Bill," Jack shook his head with a grin. "For some reason I never understood, Fanny had eyes for only one man….you!"

"What about Burnett?"

"What about that old lobsterback?"

"It seems to me that Fanny was smitten with him."

"It seems to me," Jack winked. "That you've had too much time to sit and think about things that are all in your head. You know that Burnett is loyal to the king and you also know that Fanny is as committed to the colonies as General Washington. Might I remind you that it was Fanny who orchestrated this whole thing?"

"At what cost?" William sighed. "What did she do to get Channing to come all this way?"

"Have you asked Channing?"

"I've been attempting an audience with Channing for weeks now, but he barely leaves his quarters."

"A finer captain, you'll never meet." Jack wiped some moisture from his forehead with the back of his hand. "Just ask any of the crew. He saved them all from being kidnapped, you know."

"I do believe he is a gentleman," William sighed.

"But I am curious...do you find it odd that the Irishman sleeps at his cabin door every night?"

"You mean Terrance Mooney?"

"Yes."

"It all started the night Captain Brownless tried to kill Channing. I believe he feels indebted to our good captain because he performed an act of great kindness when Mooney's mother died."

"Channing may be kind," William noted, "but I get the distinct feeling he is avoiding me."

"Maybe you should do something about that," Jack winked. "I think you might be pleasantly surprised."

⚓

On their fourth day at sea, the wind in the horse latitudes had picked up enough to allow the ships some headway as they continued on their northwest course in the Atlantic, back to Boston. William, still perplexed by Captain Channing's distance, was surprised to receive a summons from the man to report to the captain's quarters immediately after dinner that evening. Unsure of what to expect, William mulled over the reason why Captain Channing might want to see him.

All afternoon, as he stood watch, he thought about their strained relationship. Perhaps, the captain was displeased with his performance at the helm and wanted to relieve him of his duties. But why would he wait until after dinner to do that? William thought hard about all that had happened since his rescue and could not find any reason for the captain's displeasure. One thing he was sure of—if the captain didn't explain his strange behavior, William would force it out of him. He was beginning to dislike being Channing's first mate and would ask to be transferred to the *George* under Jack's command.

That night, William stood at Channing's door and took a moment to compose himself before he knocked. When the captain called out to him, he entered the cabin and saluted his superior with all of the respect due an officer of his standing. No matter their differences, William was aware of Channing's bravery at sea and the fact that he had single-handedly taken the *Constance* from Brownless and his men without firing a single shot. He also knew about the seizing of the *George*, as well as the attempted mutiny aboard that same ship where the captain had killed the rebellious Englishman. William couldn't help but be impressed with the man that stood before him, but he still had reservations. Despite his misgivings, he also wanted to thank him.

"Mr. Lovell." The captain walked over to a small wooden table that sat in one corner and motioned to a chair. "Please…take a seat."

"Thank you, sir." William sat down while Fanny took a seat across from him.

"You are looking much better. I trust you're feeling stronger."

"Yes….I feel quite a bit better thanks to you and your crew."

Fanny paused a moment studying William. "I believe you know who hired me to sail on this mission and release you and your comrade from prison?"

"Yes, sir, I do. Mr. Herbert explained that it was my Fanny. I have wished to speak with you on the subject, but you have been unavailable and I hope that I have not offended you in some way. If I have that was never my intent."

"Not at all," Fanny shook her head. "I have had a lot to think about these last several days. Your Fanny is a beautiful girl and I half envy you."

"Fanny is dearer to me than anything in this world. It was the thought of being with her that kept me going all those months in that prison. I would have given up long ago if I thought she no longer cared."

"You've been gone a long time, Mr. Lovell," Fanny hesitated a moment, paying close attention to William's reaction. "Things change. Surely, it must have occurred to you that your Fanny might have found someone else."

"I had to quash those thoughts, or I would have gone mad."

"Let's just say for talking's sake, that Fanny has changed her mind about you."

"Then why would she hire you to save me?"

"Maybe she felt it was her duty since she was the one who

talked you into leaving in the first place."

"What are you getting at, captain?" William's brow furrowed in confusion.

"Do you think I might succeed with the lady myself upon our return?"

"I beg your pardon, sir!" William stood straight up, glaring down at what he perceived to be his competition.

"Well....suppose I make you a present of this brig. Would you be willing to give up the lady in exchange for being captain and owner of the fastest privateer sailing for the colonies?"

"No, sir, I would not!"

"I assure you it would be a most profitable arrangement."

"Captain Channing." William's voice remained even as a new thought struck him. "I am beginning to think you are not really who you say you are."

"Who am I then?" Fanny goaded him.

"Your real name wouldn't be Burnett, would it?" William had never met the infamous captain of the king's cutter. He'd only heard Fanny speak of him.

"What makes you think that?" Fanny, still seated, seemed amused, which aggravated William even more.

"So I'm right," William shouted. "And you made Fanny's hand the price for your service!" William paced the length of the room angry, at the thought that Fanny could strike such a deal. "Believe me, Captain Burnett, if any other had made my girl a bargaining chip, I would meet him at the business end of my sword, but since I owe my life and my freedom to you I will make an exception this once!"

"So you assume I am Burnett?" William's sudden jealousy made Fanny smile. "Excuse my bluntness, Mr. Lovell, but I was simply insuring that you are worthy of as fine a girl as Fanny Campbell. After all, it is solely because of her that I am here."

"My only hope is that she will marry me upon my return. Whether or not I am worthy of her hand is another question that only she can answer."

"In that case—" Fanny, too, stood up, facing William directly. "Since your answers to my questions have proven satisfactory, I will now be honest with you. My name is neither Channing nor Burnett."

"I don't understand." William was totally confused by this admission.

"You are about to hold your beloved Fanny, sooner than you hoped."

"What do you know about Fanny?" William demanded.

"I know this." Fanny wiped the scar from her cheek with the back of her hand and dropped the accent. "She wants very much to marry you so the answer to your question is yes, you are worthy of her hand."

"But how do you know that?" William was bewildered.

"Because she stands before you now."

Shocked and confused, William was speechless as he stepped back to study "Channing" more closely. He did see a strange resemblance, but the darkened skin confused him.

Realizing his quandary, Fanny dipped her hand in a basin of water and scrubbed the tint from her skin. Seeing the result, William's eyes traveled up to the capatain's face—"Fanny?"

"It is only a stain....one that has fooled even you, my dear William. And, without Heaven's blessing, it all would have failed." Tears welled in her eyes as she finally gave in to all of the emotions she had kept hidden for so long. "For God's sake, William, hold me!"

And with that, William scooped Fanny up in his arms and laid his mouth on hers. With eyes closed, she took in everything about him—the feel of his skin, the warmth of his breath, the tenderness of his touch. Fanny had waited so long to feel him this close. "Tell me this isn't a dream," she gasped.

"Not a dream." William caressed her cheek. "But a dream come true." He kissed her again and she responded with an eager kiss of her own, savoring the feeling that from this moment on they would be partners for life.

"Fanny," William spoke first. "I was so worried that you wouldn't be happy to see me."

"If you think I sailed all this way, caused a mutiny, fought the redcoats, waged a war with pirates, and sneaked into La Cabana just because I wanted to....well, my dear William, your ordeal has left you more adrift than I thought."

William nuzzled the side of her neck. "I am so relieved to hear that you still love me, after all this time."

"I do love you," Fanny smiled. "There wasn't a day that went by that I didn't ache for you."

"And only the thought of returning to you kept me alive day in and day out." William leaned back and touched her short hair. "I just want to look at you! Your beautiful locks....they're gone!"

"Nothing to worry about. They will grow back."

"But how did you come to this?"

"Everyone else had given up hope. They thought you were dead, but I knew in my heart you were still alive. And knowing that, I could not sit home just hoping that someone else might bring you back to me. In fact, it was Moll Pitcher who told me I would be the one to save you and she helped me devise the plan."

"Moll Pitcher?! Then her predictions must be as accurate as they say. Thank God she saw our future and you listened to her.

But that doesn't explain how a girl your age could be brave enough and knowledgeable enough to commandeer two British ships almost single-handedly."

"I did what I had to do," Fanny shrugged. "And you would have done the same for me."

"Not half as well." William kissed her nose. "I am so proud of you, Fanny! What you did would have been a major challenge to even an experienced naval captain!"

"So...shall I continue wearing my disguise until the end of the voyage?" asked Fanny. "Or should I reveal my true identity to the men?"

"Make no concessions for me." William touched her face. "As far as I am concerned, you are still master and commander of the *George* and the *Constance* and you must continue as Captain Channing."

"Then you will go along with the charade?"

"My darling Fanny, I have never found you so enticing as I do now. William kissed her again. "But tell me how you learned to sail this ship so well and handle these old salts better than I could have, with all my years of experience?"

"After you left, my heart lay at sea with yours, so whenever I could I sailed with our fathers on their schooner, which is half brig in its rigging. Somehow, when I was on the water, I felt closer to you and I remained diligent and determined to fully understand how to sail. When I was not at sea, I read every nautical book I could find and Reverend Livingston taught me practical navigation."

"So I take it that you have been plotting this rescue for some time?"

"Yes, of course, but never in my wildest dreams did I imagine how these skills might help me, but they have certainly come in handy even though it was my heart that truly drove me to find you and bring you home."

"But why did you hide from me all this time? I would have kept your secret."

"I felt it best for you to get your bearings and your sea legs back before I revealed myself. The shock may have been too much for you at first and I felt it necessary to keep my disguise. I was worried that you might inadvertently give it away and how the men might react if they learned that they had been following a woman all this time and even committed mutiny for her?"

"Now, I understand why you were avoiding me."

"I had to," Fanny frowned. "I didn't trust myself around you, but from here on out I will continue my role here as captain."

"It's obvious that your men love you."

"At least they love Captain Channing," Fanny sighed.

"How could they not love you, Fanny?" William once again drew her close.

"That will do for now, Mr. Lovell. You must keep your distance and maintain your respect. And please….don't forget to address me as Captain Channing."

CHAPTER 19

Hanging from the Yardarm

E arly the next morning, "Captain Channing" and his first mate, William Lovell, stood together on deck, each lost in their own thoughts of the night before. After their emotional reunion, William had reluctantly returned to his quarters in order to prepare himself for the day ahead, but sleep eluded him. Instead, his mind raced with all of the newfound facts he had discovered over the last few hours. Fanny, on the other hand, slept well, finally free of her secrets, at least from William. He now knew who she really was and accepted it without question. He even agreed to support her in her role as captain.

"SAIL-HO!" a shout from the lookout in the crow's nest interrupted their personal reflections.

"Where-away?" Fanny flinched, startled by the warning call.

"Ten degrees off the starboard bow and closing fast!"

Taking her spyglass, Fanny surveyed the stranger for several moments, carefully assessing the situation. This was no time for mistakes. "An English merchant, I think." She handed the spyglass to William. "Take a look. Tell me if you agree."

"I think you're right, captain," William studied the ship through the eyepiece. "She appears to be a large vessel, possibly a rich one. How should we handle her? Shall we run or fight?"

"She may be larger, but she is surely not faster than our *Constance* and her low waterline indicates that you are right....she is heavily laden with cargo." Fanny took the spyglass from William and once again peered through it. "I cannot see any large guns on deck. It seems we just may have the upper hand."

"I'm feeling lucky, are you?" William smiled with a wink.

"Fall off the wind to converge with her course," Fanny ordered the helmsman. "Hold at least our long-gun's distance so they can't reach us with their small metal."

The helmsman obliged and adjusted their course by falling off the wind a few degrees, putting the *Constance* on a near collision course with the stranger.

As the ships drew closer, it became clear that this was an English mercantile ship of at least 500 tons—much larger than the *Constance*, but also less nimble. She seemed armed from her bows as the heavy report of her cannon came down short on the brig.

"Show them our Liberty and Union flag, Mr. Lovell," Fanny directed.

Before the flag was fully raised, another shot came from the stranger, once again falling short of the brig and the barque, which followed in the wake of the *Constance*. "Clear away the long-gun and prepare for battle!" Fanny shouted further orders. "Jibe the ship so we might follow her course. With us to her weather, we will slow to her pace. Just be sure to keep a safe distance."

All hands rushed to execute the orders, while William took his station at the gun, but not before giving Fanny a quiet warning. "Go below decks, captain, where you will be safe."

"What....? Sulk below?" Fanny frowned at her first mate. "Let me remind you who you are talking to Mr. Lovell. I am quite familiar with this game and you know it."

"As you wish, captain." William gave in, knowing how stubborn Fanny was. He took his position at the gun next to Terrance Mooney. Together, they cleared and loaded the weapon.

"Just give me that English flag as an enemy and I will fight all day," Terrance mumbled as he stripped away his shirt, eager to start the battle.

"What are you grumbling about there, Mooney?" William asked, a bit amused at the Irishman's enthusiasm.

"Just saying me prayers before going to battle, sir."

"Are you scared, Mr. Mooney?"

"Arrah...the only person who put the fear of God in Terrance Mooney was me sainted mother. She was nobody's fool and neither is her son. Just give me a place at the gun and I'll show you what us Mooneys are made of."

"Terrance, let's make your mother proud." William smiled as he handled the weapon.

"I just wish Captain Channing would step down here." Terrance mopped his brow with a worn, red rag taken from his pocket. "He has such a way with the men and it would encourage them to hear his voice. Besides, if he came down here, we might protect him better. Those blackguards could shoot him where he stands now."

"I have already tried to lure him away, but he is quite adamant about staying on deck." The idea of Fanny being so exposed left William uneasy—he hadn't come this far to lose her now.

"Forward there!" The captain's shout came between William and his thoughts. "Mr. Lovell, lay one right in her mid-ships, pronto!"

A shot was fired and the recoil of the gun shook the brig to her keel. William's first volley struck well into the middle of the stranger's deck, filling the air all around with smoke, shrapnel, and splinters, wounding many of her crew.

"Ha ha! Perhaps you might like a few more of those pills," hollered Terrance, his voice ringing with glee.

"Mr. Lovell, another shot like that one will do us nicely," Fanny called down. "It seems you hit their weak point. Keep her far enough away...so their small guns can't reach us."

"Seems they have no weapons to match our long-tom," William noted as he fired once more.

"Then we'll just sit right here and feed them their medicine until they have had enough." Fanny caught sight of the *George* coming closer. "We don't want to sink or disable her so we can't bring her to port. We just need to cripple her a bit."

The enemy kept firing at the *Constance*, but to no avail, their metal was far too short to compete.

"Brig ahoy!" Jack Herbert brought the barque up under the lee of the *Constance* so they were within hailing distance.

"Yes, Mr. Herbert!" Fanny waved.

"Shall I take a few shots at the stranger with my short pieces?"

"No, Mr. Herbert....best to keep the *George* away on your present course. We shouldn't give them a target they can reach. We'll soon bring them to their knees with our long-tom and we shouldn't risk our men in such close action."

"Aye aye, sir." Jack's disappointment was obvious as he gave a quick salute before veering away from the *Constance*, resuming a steady course.

The long-tom proved once again to be the *Constance*'s salvation, since the enemy had started the contest too far away, rendering their undersized metal ineffective. The shots that William kept hammering into the ship were quite damaging as splinters flew with every blast and angry men could be heard screaming—some in agony—others simply enraged. All the while, the stranger's shot fell short and the *Constance* remained unharmed and intact. The fight was over quickly as the damaged deck and crippled rigging, along with four dead and multiple wounded, rendered the ship at their mercy.

Like the *George* had done, the captain of this ship found it necessary to strike the king's colors in submission to the *Constance* as she steered within hailing distance of her newest prize. Fanny ordered their captain over to the *Constance* so they could discuss the terms of surrender. While the vanquished officer rode a dinghy to the victor, William and a half dozen well-armed men boarded the British merchantman. Unfortunately, they were met by the enemy ship's first-mate, a gargantuan fellow, who was not quite ready to give up the fight. He fired upon them, causing minor injuries to three of the *Constance*'s crew. Those who remained unscathed scrambled to shackle the culprit before he could do further damage.

This new ship, the *Wellington*, which had been bound from Liverpool to Boston, via the West Indies, held stores and munitions for the Royal Army—a valuable boon for the Americans. The colonists had not yet established a formal naval presence, but instead enlisted various privateers to command the seas on their behalf. The British, however, didn't know this and had erroneously assumed that while upon the open sea, their cargo was safe from the rebels. Therefore, they entrusted their vital supplies to a merchant ship rather than a heavily armed naval ship. As a result, the Crown had left its non-military sailors with little protection from rovers, pirates, and colonists, who now battled bravely on the open waters of the Atlantic.

⚓

Fanny now had a small fleet under her command with more prisoners than crew. In anticipation of trouble, she ordered the prisoners confined in chains, despite her preference to treat them more kindly. She just couldn't take that risk, especially while repairs were needed in order to bring their latest conquest back to port. Planning to keep the three vessels within hailing distance of each other, Fanny gave William command of their newest brig.

Upon a thorough search of the *Wellington*, Fanny's men discovered that she carried a rich cargo indeed. It seemed their newest ship was heavily laden with munitions to be used to suppress the rebellion. When William reported their find to Fanny, the captain was thrilled to know that they would bring back an ample contribution to the colonist's cause while at the same time stealing it away from the lobsterbacks.

Fanny ordered a vigilant guard over the English captain, as well as his oversized first mate. Despite these efforts, Fanny was still concerned about the threat of trouble. After all, it had taken four strong men to secure the Herculean first mate who had threatened the immediate destruction of the *Constance* as soon as he had the chance. To insure his confinement, he was secured in double restraints and put in isolation in the forecastle of the brig. Despite these extra efforts, he managed to free himself from his chains as well as the isolation cell.

It was Terrance Mooney who discovered the giant in the foremost part of the ship where he was starting a fire with a large amount of straw and other combustibles that he had quickly gathered before anyone noticed. Without a word, Terrance rushed in to extinguish the flames. The man reached into the Irishman's pocket and pulled out a knife and with one quick flourish, stabbed Terrance in the left arm. Enraged, Terrance swung hard and his right fist connected with other man's jaw. The punch had no effect on him and Terrance shouted for help.

Numerous crew heard Terrance's cries and rushed to his aid. Two men finished dousing the fire while the rest secured the large man who now had to be watched even more closely than before. They could not take the chance of another escape. He was obviously vindictive and blood thirsty with no concern for his own life, let alone the crew of the *Constance*. Luckily, for Terrance, he had only a flesh wound, but the thought of what might have happened put fear into the men of the *Constance* and they demanded that the captain make an example of the Loyalist.

Fanny knew that she must set a precedent to ensure that the other prisoners would not attempt anything as foolish. The crew of the *Constance* insisted on the ultimate punishment. After all, this man had knifed one of their own and had made a fiery attempt to destroy the lot of them. If Terrance had not discovered the man when he did, the *Constance* would have burned to her waterline, sending her entire crew into eternity.

Fanny called her confidantes, William, Jack, and Marion, to a meeting. She wished to discuss their next course of action and hear their thoughts on punishing the perpetrator. "The crew tells me that we should hang this man for his actions that could have proved deadly." Fanny paced the floor. "Do you concur that our only recourse is to execute him?"

"I would string him up within the hour," Jack declared. "The longer he remains among us, the more chance he has to instigate trouble."

"I regret the need for such a drastic sentence, but if we don't make an example of him, the rest of his crew and captain will think that our commander is weak and they might very well attempt to mutiny," William agreed.

"As much as I hate to say it," Marion chimed in. "Showing any mercy to this man would be like striking a match to the powder keg."

"Then the matter is settled," Fanny sighed. "There is no other choice. The man must die at high noon tomorrow."

The three captains then separated, each to tend their own vessels and spread the news amongst the prisoners and crew of the impending execution.

⚓

By now, the ships had barely reached mid-coast of the Americas. The wind was light, allowing the three vessels to stay within hailing distance while repairs were made upon the *Wellington*. The high sun warmed the men's faces, but also exposed a gloom about the ship as the *Constance's* crew prepared for the execution, which would occur upon the yardarm.

The momentous event brought no joy to the men who went about their duties with a solemn air. Their long faces and silence reflected their sorrow at having to hang a fellow sailor, despite his appalling actions. Any one of them would have gone into battle to slay an enemy without a thought, but now they found time to really think about the fact that they would soon send a man to meet his maker. It seemed cold-blooded even to Terrance Mooney, despite the knife wound to his arm. "I know he's a giant of a devil," Terrance told O'Hara. "But it might bring bad luck upon our little brig to have a man dangle by his neck up there."

"It seems the only bad luck here," scoffed O'Hara, "was bringing that devil aboard in the first place. Look what he did to you!"

"Aye." Terrance rubbed his wounded arm. "But I dreamed of my sainted mother last night. She told me of the *Constance's* near demise and that we'd all be drinking salt water if it weren't for Channing's quick thinking."

"Maybe she was trying to tell you that this hangin' business is a good thing. Maybe, it will save us from an even worse fate."

"Maybe." Terrance stared up into the sky as if his mother might be looking down at him.

The morning slid past and a somber silence reigned over the brig as she rose and fell gracefully upon the short, close swell of the Atlantic. It seemed that even the sea held its breath in anticipation of the deadly act.

A single whip hung from the yardarm and swayed back and forth in rhythm with the ship's motion. One end led inboard while the other ran along the yard through a block down to the deck. Whether they wanted to look or not, each man's eyes were drawn to it, knowing that before this day was over, they would be responsible for snuffing out a life on this very spot.

Back on the *George*, a troubled Marion stood with Jack at the helm. "Maybe you shouldn't watch the hanging today." Jack looked down at her.

"Do you think Fanny will actually go through with it?" she wondered.

"I don't see how she can't," Jack said. "What the scoundrel did was unforgivable."

"But surely the man must have some good in him." Marion tried again.

"Even if he does, by the time we find it, we could all end up dead," Jack said.

"I know all that." Marion leaned against him. "But still, I feel torn about this hanging, even though I condoned it. We are sending a man to his death and we know nothing about him."

"We know enough," Jack told her.

"How can you say that?" Marion said rather sharply. "We don't even know his name!"

"My dear." Jack slipped his arm around her shoulders. "I would protect you and keep you safe with my last dying breath. While you were tending Samuel, that man almost cost us our lives. It seems Fanny has no recourse."

"In case you have forgotten," Marion reminded him with a wistful smile, "Channing has no recourse. Fanny might feel differently."

Fanny's conscience, too, was troubled over the hanging and she asked William to come aboard the *Constance* and meet her in the captain's cabin. "I do not like this business."

"I know, Fanny." William slipped his arms around her in an effort to calm her. "It's truly a terrible thing to sentence a man to death, but it can't be helped."

"Who would have ever thought that I would be the one to execute a man like this, or shoot a mutinous man in cold blood." Fanny's face grew pale. "I never wanted to play God, William, and you know I am not some cold-blooded pirate captain."

"Courage Fanny." William pressed her against him. "If you want to be a man you must think like one...with reason, not emotion. Besides, the man sealed his own fate when he started that fire and stabbed Terrance Mooney. You were not responsible for any of that and must I remind you that he has sworn to finish the job he started if given the chance."

"Then there is no reprieve for the man?"

"None that I can see," William sighed. "You have to carry out the death sentence in order to protect your ships and your men. They must come first...at any cost."

"I have always put my men first," Fanny said. "But there is something about this man that makes me want to spare him. Maybe he has family...children who depend on him."

"And maybe you should stop dwelling on who he is and remember what he has done."

"But we don't even know his name, William," Fanny tried again.

"Does it really matter, dear? The man must pay for his crimes. I know you have your doubts." William touched her face. "But you have carried yourself nobly thus far, facing more challenges that any woman should."

"And will hanging a man be a noble deed, my love?"

"It's always noble to do our duty," William reminded her, but the sinking feeling in her stomach remained.

CHAPTER 20

The Execution

At the appointed hour, Fanny steeled herself and ordered the prisoner to be brought before her. Led by four crewmen and tightly bound, the big man was escorted above deck to stand in front of "Captain Channing". Physically, he was in fine form, but his brow was furrowed and his mouth turned down into a scowl. He stared at the deck, exuding rage against his bonds with each breath he took. Even though he was confined, the crew still feared him and most kept their distance from him.

Fanny, flanked by William and Jack, thought it was ironic that this gargantuan man now stood before a gentle-hearted girl who was about to send him to his death. Fanny inhaled a deep breath and then glanced at Marion who had just arrived from belowdecks. Despite Jack's words of caution about witnessing the execution, Marion's natural curiosity got the better of her. Seeing Marion made Fanny dismiss her own womanly feelings. Marion's safety and the safety of the crew were all that really mattered. As captain, Fanny had faced difficult decisions before, but somehow this was different.

"Prisoner," Fanny declared in a loud and steady voice. "Are

you aware that this counsel has decided that you are to die upon the yardarm within this very hour?"

"I saw the whip rigged aloft and understand its meaning." The man never looked up.

"Have you nothing to offer before your execution?"

"Nothing," he answered—his eyes still upon the deck.

"Do you have a name? Surely your parents gave you one at birth."

"My name makes no difference."

"It makes a difference to me," Fanny offered. "If you please, sir, I would like to know who you are and where you come from."

"My name is Edward Finch." The man looked up for the first time. "I was born and raised in Bath."

"Thank you, Mr. Finch," Fanny nodded. "I am sorry that we find ourselves in these unfortunate circumstances, but it seems that a man about to lose his life would have some final wishes. Speak now and if reasonable they will be granted."

"I have none." Finch's cold fixed stare remained strong.

"Are you a family man? Perhaps you have children?" Fanny continued.

The Englishman caught his breath and his shoulders slumped. Fanny's question had somehow hit a nerve and touched his hardened soul.

"Speak now, sir," Fanny encouraged him. "For soon it will be too late."

"I have both wife and children." His chest heaved with emotion, but he still refused to look up.

"How many children?" Fanny asked.

"Six...the last was born just before I left Bath to sail on the *Wellington*."

"And you have no word, or wish, to leave for them?"

"None!" Finch clenched his fists. "They will know that their father died loyal to the king unlike you sir, a rebel, as are those who surround you!"

"If given the chance, would you not wish to see your home, your wife, your children again?"

"I shall see them in Heaven," he snapped.

"And it is only your loyalty to the king that has incited your actions here?"

"Of course," the man shrugged. "What else would inspire a British sailor?"

"Loyalty is an admirable trait when given for the right reasons." Fanny clasped her hands behind her back and began pacing the deck. "Do you know why the American colonies must break away from the king? Do you know how we have been oppressed? Are you aware of the flagrant wrongs we have endured, of the servile and debasing treatment we have suffered at the hands of your king's evil advisors?"

"I only know what I am told by my superiors," Finch answered.

"Then you cannot possibly know of the unfair taxes, of homes unfairly seized by the king's soldiers, or of the disruption of free trade...all of which has caused the distress of thousands. Tell me, sir, how you would feel if your children and livelihood were threatened? If your home was taken and your family hungry and homeless? Would you not want to put an end to the persecution once and for all?"

"That I would," Finch whispered.

"Then do not let this spirit of revenge live in your heart any longer, but first consider why we have resorted to arms and then be the judge of who's wrong. Can you do that, Mr. Finch?"

The man stared down at the deck for a time, before lifting his head to stand tall. "I had no idea of the hardships inflicted upon the colonists. I only knew of the rebellion, which I was told was unwarranted."

"There are two sides to every story and we colonists are not ungrateful to the Crown, Mr. Finch." Channing continued to pace. "But we must be allowed to live our lives in freedom just as you do in England. We asked only for fair treatment and instead received persecution...both monetary and physical. No one wants a war, but living in the colonies under British rule has become unbearable. I don't suppose your king has told you that."

"He did not."

"Put yourself in our place, if you will. What would you do? Sit back and do nothing, or take up arms and try to put an end to the persecution of your wife and children? Would you not seek a better life for them?"

"Of course, I would." Finch looked Fanny in the eye. "Or I would die trying."

"Then you are an honorable man as I thought." Fanny smiled for the first time.

"I believe you are also an honorable man, Captain Channing," Finch said. "And I hope you believe me when I say I am truly sorry for the trouble I caused you and your men, and for the hardships the colonists have endured because of my king. In light of this news, it shames me to be one of his subjects."

"I think you are sincere." Fanny stopped pacing and faced the prisoner. "And if I am right, it behooves us to talk on equal terms. As captain of this ship, I now decree that you are a free man. There will be no hanging on the *Constance* today."

A collective gasp escaped from the crew. Had their beloved

captain lost his mind? Had he forgotten what this man had done? Despite their doubts, however, they didn't dare protest.

"And why would you call off my execution?" The man was immediately suspicious of Fanny's decision.

"Because I believe that deep down you are a good man who was misguided." Fanny stood quiet for a moment before speaking again. "Unbind Mr. Finch," she commanded the guard. Not one man stepped forward to carry out her orders. Then Fanny narrowed her eyes and squinted at the guard, "Do I command this vessel?!"

"Certainly sir, but we--"

"--do you hear me?" Fanny drew her sword and raised it high in the air. "I said unbind him!"

William and Jack were both surprised at Fanny's words, but they stood by quietly as the guard did as he was told. The other men drew their weapons expecting the worst. Fanny once again looked toward Marion, who faintly smiled her approval. Stunned, the Englishman, now free, stood quietly before Fanny.

"So then may I trust you, Mr. Finch?" Fanny extended her hand.

The transformed Englishman seized Fanny's small hand in his oversized one. "My own king would not have shown me such kindness. I would give my life for you, sir." He dropped to one knee, overcome with respect. "Can you forgive me for the wrongs I have done to you and your men?"

"You have already been forgiven." Fanny laid her hand on the man's broad shoulder. "Now, you must report for duty to Mr. Mooney."

The man stood tall and turned toward Fanny's first mate, whose wounded arm was still wrapped. "I also owe you an apology, Mr. Mooney. If you will allow me to report to you, I assure you that I will make myself most useful to this ship."

"If I weren't standing here to see it," Terrance shook his head. "I wouldn't believe it, but here I am and I believe there is power in forgiveness, so I accept your apology, but I will be keeping a close eye on you, Finch, just so you know."

"Understood, sir." Finch held out his hand. "I will not disappoint you."

The two men, one contrite while the other remained suspicious, shook hands.

"I came here to watch a hanging." Terrance accepted his outstretched hand. "But I leave here with a new man who I can put to good use. I'd say all-in-all it is a good day."

⚓

"Why didn't you tell me that you planned to pardon Finch?" William asked once they were alone in Fanny's cabin later that day. "Did you not trust me to keep your confidence?"

"To be honest," Fanny admitted, "I did not plan it. It just happened. Something about Finch's noble bearing and the emotion he evinced when asked about family and home struck a chord in me. I suddenly realized that his heart was in the right place and that he could be influenced by truth, kindness, and compassion."

"No one could have acted with more skill or better judgment." William was amazed at the way Fanny had detected the goodness in Finch—enough to risk trusting him.

"It just seemed the right thing to do at the time." Fanny shrugged. "I hope Finch doesn't prove me wrong."

"I don't believe he will." William pulled her closer to him. He had discovered another side of Fanny today and it resulted in a greater love and respect for her. "I couldn't be prouder of you than I am right now. You and your compassion will make a fine mother for our children."

"Proud or not, we have a charade to maintain," Fanny reminded him with a smile.

"This make-believe is getting tiresome." William pulled her against him.

"If you are not careful William, you will expose me to the crew."

"Then Heaven bless the honest man," grinned William as their embrace dissolved into a gentle kiss.

⚓

Handling three ships with eight hands each, while keeping track of even more prisoners, proved challenging. Even worse, the former captain and crew of the embattled merchantman were enraged when they discovered that such a small number of assailants had forced them to surrender so quickly and to a 'boy rebel' no less. But that 'boy' was nobody's fool. Fanny's keen vigilance prevented an uprising and surely saved them all from disaster, but the increased burdens wore heavily on her. She took heart, however every time she glimpsed William at the helm of the British ship.

As summer drew to an end and they journeyed further north, the sun loomed high, but the heat of the tropics cooled aboard the ships. It seemed that a storm was brewing and the ships ran from the leading edge of the southeast winds. The urgency to return to Lynn grew with every passing hour and the men were anxious to see their families again. Fanny and her crew had been lucky to have moderate weather and calm seas with just enough wind to fuel them back to the colonies, but it seemed their luck had run out and they guessed that a tropical storm was winding its way up from the islands toward the mainland. They were so close now they couldn't take risks and they remained focused on one thing —going home.

What they couldn't have known was that a deadly hurricane had been working its way across the Atlantic and had taken aim directly at the island of Hispaniola. From there, it headed northwest for the Outer-Banks of the Americas, causing serious damage to North Carolina, Virginia, and Washington. It was grinding its way up the east coast, wreaking havoc with the colonists' efforts against the British and it was now well on its way to Boston Harbor. Although the land had taken much of the punch out of the storm, the sea still forced many ships to ride out the storm offshore. Leaving a path of vast devastation along the shoreline from North Carolina all the way up to Newfoundland, the tempest ultimately claimed 4,000 lives and would later become known as the Hurricane of Independence.

CHAPTER 21

Friend Turned Foe

The danger for "Captain Channing's" three ships grew with every mile they sailed since the coast swarmed with British cruisers and man-of-war ships while the winds increased. To try and blend in, Fanny, while maintaining the flag of Taunton high on the stern of the *Constance*, ordered the British ensign raised on the *George* and the *Wellington*, hoping that this would be enough to deter a possible attack.

As their little fleet approached the shores of Massachusetts, Fanny's run of fortuitous luck quickly changed. They were within hours of laying down their ground tackle for the night when the wind went from a brisk breeze to a formidable blow and the seas picked up, likely washing out any anchorage ashore. Suddenly, the look-out warned of a king's cutter wearing the British ensign from the rigging. Fanny and the crew of the three vessels were prepared to face danger, but a fully equipped man-of-war carrying fifty men and twelve guns was well beyond their defense capacity. Their only hope was to outsail the enemy, but just one of their three ships was capable—the *Constance*. It should be easy for her to outrun the ship in the ever stiffening wind from the leading edge of the storm. There was no sense in risking their two prizes, so Fanny commanded William and Jack to veer off their course in opposite directions by signaling with a flare gun. It would be impossible for one British vessel to pursue all three of them. They would most likely target the *Constance* with her flag from the colonies.

William had his doubts about deserting Fanny, but only hesitated for a moment. No matter his personal feelings, he could not deny an order from his commander for fear that the men under him might rebel, and so it was with great reluctance that he changed the course of his ship. Jack, too, had second thoughts, since Marion remained on board the *Constance* and he knew that the ship might be targeted and fired upon by British guns. He had good cause for concern as the enemy ship spotted the flag of the colonies with the words 'Liberty and Union' blazoned across it and fired a warning shot almost immediately.

"Hold your stance," Fanny commanded. "And fire back a single shot. I want to let them know we are not afraid."

As her orders were carried out, Edward Finch approached. "I am sorry, captain," the burly Englishman began. "But I must ask to be excused from this fight. I cannot, in good conscience, raise arms against my countrymen. I hope you understand."

"You have been a valuable asset to this ship," Fanny sighed. "And I was hoping you would join our fight, but I understand your need to remove yourself from this situation. I only ask that you refrain from working against us."

"I would not lift a finger to harm you or your ships, but likewise, I don't wish to do battle with those you deem your enemy. I will go belowdecks and wait there until you send for me."

"Perhaps you could see to it that Miss Ashton and Mr. Breed are all right."

"It would be my honor, sir. I will protect the lady with my life if necessary." And with that, the gentle giant left the deck of the *Constance*.

"Fall off the wind! Two degrees abaft the beam!" Fanny turned her attention back to the matter at hand. "Let's out-maneuver them! At the very least, we should be able to out-run them!" Fanny then picked up her spyglass and drew in a sharp breath.

"The *Dolphin*!" She gasped as she realized that this was the ship commandeered by her spurned suitor, Captain Burnett. Her old friend and mentor had suddenly become the enemy.

Fanny knew that the *Constance* and the *Dolphin* were similar in tonnage and speed, but Fanny had a certain advantage: she had been an attentive student and confidante of Burnett's own teaching. She had listened well to his tactics and strategies, which would now allow her to anticipate his every move. If only Burnett knew that his present enemy was none other than the woman for whom he had declared his love not so long ago.

Despite knowing that the same force of wind propelling the *Constance* also propelled the *Dolphin*, Fanny prayed for increased winds as she studied the mares' tails and mackerel skies, which had been forming all morning. There was a major storm brewing and if she could only last until the wind increased and the sky grew dark, she most certainly could outsail, or lose, the British cutter.

The two ships continued their chase at sea over the next three hours as Fanny's prayers were answered and the winds grew. While the *Constance* held a safe distance, it was quite apparent to Fanny that Burnett's true advantage lay in his ability to precisely and proficiently trim his sails. Burnett's crew of four dozen outnumbered the men aboard the *Constance* who totaled eight. This tactical advantage had gradually given Burnett a leading edge and the safe distance for the *Constance* was closing quickly.

Within another hour the wind had increased, causing the *Constance* to leap from wave top to wave top on a beam-reach—the helmsman struggling to maintain control. Fanny furled sail after sail as the *Dolphin* shot forward like an arrow—better able to reef her jib, staysail, and mainsail due to sufficient crew. Before long, Fanny realized that there was no escape, at least not without a fight, but with her few men to Burnett's nearly fifty, she also knew that they stood little chance of winning at hand-to-hand combat. Fanny's quick wit, however, recognized her one great advantage with the rising swell and sea—boarding the *Constance* in those rough waters would be nigh on impossible.

"Captain Channing, sir," Edward Finch interrupted Fanny's thoughts.

"What is it, Finch?" Fanny was alarmed at the sight of the big man. "Is Miss Ashton alright?"

"Yes, sir, it was she who convinced me to come up here to the helm. She thought I should do my part to help you."

"And just what is your part since you are unwilling to fight?"

"Well, sir, I cannot fight against my own countrymen," replied Finch, "But if you order the helmsman to turn over the wheel, I will serve you faithfully and do my best at the helm during this storm."

Touched by the Englishman's sincerity, Fanny smiled. "Your service would be greatly appreciated, Mr. Finch. It will allow me to man the long-tom myself and your strength on the helm in this sea would be a fine asset."

The *Dolphin* was now within reach of her gun as Fanny aimed the weapon over the rise and fall of the swell. As she fired, Fanny's thoughts took over for a moment—if William could see her now, he would be proud of how she was about to do battle against a man he always considered a threat. Deep in her heart, however, she wished Burnett no personal harm and regretted this ironic turn of events. After all, when it came down to it, she owed William's life to Burnett's tutelage.

Barely a shot was wasted and Fanny's sound precision took Burnett by surprise as his ship was pounded by shot. Due to the distance between the two ships, Burnett's own guns remained in-effective and unable to render any damage upon the *Constance*. It didn't take Burnett long to realize that his only recourse was to run from the enemy's metal, since he knew he could never board the enemy in the ever-increasing turbulent sea. With that, Burnett steered off the wind, quickly creating distance between the two vessels.

"He does not like this gun," Fanny shouted to Finch as they watched the *Dolphin* veer off course, with the wind and sea from the south-west. "Now, fall off the wind, Mr. Finch!"

The *Constance* pursued the cutter, while Burnett made every attempt to escape the reach of the long-tom. They were clearly not safe from the storm or the present danger, but Fanny felt the rise of a victor's pride as she watched the *Dolphin* retreat, des-perate to escape further damage.

⚓

Onboard the Royal cutter, Burnett assessed the damage and took count of casualties. A single ball had dug a trough across the deck amidships and another had holed her starboard side. Lurch-ing to and fro, she quickly took on water due to the raging sea. Burnett knew he must stay on a starboard tack in order to keep the sea from filling her hull until his men below deck could make some quick repairs. This point of sail forced the *Dolphin* further offshore into even deeper waters.

"What of our men?" Burnett asked his first-mate.

"Five of our best men dead and a dozen in the surgeon's cabin," reported the first mate, as the wind howled around them.

"Keep her away another point, my good man! That devil pirate will kill us all at this rate and we are helpless to strike back with even a single blow."

"I'm afraid she won't bear another point, sir. We are already running under bare poles and a staysail in this gale!"

"Then keep her as she is and let's pray that these winds subside and that rebel doesn't sink us before morning!" He raged, much like the storm that surrounded him. "It has to be more than sheer luck that their shots in these rough seas are so accurate!"

The cutter lurched, causing the men to stumble. "Reef that staysail and strike that article!" Burnett regained his balance and pointed at the English flag flying from the rigging.

"Strike it, sir?" gasped the astonished first mate.

"Only until we can regain the upper hand," explained Burnett. "Lucky enough we can't be boarded in this sea. Night will soon set in and we can claim our own course under the cover of darkness and it may buy us some time to recover. Now take down that flag!"

And with that order, the king's flag was struck to the Taunton flag of the colonies and their rag-tag rebels, just as darkness took over, hiding the two ships from one another.

As the cutter's flag lowered, the *Constance* ceased fire and focused on the safety of the ship and her crew. The intense darkness and heavy cloud cover shrouded the two ships entirely from each other's view. It was a harrowing night for both ships and their crews, while the raging hurricane winds that decimated the eastern seaboard had finally decreased to a tropical storm level. What they didn't know was that most every king's man-of-war, merchantman, and fishing boat was also being forced to ride out the storm at sea, rather than in the precarious harbors with their huge waves and flooding coastline.

Fanny wondered how Jack and William were faring with the *George* and the *Wellington*, since neither vessel could be easily handled in such a sea. Would the two ships make it through the night? For that matter, would the *Constance*? It was a challenging night at the helm for Finch and Fanny as they ran with bare poles from the storm, hoping their fair lady would not bury her nose into the sea. The seas were so rough that the two men had to lash themselves to the helm's pedestal to keep from being washed overboard.

Aboard the *Dolphin*, Burnett focused only on keeping his ship afloat as his men struggled below decks to put a temporary patch on the ball-sized hole in his freeboard. His anger rose at the thought of how this rebel ship could have inflicted such damage on his crew and cutter.

The next day, as the storm blew over and the early morning light broke on the eastern horizon, Fanny stood next to Terrance Mooney who had just relieved Finch at the helm. The two men spotted the *Dolphin* silhouetted in the rising sun, about three miles east. Even at that distance, it was apparent that the cutter's spars and rigging were badly damaged. The storm had blown through, taking most of the wind with it, even though the sea still churned like a wash-tub without the strong gusts to give it direction.

"Mr. Mooney, do you think those Englishmen will be distraught to learn that they have been disabled by such a small crew?" Fanny asked.

"No matter how many we number," Terrance replied, "I think they are quite ready to be done with us and that lucky iron-piece of ours."

With that barely said, the *Dolphin* shook out what remained of its canvas and soon set a course directly for the *Constance*.

Looking through the spyglass, Fanny watched as the cutter rolled in the sea, slowly moving right for them, with lessened sail due to the broken rigging.

"Well Mr. Mooney....it seems they there are not quite as full of us as we thought," Fanny lowered the spyglass. "And I see they have once again hoisted the king's flag. I assume he wants revenge for his suffering."

"What should we do?"

"Prepare for battle!" Fanny shouted. "This time at close quarters, I'm afraid!"

"Shake out that canvas, men," Terrance called to the crew. "And ready the iron for battle!"

Within minutes, the *Constance* was rolling over the whitecaps under the light breeze, as it ran from the *Dolphin*. Despite its damaged rigging, the cutter slowly gained on them and before they realized it, Fanny was once again doing execution upon the *Dolphin*'s deck. Although she intended to further impair the *Dolphin*'s rigging hoping to disable her, the deck took the brunt of the damage. Eventually, as the cutter gained ground on the *Constance*, its smaller metal began doing some damage to Fanny's rigging.

"I will not give up this brig, Mr. Mooney," insisted Fanny. "Have the six carronades brought aft to the rise of the quarter-deck. Point them all forward to sweep the deck. Load them with slugs, bullets, and a few small shot each, then draw a canvas strip across to hide them from sight, but you must make sure the cloth can be dropped at a moment's notice."

"Aye, aye, captain...I understand your plan...it be brilliant, might I say."

"The brilliance of my plan is yet to be seen, Mr. Mooney. Just be lively now, we haven't a moment to spare!"

The *Dolphin* and the *Constance* wasted no time closing in on one another and by his course, it was clear that Burnett planned to lay directly alongside the brig. "Tack Mr. Mooney, and stand directly for the *Dolphin*!"

Surprised, Terrance gave the order to tack and started the *Constance* through the wind, "You seem familiar with this king's ship, captain."

"Very familiar...and I know its captain only too well. You might say he was somewhat of a mentor to me at one time and I fully understand his tactics and logic. It's to our advantage that he does not know who commands this ship. He will certainly be surprised when he discovers that I am the one who has caused so much damage to his ship and his ego."

Fanny's bold move took Burnett by surprise as the *Constance* swept the enemy's deck with her bowsprit and became entangled with the *Dolphin's* rigging. Fanny leaped down behind the canvas, while two score of Burnett's men scrambled onto the foredeck —twice the number of the *Constance's* crew, all armed with swords and boarding pikes. Finding not a single enemy to fight, the confused men paused and then gathered together in one spot to assess the situation, which gave Terrance the perfect target.

"Now, Mr. Mooney!" Fanny commanded as quietly as she could and before the enemy sailors had a chance to react, the canvas was dropped on the six cannon. Within seconds, two-thirds of the men on deck were dead and many wounded. A few were able to clamber back to the *Dolphin*. They quickly realized, however, that the crew of the *Constance* numbered only a few and after re-arming and renumbering themselves, they returned with their captain for hand-to-hand combat. Fanny pulled her pistol, aimed and fired, killing a man who collapsed a few feet away with a fatal wound to his chest. In turn, Burnett raised his sword to strike Fanny down, but she already had her gun pointed directly at Burnett. The British captain froze in place, staring at Fanny. There was something alarmingly familiar about this captain.

"Do I know you?" Burnett demanded still holding his sword over his head.

"Captain Burnett," said Fanny in her own voice. "You know me very well."

"FANNY?!" Burnett gasped and took down his blade while Fanny lowered her pistol.

"Please do not give me away to my men." She kept her gaze steady. "They know me and are loyal to me as Captain Channing. Just accept my surrender and I promise I will explain everything once we are alone."

"But Fanny," Burnett sputtered.

"I doubt that you would want your crew to know that a mere woman had given you so much resistance and caused such severe damage to your ship."

"I don't understand," Burnett spoke quietly.

"You will, I promise," Fanny assured him. "But I remember you as a man whose word meant something so all I ask is that you treat my crew fairly. They have been exceedingly dedicated and are all fine men….even Mr. Finch has done nothing, but remain loyal to your king. And my good friend, Marion, must also be let go. She has done nothing against you. Give me your word, sir, and I will go easy."

"As you wish." Burnett nodded, still perplexed. And with that, Fanny gave the order to cease fire and the *Constance* was once again in the hands of the British. Burnett then ordered Fanny to be held prisoner in his own private quarters. He also ordered the British prisoners released so they could man the *Constance* with five of his own. The Americans were locked in the *Constance's* brig. When Burnett finally returned to his cabin, Fanny was waiting, hoping that her friend and mentor would show her some mercy.

Late, after riding out the killer storm onboard the *George* and the *Wellington*, Jack and William had circled back to find the *Constance* limping toward the port of Lynn with the king's flag flying from her rigging. The two captains signaled one another and quickly planned to recapture the brig. They closed in on either side of the *Constance* and realizing they were outnumbered, the five British sailors surrendered without firing a shot. Together, William and Jack boarded the *Constance*. William freed the crew locked below decks, while Jack rushed to Marion's stateroom.

"Marion?!" Jack threw open the door.

"Yes, my dear?" Marion looked up from a book she was reading and smiled.

"I was worried sick about you!"

"I am fine." She closed her book and stood up. "Captain Burnett left orders to take me back to Boston and release me."

"No one has hurt you?"

"Not at all," she assured him with a kiss. "But I am ready to find dry land again. My sea legs are tired."

"We are almost home." Jack touched her face. "And I swear I will never put you in harm's way again."

"Now what fun would that be?" Marion grinned. "Jack, you and I are not meant for hearth and home. Maybe someday, but not while we have a war to fight."

"Fighting is a man's business, my dear wife." Jack frowned.

"Tell that to Fanny."

"Speaking of Fanny, do you know where she is?"

"Burnett took her onboard the *Dolphin* as his prisoner," Marion answered. "But I do not think he would hurt her. There was a time he wanted to marry her, you know."

"I've got to find William." Jack gave her one last hug. "You stay here until I come back for you."

"I'll do no such thing!" Marion hollered after him.

By the time Jack reached his friend, William was already aware of Fanny's fate. He had released the crew and had spoken with Terrance, Samuel, and the ever-loyal Mr. Finch, learning the details of Fanny's capture. William and Jack met privately in the captain's cabin so they could talk alone.

"What are we going to do?" William was terribly distressed. "We have to find Fanny."

"Marion says she is on board the *Dolphin* in Burnett's cabin," Jack replied. "She doesn't think he'd hurt her. He loved her once."

"That's what I'm afraid of! We have no idea what Burnett might or might not do." William nervously paced the length of the room. "I didn't come this far to lose her now, either to his sword or his hand. I do believe that Marion is right and that he would not harm her. What concerns me is that he is still in love with her and he may force her into a marriage in return for her freedom."

CHAPTER 22

A Captain's Shame

When Burnett returned to his cabin after capturing the *Constance*, he found an unnerved Fanny waiting. "I believe you owe me an explanation, young lady," Burnett demanded.

"I don't owe you anything," Fanny replied, trying to sound firm, yet tempering it with a smile. "But I will tell you my story so that you understand how I got to this position."

"I am listening." Burnett pulled out a chair and sat down while Fanny described her adventures, starting with how she had arranged the Bartholomew Channing disguise. She was careful not to mention Moll Pitcher's participation, as she did not want to jeopardize Moll's safety and her ability to spy for the Sons of Liberty. Burnett took it all in without a word. By the time Fanny finished her story, he was too stunned to even speak.

"I wish you'd say something," Fanny prodded him.

"I don't know what to say." Burnett shook his head. "I know you are incapable of lying, as my ego has suffered from your truthful sermons in the past, but I can hardly believe this tall tale of yours."

"It's not a tall-tale," Fanny insisted.

"But it's outrageous," he contended. "And hearing you tell it...well, I've never been so intrigued by a woman in my life. I always knew you were a most unusual girl, but--"

"--so you have told me before," Fanny interrupted him.

"But did I also tell you how much I love you?"

"Captain Burnet--"

"--just listen!" he silenced her. "You have proven yourself to be my equal on both land and sea. In fact, you have even surpassed me in shrewdness, cunning, and strategy. My damaged ship and dead crewmen are proof of that."

"I did what I had to do for William," she shrugged. "Not because I was trying to compete with you, or any man."

"William!" Burnett stood and began pacing the cabin. "It has always come back to William, but my dear....now that you have liberated your William, let his freedom satisfy you. Surely you can see that only I am your equal and it's time that you become my wife."

"Your wife?!" Fanny was both shocked and revolted at the thought of marrying Burnett.

"Think about it, Fanny." Burnett stopped directly in front of her. "My commission, my property, and my rank can only elevate your standing."

"You mean my lowly standing. But sir...I am your prisoner." Fanny's voice softened.

"No Fanny....I'm your prisoner. You captured my heart the first day I met you. I truly love you and I always have."

"Captain Burnett." Fanny chose her words carefully. "I have respected you and considered you a friend....a good friend....but I could never love you as a wife should. My heart belongs to

William and has since I was a child. I have never plotted to keep that a secret from you. Besides, you are high-born and such a man deserves to be with a woman entirely devoted to him....a woman of the same rank and class. A woman who could give you her undivided love and loyalty....Captain Burnett....I am surely not that woman."

⚓

Back aboard the *Constance*, William's and Jack's first decision without Fanny was a crucial one—which harbor to sail into without encountering the British navy? The harbor at Boston was still under siege, and now littered with sunken ships from the storm. As luck would have it, however, one of the sailors from the *Dolphin* requested a meeting with the two captains. The man was brought to the captain's quarters where William and Jack awaited him.

"You have information for us?" William was curt.

"Aye," the man nodded, his hands cuffed in front of him. His long dark hair and rumpled clothes made him appear older than he really was.

"Out with it, man!" Jack's voice rang with impatience. "We have no time to waste on foolishness."

"I am not the enemy," he began. "My name is John Walden. I am a Patriot and a spy. I report directly to Lieutenant Nathan Hale. I was given the assignment to sail with the *Dolphin* in order to gather information about the British."

"How do we know you are telling us the truth?" William asked.

"Believe me," Walden said. "I am on your side. You cannot sail into Boston Harbor and the harbor of Lynn is no safer. British ships are everywhere."

"So where can we go?" Jack seemed skeptical, but intrigued. "Marblehead?"

'No, not there either." Walden leaned in. "You will only be safe in Beverly Harbor. General Washington has been given a wharf in Beverly and he's begun to acquire ships. He has sent his first schooner there. She's called the U.S.S. *Hannah* and she was outfitted in Marblehead."

"Isn't that John Glover's fishing schooner?" William inquired.

"Yes, I believe he named the boat after his daughter," Walden confirmed. "And from what I've been told, General Washington plans to have four more ships join her. Of course with this storm, I'm not sure what remains of them, but he's bound and determined that we have our own navy and thanks to the experienced fisherman in Marblehead, it just may happen soon."

"What else can you tell us about the war effort?" Jack was eager to hear more.

"I can tell you this. General Washington could put your three ships and the supplies you have captured to good use....and if I weren't a true Patriot, I wouldn't be saying this. I can get word to several men in Beverly who can help you, but first I have to go back to the holding cell so the lobsterbacks don't grow suspicious of my loyalties."

After their meeting with Walden, William and Jack agreed upon their next course of action. The three ships then sailed through Salem Sound. With no British ships in sight and swells still high in the harbor, they anchored in Beverly Harbor after exchanging their British ensign for the flag of Taunton. Putting their trust in Walden, he quickly rowed ashore and arranged for the much-needed provisions to be taken ashore and delivered to Washington's troops.

Leaving Jack to oversee the work, William had a man row him

to the Salem shore, where he borrowed a horse and rode as hard as he could to Lynn, about eight miles south. Time was of the essence. Frantic with worry, he feared that Burnett might sway Fanny to marry him in exchange for her freedom if William didn't get to her in time. As he rode up to his home, he wasn't prepared for the emotions that raged through him when he caught sight of the house.

Nothing much had changed. The garden was still there, although it was in the last throes of summer. The grass was neatly trimmed and the windows were clean—clothes hung on the line, fresh and spotless. William took a moment to breathe before dismounting his horse. Walking up the pathway, panic seized him. How could he tell the Campbells that Fanny had been taken prisoner? Even if they were glad to see him, the news would devastate them. Maybe they would blame him. Maybe they would be right.

He didn't knock, but tried the doorknob, which easily turned. The smell of baking bread greeted him, but no one was there. "Mother? Father?" he called out. "Agnes? Henry? Is anyone home?"

"What's all the yelling about?" Agnes came from her side of the house, where she had been tending Mrs. Herbert. She carried a yellow pillowcase in her hand. "Oh, my saints!" she gasped and dropped the sham as she recognized the stranger standing in her kitchen.

"It's me, Agnes!" He stepped toward her. "It's William. I've come home."

"My William?" Sarah appeared in the doorway of the Lovell household.

"Mother!" William scooped the shaken woman up in his arms. "I'm back!"

"I never thought I'd see you again," Sarah sobbed in her son's arms. "It's been so long. I'd given up, but you're really here!"

"I am here," William smiled. "But where is father? And Henry?"

"They are working on the boat. It was badly damaged in the storm," Agnes answered, tears spilling down her cheeks. "How did you get here?"

"It was Fanny." William reached out to her, but kept one arm around his mother. "Oh, Agnes, Fanny came for me."

"Where is my Fanny? Why isn't she with you?" Agnes drew back, afraid to hear William's answer.

"Fanny is alive." William prayed he was telling the truth. "But she is being held by Captain Burnett."

"Burnett? Why would he hold her?"

"Her ship was captured by the *Dolphin* and she is being held prisoner. I was so hoping she had escaped and found her way home."

Agnes fell into a chair next to the table, too overcome to speak.

"Listen to me." William left his mother to tend to Fanny's. "She is with Captain Burnett and we all know how he feels about her. I don't believe he would harm her."

"What are we going to do?" Agnes finally found her tongue.

"Let me go find father and Henry," William suggested. "And when we return I will explain everything and I promise to answer all of your questions."

"I don't want you to go." Sarah pulled on his arm.

"It won't take long," William assured her. "Besides, I need to see if the *Dolphin* is in the harbor at Lynn."

William once again mounted his borrowed horse and galloped off to the waterfront, hoping against hope he'd find Fanny there, even though it had appeared that the cutter might have been headed toward Boston. He spotted Henry and William aboard their boat, but to his great disappointment, there was no sign of the *Dolphin* in the cluttered harbor. So Burnett hadn't brought Fanny home after all.

When the *Dolphin* entered Boston Harbor, Captain Burnett stood on deck, where he observed a few of the king's fleet still patrolling the port. It seemed that many had fled offshore to weather out the storm, while others had sunk where they lay, with their masts rising out of the water. The *Dolphin* quickly dropped anchor and Burnett's crew busied themselves refitting and repairing the vessel as best they could, while they awaited the *Constance* that they believed was following.

Burnett took some time to read the surgeon's report and only then did he realize the extent of his losses. How could he explain to his superiors that a handful of men, led by a woman no less, had caused all of this damage? He was even more moved when he heard the groans of his wounded men. How could he explain what had happened to them? And where was the *Constance*? He scanned the horizon, but the brig was nowhere to be seen. If she had been retaken, even more of his men would be at risk. His anger flared. He didn't even have one captured stick of timber to show for his trouble and loss.

It was dark by the time an angry and bitter Burnett returned to his cabin where Fanny awaited him.

"Where is the *Constance*?" Fanny asked already suspecting the answer. "She hasn't showed has she?"

"Not yet," Burnett snapped.

"Then it seems my loyal men have retaken her and most likely raised the Taunton flag by now."

"I will not be made a fool of!" Burnett seethed. "Not by anyone, especially you!" He strode to Fanny and pulled her to her feet with a rough jerk. "If I cannot have anything else, I will take for myself what your William holds dearest!" He grabbed her by the waist and pressed her against him, his lips probing hers. Fanny tried to resist, but she saw the cold, deliberate lust in his eyes and it frightened her.

"Let me go!" she gasped, trying to break free from his clench.

"You cannot command me! I am captain of this ship and you are in no position to make demands." Burnett drew her in closer, hurting her, until with a mighty shove she pushed him away and sprang to the other side of the cabin.

"Stay away from me!" she warned. "I will defend myself and hurt you if I have to." She picked up a sharp set of brass navigational dividers which lay upon the chart table.

"You are a little too bold, my dear," Burnett bellowed. "How dare you threaten me?!"

"Have you forgotten who caused you all this trouble to begin with?"

"You were just lucky to have a ship better armed than mine!" he growled.

"Luck? Luck!" Fanny laughed still clutching the sharp brass instrument. "Do you honestly think that luck allowed me to outnavigate and outmaneuver you?"

"How else could you have anticipated my every move?"

"I knew because you taught me how! Do you think your superiors or your men would understand that? In trying to woo me you disclosed all of your tactical secrets."

As the irony of Fanny's words struck him, Burnett's fury erupted. He seized her again and ripped at her clothing. Fanny struggled with him and then brought the dividers down, effectively lodging the two sharp points deep into his right shoulder. Dazed, Burnett staggered backwards then fell upon the couch staring at her in disbelief. Fanny rushed over to one of the aft stateroom's port lights, broke it, and then climbed through. She dropped onto a narrow rail that ran on the outside of the aft-deck, and made her way around the cabin until she spotted a small tender tied to the stern of the ship. She scrambled down to it, freed the ropes, and rowed towards the shore as fast as she could against the outflowing tide.

Burnett chose to let Fanny go. He used the excuse that his wound was severe enough to prevent him from pursuing her, but it was his ego that was more severely damaged. With Fanny gone, he did not have to admit to his men that he had been beaten by a woman. "That damn Channing overpowered me!" Burnett told the ship's doctor as he tended the captain's shoulder.

"Too bad he got away," the doctor said. "But I'm happy to tell you that your wound is superficial. You'll be back on your feet in no time. You can even go after that bastard if you want to."

"I want to go home," Burnett admitted.

"To England?" The doctor seemed surprised.

"Yes, England," Burnett repeated. "I never want to see these colonies again!"

Fanny may have escaped Burnett's wrath, but she was now at the mercy of the large swells and the outflowing current. She was close enough to make out several figures onshore, but it took all she had to inch the little tender closer to land in the raging waters. Fanny rowed for what seemed like hours, doing her best to reach shore before her strength ebbed and the powerful current swept her out to sea. When she finally realized that she could not safely navigate the tender to the docks without it being turned into matchsticks, she removed her jacket and swam the rest of the way, hoping she would not be turned into tinder herself.

Carefully, she used the momentum of the waves to move her along toward shallow water. Wet and bedraggled, with no trace of golden stain remaining on her skin, Fanny dragged herself onshore just north of the docks at Boston Harbor, where she collapsed—exhausted from the physical and emotional strain of the last forty-eight hours.

She awoke several hours later with her clothes somewhat dry and the sun lowering on the horizon. She got to her feet and assessed her situation, happy to find a few coins still in her pocket. Since everyone would be looking for an escaped Barbadian captain, she must find some women's clothing. Fanny made her way down the back streets of the wharf to an open air market where she quickly spotted a dark-haired woman selling dresses, the kind that her mother might wear at home. Fanny chose a plain gray dress with a matching bonnet and as she handed over the coins, she asked if she could change in the woman's wagon.

"Yes, of course," the lady nodded, a bit curious at Fanny's rumpled clothing, yet pleased with the sale. "Go right ahead and take your time."

"Bartholomew Channing" then slipped into the wagon and Fanny Campbell emerged. Climbing down and straightening her skirts, she thanked the woman and walked towards the wharf hoping to find someone from Lynn willing to take her home. The old farmer, Josiah Pettibone, who had once brought her and Marion to Boston to call on the Breeds, was packing up his wares. "Mr. Pettibone, might I hitch a ride with you back to Lynn?"

"Fanny Campbell?!" Pettibone gasped. "Where on earth have you been, young lady? Your mother is worried sick about you."

"Oh, I've just been visiting cousins at the Cape," Fanny lied with the first story that popped into her head.

"In this storm?!" Pettibone shook his head.

"Yes, sir, it was foolish of me." Fanny looked contrite. "But I really would like to go home now."

Pettibone climbed into the wagon and pulled her up next to him. "Take care of this, my girl." He handed her a small wooden box. "This is all of the money I earned today."

"I'll guard it with my life." Fanny grinned resting the box on her lap.

Pettibone cracked his whip to start his team back to Lynn. He hoped to be there before dark. They rode mostly in silence and with each passing mile, Fanny's excitement grew as she recognized familiar landmarks. Soon she would be home safe with her family, and hopefully, in William's arms. She prayed that he had made it back and was not still at sea looking for her. The ride seemed longer and bumpier than she remembered, or maybe she was just impatient to get home. Finally, she saw the house in the distance. "Stop the wagon," Fanny said. "I think I can run faster."

"I'll take you to the door," the farmer answered.

She handed him the money box, kissed him on the cheek and jumped out before Petibone could say more. As soon as her feet hit the ground, she darted toward the house as if a wall of fire chased at her heels.

"Well, if that don't beat all," the old farmer said, smiling as he watched her race off. "She must have really missed home!"

"Mother! Father!" Fanny shouted as she reached the door and pounded her fists against the familiar wood. "Mother! Father! Open up, it's me! It's Fanny! I'm home!"

But neither her mother nor her father answered. Instead, William opened the door. Without a word, he took her in his arms and kissed her, a long, lingering kiss. The Lovells and the Campbells quietly gathered behind him, not daring to interrupt until

Agnes felt as if she might burst.

"Do you think you have a peck to spare for your old mother who has been sick with worry for months on end now?"

"Oh, Mother, I've missed you!" Fanny broke free from William and fell into Agnes's arms, sobbing like a little girl.

"There, there, daughter." Henry pulled her into his embrace. "You're home now and safe with the people who love you. Nothing else matters."

"But my ships?" she suddenly gasped, remembering the *Constance*, the *George*, and the *Wellington*. "Where are my ships and my men?"

"You can rest easy." William took her hand. "They are all safe in the harbor at Beverly."

"Why Beverly?" she asked.

"That's where General Washington and John Glover are forming an armed fleet. Glover has given us inside information that the Continental Congress is working on legalizing the use of privateers against British supply ships and, as privateers, our ships will make a fine addition to this new navy. I am to meet him there myself in a few days to discuss everything."

"But not the *Constance*," Fanny spoke up. "The *Constance* is ours. We earned her and we should be the ones who sail her. No one else."

"You are right, my dear. The *Constance* will remain in our hands and I plan to request a letter of marque on her behalf."

"Letter of Marque?" Fanny questioned the term.

"Yes, an official document issued by the Continental Congress that will allow the *Constance* to take on the enemy. It will give us the legal right to attack British ships and bring the spoils back to General Washington....if you are ready for a new challenge."

"Of course, I am ready, but then what, William?" Fanny asked. "What's next for us?"

"A proper marriage," he grinned with a wink. "And a war to win."

EPILOGUE

A Secret Kept

None knew the secret of Fanny Campbell—the female pirate captain—except for a chosen few. Of course, there was also Captain Burnett, but he was not talking. Not even Terrance Mooney, Channing's loyal mate, ever knew the truth. As for Moll Pitcher, who orchestrated the entire charade, her lips were sealed. So, as lore would have it, the Barbadian man, known as Bartholomew Channing, would go down in history as a heroic captain who mysteriously disappeared at sea, but lived and died by the unwritten code of the seafarers—an honorable and worthy leader.

Perhaps it was Terrance Mooney who summed it up best. Once he recovered from his stab wound, he went in search of Channing, but never found him. "I always said that the good captain was a holy spirit, not a man after all. He did what he came for, but I only wish he might have given me a handshake and said goodbye. Yes, it's clear to me that he came straight from heaven to help me bury me mum, liberate William and Samuel and help those American sailors who were about to be taken away. Sometimes I think his spirit has gone into Mr. Lovell's sainted wife, for she's so beautiful that it does me heart good to look at her. Her gentle kindness reminds me of the good Captain Channing."

The *Constance* was refitted and renamed the Fanny with William Lovell named captain. Fanny, herself, often accompanied him to sea, not only as his companion, but also his counselor in many hard fought contests to come.

Moll Pitcher continued spying, prophesying, and working for the colonists by hiding munitions and supplies. She also carried on with readings for the British soldiers seeking her counsel. Any valuable intelligence she gleaned as a result of these sessions, she turned over either to the Sons of Liberty or directly to General Washington under the pretense of having tea with the general's wife, Martha.

THE END

ADDENDUM

Just who was Fanny Campbell? Was she inspired by a real woman....? Only her creator, Maturin Murray Ballou who authored the original book, Fanny Campbell, the Female Pirate Captain in the 1840s can definitively answer that question. But we do know that before Fanny Campbell, there were two famous female pirates who disguised themselves as men—Ann Bonny and Mary Read—and went to sea. Perhaps, they inspired the whole idea or just maybe, Fanny Campbell, herself was inspired and took to the open waters following in their footsteps.

Whoever, she was—a real woman forced to hide her true identity lest she be hung as a pirate by the British Navy, or simply a product of Ballou's imagination, Fanny Campbell stirred up excitement and inspired women to take charge. Evidence of this lies in the many Fanny Campbell items that sprung up for sale after the original novel's release, including scrimshaw likenesses still available today.

In addition, real people like psychic Moll Pitcher, General John Glover, future U.S. Vice President Elbridge Gerry, and George Washington were all part of Fanny's story. Some historians believed that Fanny was also real, yet there is no trace of her genealogical lineage.

The mystery of the real Fanny Campbell remains, but either way, we hope that this modern re-telling of her story will inspire women today—both young and old—to find the bravery and passion to pursue their own dreams.

⚓

With the founding of the U.S. Navy, the first U.S. military ship, the *U.S.S. Hannah*, was outfitted at Glover's Wharf and sailed from Beverly, Massachusetts on September 5, 1775. The fishing schooner was originally owned by John Glover of Marblehead, Massachusetts and named after his wife.

The Second Continental Congress officially created the U.S. Navy on October 13, 1775. In addition, letters of marque were issued to privately owned vessels and commissions assigned to those privateers who agreed to fight enemy ships. Experienced seamen from Boston and the surrounding areas were recruited to sail these vessels.

The 1,697 privateer vessels well outnumbered the U.S. Navy whose total ships eventually equaled 64. As for weaponry, the privateers had 14,872 guns while the Navy had only 1,242. In battle, the Navy captured 196 enemy ships and the privateers seized 2,283, proving that these merchant marines played a significant part in winning the Revolutionary War. Their selfless contributions for our freedom should not be forgotten.

ACKNOWLEDGEMENTS

Cheryl Bartlam du Bois

In a time when no woman could speak her mind, travel alone, go to sea as a captain, or battle pirates, it took guts for Fanny Campbell to don the guise of a man, stage a mutiny, rescue the man she loved from a Cuban fortress, sink a pirate ship, and seize three British merchant ships—almost single handedly.

Having fought to get my own Captain's license when only one other woman on the east coast had received one, I can only admire the guts and guile it took for Fanny to lend her bravery to a revolution. Sharing her love of the sea, I can truly understand her desire to master the oceans, the Tradewinds, and the love and mastery of her vessel. During the years that I chartered a sailing yacht in the West Indies, I developed my own passion for the art of sailing.

I would like to thank Jon Westmoreland, the man who truly taught me to sail and instilled in me the love for my dear little 50-foot catamaran; Buddy Bond for inspiring me to become a U.S. Coast Guard Merchant Marine Captain; and last, but not least, my dear friend, Randy West, who taught me to respect the sea and mother nature when he loaned me his hurricane stories for my first novel, "WEST OF THE EQUATOR." May your sails be full and your winds be fare as you journey through an endless sea of stars on the Otherside. We miss you and your crazy sense of humor and tall tales.

Most of all, I want to thank all brave and inspiring women who have sailed through my life as inspiration to achieve all that I am capable of, whether they have touched my life in person, or from the page. I only hope that our resurrected version of Fanny Campbell's story will continue to inspire women around the world.

Debra Ann Pawlak

Writing an historical novel is not for sissies. Even though it may be considered 'fiction', it is important to get your facts straight. There were many frustrating moments that occurred when research didn't quite go the way I wanted. It was during those moments that I counted on my best buddy, Linda Wells, to keep me straight! I would be lost without ya! Sadly, my other BFF, Therese Kushnir, who always cheered me on, is not here to see this book's publication. I miss you, buddy! And then there is Alberta Asmar who seems to point me in the right direction whenever I am looking for answers. You are the best of the best! A special shout-out to author Martin Turnbull who so patiently walked me through the world of self-publishing and who 'introduced' me to one fabulous editor, Leigh Carter. Leigh provided invaluable input with her editing skills and know-how. I also want to thank my writing partner, Cheryl Bartlam Du Bois, for making this journey not only interesting, but fun. And finally— we are both living in the same time zone! Just proves that miracles do happen!

I must also give a nod to Michigan's own, Sarah Emma Edmonds, who disguised herself as a man, joined the Union Army and fought for her country during the Civil War. It was Sarah who led me to Fanny Campbell in the first place. She was just one of many women who were inspired by Fanny's adventures.

I also need to say a special thanks to my family. My daughter,

Rachel, and my favorite son-in-law, Jon, along with my son, Jonathan, and my favorite daughter-in-law, Stacey. You are always in my corner and I love you tons! Then there are my 'little people': Madeline, Olivia, Michael, and Lucas. I am the luckiest GiGi in the world to have the four of you to snuggle with! Last, but hardly least, my husband, Michael, who somehow manages to put up with me on a daily basis! I don't know how you do it!

UP NEXT!

SNEAK PREVIEW!

THE REVOLUTION

(PART II):

SEER, SPY, HEROINE

BY

CHERYL BARTLAM DU BOIS

AND

DEBRA ANN PAWLAK

CHAPTER 1 – A Psychic Inheritance (1775 – Lynn, Massachussetts)

It had been a long, unforgiving summer for the people of Boston and its surrounding areas. The British siege began that spring and Redcoats dominated the streets. Residents were forced to give up their arms and many patriots fled the city in fear. Loyalists then moved in, with some even enlisting in the King's army. The isolation of the city and the blockade of the harbor caused a food shortage for the populace and a lack of hay for the horses. Businesses were shuttered and the Colonists lived in constant fear for their very lives as the British soldiers plundered their homes and shops helping themselves to whatever they wanted.

In early June of 1775, a group of Colonists stormed the British-held Little Brewster Island, where a strategic lighthouse overlooked Boston's outer harbor. They removed the lamps and oil before setting the structure on fire in an effort to render the lighthouse useless to English ships. Caught off-guard, the Redcoats immediately went to work repairing the damage.

On July 31, 1775, General George Washington sent Major Benjamin Tupper and about 300 defiant Americans to Little Brewster Island with orders to attack and stop the lighthouse repairs. The raid was successful with only one casualty under Tupper. Several Lobsterbacks, however, were killed and many others taken prisoner, unnerving those still faithful to the King. Patriot or Loyalist, everyone was on edge and wondering what would come next.

Moll Pitcher, known as the Psychic or Fortune-Teller of Lynn, Massachusetts, came by her intuitive abilities and world-renowned reputation honestly through her linage as the grand-daughter of Edward Dimond, the great Wizard of Marblehead. Thanks to the respect he garnered due to his accurate predictions, the Psychic of Lynn became a trusted source for even the British military, who sought her out hoping to learn about their future fate in battle, as well as their place in history.

As such, Moll was fully aware of the struggle and hardship to come. She was also mindful of Fanny Campbell's every step, or perhaps it's better to say, Captain Bartholomew Channing's every conquest. Moll felt responsible for Fanny's situation as she was the one who sent Fanny to the West Indies disguised as the male, Barbadian sailor, named Channing. Moll's visions of Fanny started when the girl was just a child and when the time came to save William Lovell, Fanny's lover, from certain death, she found Fanny to be a willing and dedicated student, able to step up to the most dangerous task at hand.

Although Fanny had been gone for months, Moll knew exactly when she had overthrown the *Constance*, a British vessel, and, as Captain, made her an American Brig bound for the West Indies. She also knew when Fanny won her second British ship, the *George*. In addition, Moll had seen Fanny's daring rescue of William Lovell and Samuel Breed from Cuba's notorious La Cabana prison, as well as the taking of Fanny's last prize, the *Wellington*. She also saw the sinking of the *Crimson Blade*, a notorious Pirate ship. Her visions appeared both in the clouds and in her tea leaves, giving her unwavering confidence that Fanny, as Captain Channing, would soon return to Lynn triumphant.

Just before midnight on the eve of September 3, 1775, Moll's thoughts of Fanny were replaced by a more immediate danger—a terrible storm that would be remembered as one of the worst ever to hit the East Coast. It began in Martinique, which was very low in the West Indies and an unusual place for such a violent tropical tempest to evolve. Two days after leaving Martinique, the hurricane hit Santo Domingo, causing major damage and spawning a second storm.

From there it had plenty of ocean to strengthen over, but no one in America realized that they were in the path of such a formidable storm until it slammed into the North Carolina coast at New Bern. Residents of The Outer Banks were totally unprepared for the danger they faced, when the rains started shortly after midnight. By the next afternoon, the storm had gone from gale to hurricane proportion. More than 200 people were killed, trees were uprooted, corn and tobacco fields laid flat, and warehouses filled with goods destroyed as angry waves crashed upon the shore and rivers overflowed their banks. A 30-foot storm surge sunk ships as they lay anchored in the many coastal harbors, while huge swells at sea, forced many vessels to the bottom of the Atlantic. The mountainous surfs and fierce winds continued northward to Norfolk and by that night, Virginia and Maryland also felt the brunt of the hurricane. When the tempest reached Boston, the seas still rampaged like a herd of mad stallions, pummeling the coastline and wreaking havoc with not only the ships at sea, but also those unlucky enough to be caught in the unprotected harbors that dotted the coastline.

Moll knew that the *Constance*, the *George*, and the *Wellington*, along with every other ship out there, were all in trouble. Like her grandfather before her, she felt duty-bound and knew she must try to save them. Taking her warmest cloak, she covered her head and stepped outside looking skyward as the rain beat down around her. No one in their right mind was out on such a night, but lives were at stake. The powerful storm grew even more furious, as she slowly made her way up the hill to the cliff at High Rock, dodging blowing branches and debris with every step. The small-framed woman was barely able to stand in the relentless winds as she clung to the outcropping of rock, clutching her grandfather's curlew-peewit whistle against her chest. When she finally reached the top, she called on the Wizard's powers, then put the black whistle in her mouth and blew as hard as she could, but the screeching winds drowned out the sound. With everything she had, she blew it again—"Do you hear me Fanny?! Run with the wind... stay offshore and you will be safe!"

Moll, sheltered behind the rock, waiting for an answer. She must reach not only Fanny, but the other seamen whose lives now lay in the hands of Mother-Ocean. She blew the whistle again and again. Suddenly, the howling winds grew silent, the pelting rain slowed and the cloud-filled sky started to clear. It was the sign she'd been waiting for. Again Moll put the whistle to her lips and blew as long and hard as she could one more time. She knew the tranquil moment wouldn't last as it was only the eye of the storm. Moll closed her eyes and listened.

"I hear you, Moll," came Fanny's answer—faint at first. "We will run for our lives as you said."

"Beware of a friend turned foe!" Moll called back as loud as she could. "And remember, he has given you the very tools you will need to outwit him at his own game!"

"Yes, Moll, and I promise you he will not win." Fanny's voice was now strong and self-assured. "I will be ready for him!"

Relieved, Moll looked up just as the first quarter moon broke through an eagle-shaped cloud. It was a message from the heavens telling her that her friends would be safe from the storm, as well as their enemies. She then closed her eyes, remembering the other sailors unlucky enough to be at sea on such a terrible night, and quickly whispered a prayer to St. Elmo asking for their safe return. Moll knew in her heart that was exactly what the Wizard would have done.

The damp night air sent a shiver right through her despite her heavy cloak now soaked through from the rain. There was nothing more she could do here, but just as she began her descent down High Rock, a disturbance over in Lynn Harbor caught her eye. A large waterspout formed just offshore, churning near the docks. She watched as it tossed aside everything in its path like matchsticks.

"Amen and Godspeed," Moll gasped with a shudder before returning to the safety of her cottage. Once inside, she bolted the door, struggling against the increasingly powerful wind as the storm's eye passed. Her worried husband, Robert, waited inside, pacing in front of the hearth.

"HAVE YOU LOST YOUR MIND WOMAN?!" he bellowed as fear and relief intermingled inside him.

"How long have you known me, Mr. Pitcher?" Moll scolded him with a smile as she removed her dripping cloak.

"Too long, I think." he frowned taking the wet garment from his wife.

"Then by now you should know that I had to guide the sailors to safety and ask St. Elmo to save them."

"And did St. Elmo hear you?" He hung her wrap on a hook near the fire.

"I did what I could, but I left them all in the divine hands of our saint, but even he may need to call upon his holy helpers tonight."

"You're a funny girl, Moll Pitcher." Robert pulled her in front of the fire.

"But you married me anyway," she grinned.

"That I did," Robert sighed. "And by now, I should know better than to argue with the famed Psychic of Lynn."

⚓

As the next morning dawned, much of the wind subsided, but a drizzle of enduring rain continued to fall, while the angry waves still crashed against the rocks near the harbor. It wasn't often that Moll was surprised by events, but when she answered a knock at her door, shortly after sunrise, the unexpected visitor shocked her. There, on her doorstep stood Fanny Campbell's mother, Agnes, wet to the bone, bedraggled, and nervously wringing her hands.

"Agnes, what on earth are you doing out in this weather?" Moll reached for the woman's arm and tried to pull her inside. Despite the rain and her disheveled condition, Agnes resisted as if she were entering a witch's lair.

"Please, come in," Moll tried again. "And tell me what's brought you out here on such a terrible day. Is it our Fanny?"

"MY Fanny," Agnes corrected as she reluctantly stepped inside. "She's MY Fanny and I need to know if she's safe!"

"Come and warm yourself by the fire." Moll led Agnes toward the hearth, where the gaunt woman broke down, distraught and sobbing.

"I can't take any more! Not knowing where she is and if I'll ever see her again! Day after day, month after month! Mrs. Pitcher, can you please help a poor mother who is worried sick about her only child?"

Moll was stunned. Before today, this trembling woman had never once entered her cottage at High Rock. Agnes had always made it quite clear that she didn't believe in Moll's prophesies even if she did occasionally buy an herbal potion or two from Lynn's well-known mystic. No matter, Agnes fell just short of thinking that Moll consorted with the devil himself.

"By the grace of God," Moll winked at Agnes. "I never expected you to come here and seek council from me, a real witch!"

"Oh please, Mrs. Pitcher! I am at my wit's end with worry. It's bad enough that my Fanny is gone, but knowing she is out there somewhere in this storm is more than I can bear."

"I know, my dear." Moll took Agnes's hand in a sympathetic gesture. "I'm a mother, too, and I'm very fond of Fanny. So from one mother to another, please call me, Moll."

"Can you ever forgive me for having such evil thoughts about you?" Agnes shivered and her voice shook. "I know you have done many good things for others and that you're a God-fearing woman."

"That I am, Agnes." Moll put an arm around her and offered her a seat at the small Queen Anne table she used for her readings. "Sit down and join me in a hot cup of tea. We can talk and I will try to put your mind at ease."

Agnes took a seat, watching as Moll opened the top drawer of a large wooden chest and retrieved a thick blue shawl.

"Becky, come here with some tea," she called as she carefully placed the woolen wrap around the anguished woman before sitting directly across from her visitor.

Moll's daughter, Becky appeared and took two small blue cups from over the fireplace and placed them on the table.

"You remember my girl, Becky?" The young, dark-haired girl smiled shyly at Agnes as she set out the cups and prepared the tea.

"Yes, of course, I remember her," Agnes smiled feeling slightly relaxed for the first time since she'd arrived. "Thank-you, child. I'm sorry if I seem abrupt, I'm just beside myself with worry. How old are you now?"

"I'm ten, ma'am," Becky smiled warmly. "But you mustn't apologize. I know you are worried about Fanny."

"That I am," Agnes sighed. "But I shouldn't take it out on you. You and your older sister, Ruth, are always so pleasantly polite."

"If only the younger two were as good," Moll grinned. "Lydia and John are much more of a handful. I'm afraid they are spoiled by the older girls—especially John being the only boy and all." Moll sipped her tea encouraging Agnes to do the same. "Drink up... the lavender will help calm your nerves."

Agnes tried to steady her trembling hands as they gripped the warm tea cup. She found the heat soothing and for the first time felt hopeful as she looked around the unfamiliar room and noticed Moll's black cat, Percy, sleeping in one corner. The room itself was small, but the walls were lined with shelves filled with jars, marked with various herbs and potions. She breathed in the steam from the tea before taking a sip and speaking. "Please, Moll, can you just tell me if my daughter is safe and whether I will live to see her again?"

"I can assure you that Fanny is safe," Moll smiled. "I went up to High Rock last night to guide her myself."

"You went out in that storm last night for my Fanny?!" Agnes slumped in her chair feeling even worse about all of the terrible things she'd said about Moll in the past.

"Of course, I did and I called upon St. Elmo and his helpers to bring them all home." Moll patted Agnes's arm. "Now finish your tea."

Agnes took a deep breath before lifting her cup and taking another sip. For the first time since the storm began, she felt a sense of calm slip over her.

"Please tell me what you know. Don't keep me in suspense any longer. I can pay you for your trouble."

"I'll not take money from a friend, Agnes." Moll too sipped her tea then set the cup down. She paused for a moment, thinking.

"Tell me what you see, Moll." Agnes held her breath, waiting for an answer.

"Well… William has been rescued from the prison and they are very close to home now, but I see they are onboard different ships." Moll closed her eyes in an effort to focus on what was to come. "I suspect you will find William at your door before another day passes."

"But what about my Fanny? When will I see her?"

"It may take a bit longer for Fanny to find her way home. But, you will see her within a fortnight."

"But why aren't they together?"

"It's a long story, Agnes… one that should be told by no one, except Fanny herself and I can assure you that she will come home safe and sound with adventures of a lifetime to tell you and your grandchildren."

"Grandchildren?!" Agnes echoed. "Are you saying that Fanny and William will marry and have children?"

"Yes, they will marry soon after their homecoming, but children will wait until the fight for independence is over."

"What does that mean, Moll?" Agnes asked.

"There are dark years ahead," Moll offered. "But we will triumph and become a great nation of power and might. In the meantime, rejoice in your daughter's homecoming. Be glad that she will find her way back to you."

Agnes finally stopped trembling. She couldn't decide whether it was the hot tea or Moll's comforting words, but she felt her body relax and even started to enjoy her drink, as well as Moll's company. The Psychic of Lynn had given her hope and restored her faith in Fanny's return. There was nothing wicked about this woman and there were no signs of the devil inside her home. Moll Pitcher had proved herself to be a kind and compassionate person—not a witch at all. She had been totally wrong about Moll and felt very embarrassed by her wicked thoughts.

⚓

Due to the Second Continental Congress's ban on trade with Great Britain, which was to take effect on September 10th, there had been a flurry of activity in every port along the eastern seaboard, Lynn included. Merchants and sailors alike all tried making one last shipment from places like Pamlico Sound, Charleston, Norfolk, Philadelphia, New York, Rhode Island, and Boston. As a result, warehouses on the wharves overflowed with tobacco, lumber, naval stores, corn, salt, molasses, rum, sugar, and other staples before the storm. Now, most of these stockpiled goods were ruined, or gone altogether. The once-filled structures had collapsed in place, cluttering the shoreline and the valuable goods they once held floated out to sea.

After Agnes's visit, Moll walked to the docks of Lynn where she viewed the destruction. Much had been lost as pieces of splintered fishing boats crashed upon the shore, while debris and flotsam littered the harbor. Moll shook her head, overwhelmed by the loss, but as she looked up at the sky, she saw an eagle-shaped cloud pointing toward Beverly Harbor. She realized then that Fanny and William would soon bring their ships to safety there. Moll also knew that just before the storm hit, General Washington, under strict secrecy, had acquired a wharf at that very harbor where his newly-formed American Navy would launch. Despite the devastation, the Seer of Lynn smiled to herself. All was as it should be. The fallout from the storm would serve as a good distraction while Fanny and William brought their ships home right under the very noses of the British.

Not everyone, however, was as fortunate as Fanny Campbell and William Lovell. In the aftermath of the hurricane and as the storm surge subsided, bodies washed ashore amongst the wreckage of sunken ships. The huge swells lasted for days while, fishermen, lucky enough to survive, brought in, along with their catch, pieces of flotsam and bloated bodies. The massive damage prompted the Provincial Congress to help with disaster relief, but there was no funding for lost ships or rebuilding along the waterfront. Due to an 'Act of God', the Revolutionary Assembly granted an extension to those merchants attempting to ship goods in advance of the September 10th boycott. By the time the great storm finally blew itself out in Newfoundland, many English and Irish ships were lost or damaged. Between America and Canada, more than 4,000 lives were snuffed out and this 'Act of God' would come to be known as the Hurricane of Independence.

⚓

Just as Moll had promised, William came home after leaving his ships with Colonel John Glover in Beverly Harbor, but it took Fanny a while longer. After heading a mutiny, she rescued William and Samuel, from La Cabana, the deadly Cuban prison, captured three British ships, and took on a bevy of cut-throat pirates all the while dressed as Bartholomew Channing. On the sail back to Lynn, however, the three ships were attacked by the *Dolphin*, a British Royal Cutter captained by Fanny's old suitor, Ralph Burnett, who took Fanny prisoner aboard his ship. Angry at her refusal to be his wife, Burnett assaulted her, causing Fanny to stab him in order to escape, and escape she did. As Fanny found her way to her parents' doorstep, the ocean was still churning up its dead.

Now that Fanny and her ships filled with weaponry were home, Moll Pitcher had serious work to do. It was imperative that these invaluable supplies, weapons, and gunpowder did not fall back into British hands.

Some of the captured booty from Channing's three ships was easily disguised as stores and cargo within the warehouse at

Glover's wharf. The weapons and gunpowder had to be hidden as quickly as possible in order to keep them from the British. It would be nearly a week before the crew could safely unload the ships, but it gave the men in charge time to make transportation arrangements. Elbridge Gerry, elected to the Massachusetts Provincial Congress, and John Glover, both men of Marblehead, hired freight wagons to carry the munitions to Lynn where Moll and the young men who helped her would hide the goods deep inside the wolf pits of Lynn Woods and other places such as the old Western Burial Ground.

Before turning their attention to the task of repairing their damaged cities and wharfs, residents along the Atlantic Coast, began their recovery by burying their dead. The increased number of graves being dug, due to deaths from the storm, provided a perfect cover for hiding weapons in plain view of the enemy until General Washington and his Continental Army needed them.